Frederick E. Hulme

Myth-Land

Frederick E. Hulme

Myth-Land

ISBN/EAN: 9783337180508

Printed in Europe, USA, Canada, Australia, Japan

Cover: Foto ©Andreas Hilbeck / pixelio.de

More available books at **www.hansebooks.com**

MYTH-LAND.

Ballantyne Press
BALLANTYNE, HANSON AND CO.
EDINBURGH AND LONDON

MYTH-LAND.

BY

F. EDWARD HULME, F.L.S., F.S.A.

AUTHOR OF
"FAMILIAR WILD FLOWERS," ETC. ETC.

" Far away in the twilight time
Of every people, in every clime,
Dragons and griffins and monsters dire,
Born of water, or air, or fire,
Or nursed, like the Python, in the mud
And ooze of the old Deucalion flood,
Crawl, and wriggle, and foam with rage,
Through dark tradition and ballad age."

WHITTIER.

LONDON

SAMPSON LOW, MARSTON, SEARLE, & RIVINGTON,

CROWN BUILDINGS, 188 FLEET STREET.

1886.

PREFACE.

HE nucleus of the following pages was originally written in the form of two short papers to be read at the meetings of a Public School Natural History Society. Since then, finding materials rapidly growing on our hands, we have been gradually amplifying our notes on the subject until they have grown to the present dimensions; for, to quote the quaint words of Thomas Fuller, "when there is no recreation or business for thee abroad, thou may'st then have a company of honest old fellows in leathern jackets in thy study, which may find thee excellent divertisement at home." Our researches in pursuit of the marvellous, through the works of divers and sundry old writers, have been so far entertaining and interesting to us that we would fain hope that they may not be altogether received without favour by others.

Our subject naturally divides itself into two very obvious sections—the one dealing with wholly untrue and impossible creatures of the fancy, the other with the strange beliefs and fancies that have clustered round the real creatures we see around us. It will readily be discovered that we have confined ourselves in the present volume almost entirely to the first of these sections. Should our present labours prove acceptable they may readily be followed by a companion volume, at least as entertaining, dealing with the second section of our subject.

CONTENTS.

CHAPTER I.

CHAPTER II.

CHAPTER III.

LIST OF ILLUSTRATIONS.

MYTH-LAND.

CHAPTER I.

ALL science is a gradual growth. Travellers
as they toil up a long ascent turn round
from time to time, and mark with satisfaction the ever-lengthening way that stretches
between them and their distant starting-place, and
derive a further encouragement from the sight to press

onward to the yet unknown. So may we in this our day
compare ourselves, in no offensive and vainglorious way,
with the men of the past, and gain renewed courage
in the future as we leave their ancient landmarks far
behind us. Shame, indeed, would it be to us had
we not thus advanced, for our opportunities of gaining
knowledge are immeasurably greater than those of any
preceding generation.

The old herbals and books of travels abound in
curious examples of the quaint beliefs of our forefathers,
while their treatises on natural history are a still richer
storehouse. Many of the old tomes, again, on the science
of heraldry give other curious notions respecting the
different animals introduced. Some of these animals, as
the dragon or the griffin, are undoubtedly of the most
mythical nature, yet we find them described in the most
perfect good faith, and without the slightest suspicion as
to their real existence. We shall have occasion to refer
to several of the works of these old writers, and we will,
without further preface, take down from our book-shelf a
little book entitled "A Description of 300 Animals."*

No one person appears on the title-page as author,

---

* The name of Thomas Bewick is to all book-collectors "familiar in
their mouths as household words," and we rarely read the account of
the dispersal of any large library or the choice collection of some
bibliophile without finding that it contained a choice edition of Bewick's
"quadrupeds" or "birds"—a "lot" that always calls for a keen com-
petition. It is interesting to know that the book we have named above
considerably influenced him, and in no slight degree led to the production of the works that will always remain his monument, for we find
him writing to a friend of his—"From my first reading, when a boy
at school, a sixpenny history of birds and beasts, and then a wretched
composition called the 'History of Three Hundred Animals,' to the time
I became acquainted with works of natural history written for the
perusal of men, I was never without the design of attempting something
of this kind myself."

but it is stated that it is extracted from the best authorities and adapted to the use of all capacities. It is also illustrated with copper-plates "whereon is curiously engraven every beast, bird, fish, serpent, and insect, described in the whole book." The word "curiously" is very happily chosen, and most happily describes the extraordinary nature of the illustrations. The preface shows us that the primary intention of the book was the instruction and entertainment of the young, and after wading painfully through the cumbrous Roman figures, the long array of C's, X's, and the like, we find that the date of the treatise was 1786, or just a hundred years ago. Let us, then, dip here and there into it and see what "the best authorities" could teach our grandfathers when their youthful minds would know something of the wonders of creation. The lion, as the king of beasts, heads the list. "He is generally of a dun colour, but not without some exceptions, as black, white, and red, in Ethiopia and some other parts of Africa." The red lion, then, it would appear, is no mere creation of the licensed victualler or Garter King-at-Arms, no mere fancy to deck a signboard withal or emblazon on a shield of honour, but a living verity; and we may pause to remark that almost all the most wonderful things in the book have their home in Africa, not as now the playground of the Royal Geographical Society, but an unknown land full of wonder and mystery, of which nothing is too marvellous to be impossible. We are told, too, that the lion sleeps with his eyes open, and many other curious details follow. On the next page the unicorn is in all sober seriousness described. "His head resembles a hart's, his feet an elephant's, his tail a boar's, and the rest of his body a horse's. The horn is about a foot and a half in length, his voice is like the lowing of an ox, his horn is as hard as iron and as rough as any file." Burton in his "Miracles of Art and Nature," published in 1678, says that in Ethiopia "some Kine there are which have Horns like Stags; other but one Horn only, and that in the Forehead, about a foot and a half long, but bending backward." It will be seen that Burton does not identify these with the so-called unicorn, but the passage is in some degree suggestive. Any one who has noticed the fine series of antelopes in the collection of the Zoological Society of London will scarcely have failed to observe the length and straightness of the horns of some of the species, while they are often so close together and so nearly parallel in direction, that any one seeing the animals at a little distance away, and so standing that one of their horns covers the other, might well be excused for starting the idea of single-horned animals. Great virtues are attributed to the horn of the unicorn, as the expelling of poison and the curing of many diseases. The unicorn is very familiar to us as one of the supporters of the royal arms, but the form we know so well does not altogether agree with that described. The heraldic unicorn is in all respects a horse save and except the horn, while our old author tells us of the head of a stag and the feet of an elephant. The creature is sometimes referred to in our English version of the Bible, and has thus become one of the animals introduced in symbolic and religious art. In some of the passages it would clearly seem to indicate that in the very early days dealt with in some of the books of the Bible there was a general belief in some such creature, while in others probably the word is rather introduced in error by our translators—an error that may very well be pardoned when we find the animal gravely described in the much more recent book before us. In the book of Job, the earliest in point of time in the whole Bible, the belief in some such animal seems very distinctly indicated in the words, "Will the unicorn be willing to serve thee or abide by thy crib? Canst thou bind the unicorn with his band in the furrow, or will he harrow the valleys after thee?" In the 92d Psalm the peculiar feature that gives the creature its name is especially referred to in the words, "My horn shalt thou exalt like the horn of a unicorn." The reference is always to some wild and powerful animal; thus in Exodus we

read, "His horns are like the horns of unicorns;" and again in one of the psalms we find David crying, "Save me from the lion's mouth, for Thou hast heard me from the horns of the unicorns." Other passages might be quoted, but these will amply suffice to indicate the very early belief in some such creature. The form is frequently seen in the earliest Christian art, as in the catacombs of Rome, the havens of refuge for the living and the resting-places of the dead followers of the new

faith. Our illustration is a facsimile of that in the
" Description of 300 Animals."

For some reason that we cannot now discover, the
unicorn was an especial favourite with the Scotch heralds,
and it is from them that we derive it in our royal arms.
Before the union of the two monarchies the supporters
of the arms of the English monarchs had been very
various, though in almost every case a lion had been one
of the two employed,* while in Scotland for several reigns
before the amalgamation of the two countries the supporters had been two unicorns. It was very naturally
arranged, therefore, when the two kingdoms were fused
together on the death of Elizabeth, that the joint shield
should be supported by the lion of England and the
unicorn of Scotland. The creature freely occurs as a
device on the Scottish coinage; one piece especially is
by collectors called the unicorn, from the conspicuous
introduction of the national device.

We have already indicated that potent virtues were
believed to reside in the horn of the unicorn. In the
Comptes Royaux of France in 1391 we find a golden
cup with a slice of this horn in it for testing the food of
the Dauphin, and again in the inventory of Charles V.—
" Une touche de licorne, garnie d'or, pour faire essay."
Decker, again, in 1609 speaks of "the unicorn, whose
horn is worth a city." In Mrs. Bury Palliser's most interesting work of " Historic Badges and Devices " we find
an illustration of the standard of Bartolomeo d'Alviano.
He was a great champion of the Orsini family, and took
a leading part in all the feuds that devastated Central

* As for example :—Henry VI., Lion and Antelope ; Edward IV.,
Lion and Bull ; Edward V., Two Lions ; Richard III., Lion and Boar ;
Henry VII., Lion and Dragon ; Henry VIII., Lion and Dragon ;
Mary, Lion and Greyhound ; Elizabeth, Lion and Greyhound.

Europe during his lifetime. His standard bears the unicorn, surrounded by snakes, toads, and other reptiles then rightly or wrongly held poisonous; these he is moving aside with his horn, and above is the motto, " I expel poisons"—he, d'Alviano, of course, being the lordly and potent unicorn, his foes the creeping things to be driven from his face.*

In the "Display of Heraldry" published by John Guillim in the year 1679 we read—" It hath been much questioned amongst naturalists, which it is that is properly called the Unicorn; and some have made doubt whether there be any such Beast as this or no. But the great esteem of his horn (in many places to be seen) may take away that needless scruple." Having thus satisfactorily established the existence of such a creature he naturally feels at full liberty to group around the

---

* The English Cyclopædia of Natural History gives a description by Ctesias of the Indian ass. He says that these animals are as large as horses, and larger, having a horn on the forehead, one cubit long, which for the extent of two palms from the forehead is entirely white; above, it is pointed and red, being black in the middle. Of this horn drinking-cups are formed, and those who use them are said not to be subject to spasm or epilepsy, nor to the effects of poison, provided, either before or after taking the poison, they drink out of the cup wine, water, or any other liquid.

One of the Arabian annalists, El Kazwini, has much to say about the magical and curative properties of these cups; and a yet fuller notice of them appears in Lane's "Arabian Nights," chap. xx. note 32. It is also stated that most of the Eastern potentates possessed one of these cups. In Hyder Ali's treasury at Tanjore was found a specimen.

In "Uganda and the Egyptian Soudan," by the Rev. C. T. Wilson and R. W. Felkin, vol. ii. p. 275, we read :—

"Cups made of rhinoceros horn are supposed to have the peculiar virtue of detecting poison in coffee and sherbet. Often, when drinking for the first time in a strange house, one of these cups is offered to assure the visitor that no foul play is contemplated. These are considered most valuable presents and a mark of lasting friendship and esteem."

central fact divers details, as, for instance, that "the wild
Beasts of the wilderness use not to drink of the Pools,
for fear of venomous Serpents there breeding, before the
Unicorn hath stirred it with its horn."

It seems to have been a debateable point whether the
unicorn had ever been taken alive, but Guillim decisively
negatives the idea, and naturally avails himself of it for
the greater glorification of the creature and of its service
in his beloved science of heraldry.   He lays down the
broad fact that the unicorn is never taken alive, and
here surely we can thoroughly go with him ; but "the
reason being demanded, it is answered that the greatness
of his mind is such that he chuseth rather to die, wherein
the unicorn and the valiant-minded soldier are alike,
which both contemn death, and rather than they will
be compelled to undergo any base servitude and bondage
they will lose their lives."

Philip de Thaun, on the other hand, not only admits
the idea that the unicorn may be captured alive, but
gives the full receipt for doing so.   It would appear
that, like Una's lion, the animal is of a particularly im-
pressionable nature, and is always prepared to do homage
to maiden beauty and innocence, and this amiable trait
in its character is basely taken advantage of.   " When
a man intends to hunt and take and ensnare it he goes
to the forest where is its repair, and there places a virgin.
Then it comes to the virgin, falls asleep on her lap, and
so comes to its death.   The man arrives immediately and
kills it in its sleep, or takes it alive and does as he will
with it."   The young ladies of that very indefinite date
must have possessed considerably more courage and nerve
than some of their sisters of the present day, who show
symptoms of hysteria if they find themselves in the same
room with a spider—a considerably less severe test than

an interview in the dark shades of the forest with an amorous unicorn. One cannot, however, help feeling that the victim of misplaced confidence comes out of the transaction most creditably, and that both man and maiden must have felt what schoolboys call "sneaks."

The unicorn, alive or dead, seems to have eluded observation in a wonderful way, and the men of science were left to extract their facts from the slightest hints, in the same way that distinguished anatomists and geologists of these later days are enabled to build up an entire animal from one or two isolated bones. The process, however, does not seem, in the case of the earlier men, to have been a very successful one, and there is consequently a great clashing amongst the authorities, and one of the mediæval writers, feeling the difficulty of drawing any very definite result from the chaos before him, adopts the plan, in which we humbly follow him, of simply putting it all down just as it comes to hand, and leaving his readers to make the best they can of it. He writes as follows :—

"Pliny affirmeth it is a fierce and terrible creature, Vartomannus a tame animal : those which Garcias ab Horto described about the Cape of Good Hope were beheld with heads like horses, those which Vartomannus beheld he described with the head of a Deere : Pliny, Ælian, Solimus, and Paulus Venetus affirm the feet of the Unicorn are undivided and like the Elephant's, but those two which Vartomannus beheld at Mecha were, as he described, footed like a Goate. As Ælian describeth it, it is in the bignesse of an Horse, that which Thevet speaketh of was not so big as an Heifer, but Paulus Venetus affirmeth that they are but little lesse than Elephants."

On turning to the records of a distinguished French

Society established in 1633 we come across many strange items. These records are entitled " A general collection of the Discourses of the Virtuosi of France, upon questions of all sorts of philosophy and other natural knowledge, made in the Assembly of the Beaux Esprits at Paris by the most ingenious persons of that nation." Their meetings were termed conferences, and there are notes of two hundred and forty of these. The subjects discussed covered a very wide field, the following being some few amongst them—Of the end of all things, of perpetual motion, of the echo, of how long a man may continue without eating, whether is to be preferred a great stature or a small, of the loadstone, of the origin of mountains, and who are the most happy in this world, wise men or fools. Some of these subjects are now definitely settled, while others are as open to discussion as ever, as, for example, the questions whether it be expedient for women to be learned, and whether it be better to bury or to burn the bodies of the dead. In this great accumulation of the notions of the seventeenth century we find, amongst other items that more especially concern our present purpose, discussions on genii, on the phœnix, and on the unicorn.

In the early days of a similar institution, our own Royal Society—a body which is now so staid, and which focuses all the most important scientific results of the day to itself—many points were discussed in perfect good faith that are now consigned to oblivion—the trees that grow diamonds, the rivers that run precious gems, and the seeds that fell from heaven being amongst these ; while at another meeting we find the Duke of Buckingham presenting the Society with a piece of the horn of the unicorn.

The old writers had no very definite system, and though

the author of the "Book of the 300 Animals" may seem to have exercised a certain fitness in discussing the unicorn directly after the lion, the conjunction is probably wholly accidental, as the creatures dwelt on succeed each other in all such books in the most arbitrary way. The next animal to which we would refer is the wolf. He is not absolutely the next in the series, but we manifestly cannot deal with the whole three hundred, so we pick out here and there divers quaint examples of what we may be allowed to term this unnatural history. We are told that "the wolf is a very ravenous creature, and as dangerous to meet with, when hungry, as any beast whatever, but when his stomach is full, he is to men and beasts as meek as a lamb. When he falls upon a hog or a goat, or such small beasts, he does not immediately kill them, but leads them by the ear, with all the speed he can, to a crew of ravenous wolves, who instantly tear them to pieces." We should have thought that the reverse had been more probable, that the wolves that had nothing would have come with all the speed they could upon their more successful companion ; but if the old writer's story be true, it opens out a fine trait of unselfishness in the character of this maligned communard. It was an old belief, a fancy that we find in the pages of Pliny, Theocritus, Virgil, and others, that a man becomes dumb if he meets a wolf and the wolf sees him first. A mediæval writer explains this as follows :—"The ground or occasionall originall hereof was probably the amazement and sudden silence the unexpected appearance of Wolves doe often put upon travellers, not by a supposed vapour or venemous emanation, but a vehement fear which naturally produceth obmutescence and sometimes irrecoverable silence. Thus birds are silent in presence of an Hawk, and Pliny saith that

Dogges are mute in the shadow of an Hyæna, but thus could not the mouths of worthy Martyrs be stopped, who being exposed not only unto the eyes but the mercilesse teeth of Wolves, gave loud expressions of their faith, and their holy clamours were heard as high as heaven." Scott refers to the old belief in his " Quentin Durward." In the eighteenth chapter our readers will find as follows : —"'Our young companion has seen a wolf,' said Lady Hameline, ' and has lost his tongue in consequence.' " The thirteenth animal is the " Rompo " or Man-eater ; he is " so called because he feeds upon dead men, to come at which he greedily grubs up the earth off their graves, as if he had notice of somebody there hid. He keeps in the woods ; his body is long and slender, being about three feet in length, with a long tail. The negroes say that he does not immediately fall on as soon as he has found the body, but goes round and round it several times as if afraid to seize it. Its head and mouth are like a hare's, his ears like a man's, his fore feet like a badger's, and his hinder feet like a bear's. It has like-wise a mane. This creature is bred in India and Africa." Concerning the buffalo we read, " It is reported of this creature that when he is hunted or put into a fright he'll change his colour to the colour of everything he sees ; as amongst trees he is green, &c." The Manticora is one of the strange imaginings of our forefathers. In the illustration in the book (of which our figure is a reproduction) it has a human head and face and a body like that of a lion ; a thick mane covers the neck ; its tail is much longer in proportion than that of a lion, and has at its extremity a most formidable collection of spiky-looking objects ; these in the description are said to be stinging and sharply-pointed quills. He is as big as a lion. " His voice is like a small trumpet. He is so wild that it is very difficult to catch him, and as swift as an hart. With his tail he wounds the hunters, whether they come before him or behind him. When the Indians

THE MANTICORA

take a whelp of this beast they bruise its tail to prevent it bearing the sharp quills; then it is tamed without danger."

The Lamia, too, is an extraordinary creature, and one that our not remote forefathers seem to have thoroughly believed in, for though the author says that there are many fictitious stories respecting it, he goes on to describe it, and gives an illustration. It is thought to be

THE LAMIA

the swiftest of all four-footed creatures, so that its prey can seldom or never escape it. It is said to be bred in

Libya, and to have a face like a beautiful woman, while
its voice is the hiss of a serpent. The body is covered
with scales. The old author tells us that they sometimes
devour their own young, and we may fairly hope that
this cannibal propensity of theirs is the cause of their
disappearance. In earlier times men believed in a
monstrous spectre called an Empusa. It could assume
various forms, and it was believed to feed on human
flesh. The Laimæ, who took the forms of handsome
and graceful women for the purpose of beguiling poor
humanity, and then sucked their blood like vampyres
and devoured their flesh, were one form of Empusa.
The belief in some such creature seems to have been
widespread ; the myth of the Sirens is, for example, very
similar in conception. In Mansfield Parkyns' " Life in
Abyssinia " we read—" There is an animal which I know
not where to class, as no European has hitherto suc-
ceeded in obtaining a specimen of it. It is supposed by
the natives to be far more active, powerful, and dangerous
than the lion, and consequently held by them in the
greatest possible dread. They look upon it more in
the light of an evil spirit, with an animal's form, than
a wild beast ; they assert that its face is human." We
learn, however, from the rest of the description, that this
creature possesses itself of its prey by force alone ; the
human face is one further feature of terror, but does not,
as in the previous case, serve to beguile mankind and
lure them by its beauty to their fate.

The stag is said to be " a great enemy to all kinds
of serpents, which he labours to destroy whenever he
finds any, but he is afraid of almost all other creatures."
Many of these old beliefs were simply handed down
from generation to generation without question, or the
opinions of the ancients accepted without experiment

or inquiry. This belief of the natural enmity of the stag to the serpent is at least as old as Pliny, and may be found duly set forth in the thirty-third chapter of his eighth book :—" This kind of deere make fight with serpents, and are their natural and mortal enemies ; they will follow them to their verie holes, and then by the strength of drawing and snuffing up their wind of their nostrils, force them out whether they will or no. The serpent sometimes climbs upon its back and bites it cruelly, when the stag rushes to some river or fountain and throws itself into the water to rid itself of its enemy." This old belief made the stag a favourite in the mediæval days of exaggerated symbolism, its ruthless antipathy to the serpent rendering it not inaptly an emblem of the Christian fighting to the death against sin, and finding an antidote to its wounds in the fountain of living water. It was also believed that stags " passe the seas swimming by flockes and whole heards in a long row, each one resting his head upon his fellow next before him ; and this they do in course, so as the foremost retireth behind to the hindmost by turnes, one after another." In this supposed fact the seekers after symbol and hidden meaning found no difficulty in recognising that comfort and support in all their trials that all good men should at all times be ready to afford their fellows.

The tusks of the wild boar, we are told, cut like sharp knives when the animal is alive, but lose their keenness at his death. It is said when this creature is hunted down his tusks are so inflamed that they will burn and singe the hair of the dogs. The wild ox has a tongue so hard and rough that it can draw a man to him, "whom by licking he can wound to death." The elephant, we are told on the same authority, has two tusks. " One of them it keeps always sharp to revenge injuries, and with the other it roots up trees and plants for its meat. These they lose once in ten years, which, falling off, they very carefully bury in the earth on purpose that men may not find them." The liver of a mouse our forefathers believed to increase and decrease with the waxing and waning of the moon. " For every day of the moon's age there is a fibre increase in their liver." This rash and random assertion it would be manifestly impossible either to prove or disprove, though one may have one's own strong opinion on the matter. It would be necessary to kill the mouse to count the aforesaid fibres, and having killed it, the morrow's extra age of the moon would bring no added fibres to the victim of our credulity. Presently we come to the Potto, a creature that is probably the same as we now call the sloth. The illustration shows us a most hopelessly helpless-looking animal, and in the description that accompanies it we are told that a whole day is little enough for it to advance ten steps forward. We are also informed that when he does climb a tree he does not leave it until he has eaten up not only the fruit but all the foliage, when " he descends fat and in good case, but before he can get up another tree he loses all the advantages of his previous good quarters and often perishes of hunger." Eighty-seven quadrupeds are dealt with, so it will be readily seen how little we have drawn upon the wealth of information the book affords.

Book IV. of the treatise is devoted to the consideration of serpents and insects. Amongst serpents and insects the dragon naturally takes the place of honour. The writer evidently has his doubts, and carefully qualifies his description by a free use of the responsibility evading formula "it is said." He gives three illustrations. One

of them represents a biped monster, crested and winged;
the second has lost his legs, though he retains crest and
wings; while the third creature is of serpentine nature,

has neither wings nor legs, and only differs from the
serpent forms in the book by the addition of his crest.
The description runs as follows:—"The dragon, as described in the numerous fables and stories of several

writers, may be justly questioned whether he really exists. I have read of serpents bred in Arabia, called Sirenas, which have wings, being very swift, running and flying at pleasure; and when they wound a man he dieth instantly. These are supposed to be a kind of dragons. It is said there are divers sorts of dragons or serpents that are so called, which are distinguished partly by their countries, partly by their magnitude, and partly by the different form of their external parts. They are said to be bred in India and Africa; those of India are much the largest, being of an incredible length; and of these there are also said to be two kinds, one of them living in the marshes, which are slow of pace and without combs on their heads; the other in the mountains, which are bigger and have combs, their backs being somewhat brown and their bodies less scaled. Some of them are of a yellow fiery colour, having sharp backs like saws. These also have beards. When they set up their scales they shine like silver. The apples of their eyes are (it is said) precious stones, and as bright as fire, in which it is affirmed there is a great virtue against many diseases. Their aspect is very fierce and terrible. Some dragons are said to have wings and no feet; some, again, have both feet and wings; and others neither feet nor wings, and are only distinguished from the common sort of serpents by the combs growing upon their heads and by their beards. Some do affirm that the dragon is of a black colour, somewhat green beneath and very beautiful, that it has a triple row of teeth in each jaw, that it has also two dewlaps growing under the chin, which hang down like a beard of a red colour; and the body is set all over with sharp scales, and on the neck with thick hair, much like the bristles of a wild boar." It will be seen by the foregoing that the imagination of our ancestors was allowed free play, abundant variety of form, magnitude, colour, and so forth being possible.

The dragon or winged serpent has formed a part in many creeds, and the dragon-slayer has been the hero of countless legends. The legend varies with climate and country, and with the development of the race in which it is found; and yet the prophecies of the Bible of the ultimate bruising of the serpent's head and the final victory over the dragon ("That old serpent, which is the Devil and Satan" Rev. xx. 2); the legends of classic days, such as that of Perseus and Andromeda; the still older struggles recorded in the slabs of Nineveh and Persepolis; the stories narrated to awed rings of listeners in the stillness of the Eastern night, or listened to by our children with eager eyes and rapt attention in the homes of England; the mass of legend that in mediæval times clustered around the names of God's faithful ones; and the local traditions of every land, from the equator to the poles, all dwell on the mischievous presence of some evil principle and record the ultimate triumph of good. Beneath the mass of ever-varying fable stands the like foundation, the strife between the two antagonistic principles; and thus the wide world over, in every age and in every clime, the mind of man, in broken accents, it may be, and with faltering tongue, records with joy its upward struggle, feels the need of help in the sore conflict, registers its belief in final triumph. Though the dragon-conflict occurs in many literatures, the same incidents occur over and over again, and we find in almost all the power and subtlety of the monster, the innocence and helplessness of his victims, the suddenness of his attack on them, and the completeness of his final overthrow, the dragon-slayers being the

conquerors over tyranny and wrong, over paganism and
every form of godless evil.

In Egypt he was Typhon, in Greece, Python.   In
India he is Kalli Naga, the thousand-headed, the foe and
the vanquished of Vishnu.   In Anglo-Saxon chronicles
he is Lig-draca, the fire-drake or godes-andsacan, the
denier of God—always unsleeping, poison-fanged, relent-
less, the terrible enemy of man, full of subtlety and full
of power.

On the advent of Christianity these ancient legends
were not wholly discarded, but suggested others of a like
character, and a slight alteration transferred to saint or
martyr those feats and victories which had formerly been
ascribed to gods and demigods.   It only remained for
the new religion to point out the analogy, and to incor-
porate into itself the lessons they taught, the conflict won,
the abnegation of self for the good of others.

It would take up far too much space if we were to
endeavour to give many of these legends in detail.   In
some cases they were doubtless intended as descriptions
of an actual conflict, by force of arms, with some real
monster; but in others the conflict is allegorical; thus
St. Loup, St. Martin of Tours, St. Hilary, and St.
Donatus are all notable dragon-slayers, though the conflict was a mythical one, and their claim to regard on
this score is based really on their gallant fight with
either the heathenism of those amongst whom they
laboured or the heresy of false brethren.   The popular
saint, too, receives often more than his due at the hands
of his admirers, and legends gather thickly round his
name, and his so-called biography is often romance and
hero-worship from beginning to end.   St. Romanus at
Rouen, St. Veran at Arles, and St. Victor of Marseilles
are all accredited with feats of dragon-slaying; but leaving

them, St. Martial, St. Marcel, and many others to other
chroniclers, we content ourselves with referring to two
illustrious saints alone—the first because she is a lady,
and may therefore well claim our courtesy, the second
because he is our own patron saint.

It may not be generally known that the sister of
Lazarus, the St. Martha of our legend, together with Mary
Magdalene and two companions, Maxime and Marcellus,
wandered so far away from Palestine as the shores of
France. How much farther they may have intended
to go the history does not tell us, but the untoward
accident that stranded them on the shores of Languedoc
was a most fortunate circumstance for the people of the
district. The inhabitants of that region had been for
some time tormented by a monster who fed on human
flesh and had a most draconic appetite, and they at once
appealed to these strangers to help them. This alone
would seem to indicate the extremity in which they found
themselves, or they would scarcely have applied to four
shipwrecked strangers, half of them women, for aid in
the hour of their necessity. St. Martha, however, in
pitying consideration for their sad plight, at once agreed
to help them. She had hardly entered the wood where
the monster dwelt before the most frightful bellowings
were heard, at which all the people sorely trembled and
naturally concluded that this unarmed woman had fallen
a victim to her temerity; but this alarming bellowing
shortly ceased, and soon after St. Martha reappeared,
holding in one hand a little wooden cross, and in the
other a ribbon, with which she led forth her interesting
captive. She then advanced into the middle of the
town and presented the people with the dragon, as embarrassing a present as the proverbial white elephant; but
they seem to have risen to the occasion, for we find

afterwards an annual festival held in honour of the
Saint, while good King Réné of Anjou instituted an
Order of the Dragon for the more effectual keeping alive
of the memory of the event.   As St. Martha is more
especially set down in the "Lives of the Saints" as the
patron saint of good housewives, she might well have
been excused had she declined a service in itself so
dangerous and so far removed from the daily round,
the trivial task ; but the overthrowing of the mighty by
an instrument so weak gives additional point to the
story, and vindicates triumphantly the power of faith
over evil.

The "Legenda Aurea," written by Jacobus de Voraigne,
Archbishop of Genoa, in the year 1260, is what Warton
termed "an inexhaustible repository of religious fable."
For some centuries it was considered to have an almost
sacred character, and its popularity was so great that it
passed through an immense number of editions in the
Latin, Dutch, German, and French languages.   It should
have the more interest to us, too, from the fact that it
was one of the earliest of English printed books, Caxton
publishing the first English edition in 1493.   This was
followed by other editions by Wynkyn de Worde in the
years 1498, 1512, and 1527.   The following account of
our patron saint is taken from this source, a much less
favourable history being found in Gibbon's "Decline and
Fall of the Roman Empire." *

Once upon a time the neighbourhood of the city of
Sylene was infested with an enormous dragon, who,
making a "ponde, lyke a sea," which skirted the walls,
his usual residence, was accustomed to envenom the
miserable citizens with his pestiferous breath, and there-

* Appendix A.

fore they gave him every day two sheep for his dinner, and when these were spent they chose by lot a male and female, daily, whom they exposed to the monster. At length, after many of the rich had been compelled to sacrifice their offspring, the lot fell upon the king's daughter, a lovely maiden, and the idol of a fond father, who, in the bitterness of his grief, entreated his subjects for the love of the gods to take his gold and silver, and all that he had, and spare his child; but they replied that he had himself made the law, and that they had suffered in obeying it, and concluded by telling him that unless he complied with his own mandate, they would take off his head. This answer only increased the king's affliction; but being anxious to defer, if he could not avert, his daughter's death, he craved that a respite of eight days might be given her; and his people, moved, apparently, by the groans and tears of the sorrowful old man, granted his request. When the stipulated time had elapsed, they came and said to him, "Ye see how the city perisheth!" So the monarch bade his child array herself in her richest apparel, and led her forth to "the place where the dragon was, and left her there."

It chanced that St. George, who, like a true knight-errant, was travelling in quest of dangerous adventures, arrived at the spot not long after the king's departure, and was much astonished when he beheld so fair a lady lingering there alone and weeping bitterly, and riding up he asked the cause of her sorrow. But she, unwilling to detain him in a place so perilous, entreated him to leave her to her fate. "Go on your way, young man," she said, "lest ye perish also." But St. George would know the truth, so the maiden told him. Then was the knight's heart merry within him, and he rejoined, "Fayre doughter, doubte ye no thynge hereof, for I shall helpe thee in the name of Jesu Christe." She said, "For Goddes sake, good knyght, goo your waye, and abyde not wyth me, for ye may not deliver me." St. George, however, was of a different opinion, and indeed, had he resolved, upon second thoughts, to escape, he could not have done so, for the dragon, smelling human flesh from afar, emerged from the lake while the lady was speaking, and now came running towards his victim. Not a moment was to be lost, so St. George crossed himself, drew his sword, and placing his lance in the rest, rushed to meet the monster, who, little expecting such a rough greeting, received the weapon "in his bosom," and rolled over in the dust. Then said the victor to the rescued virgin, "Take thy girdle, and bind it round the dragon's neck;" and when the lady had obeyed her champion, the monster followed her as if it had been "a meek beeste and debonayre." And so she led him into the city; and when the people saw her coming they fled with affright, expecting to perish all of them; but St. George shouted, "Doubt nothing, believe in God Jesus Christ, consent to be baptized, and I will slay the dragon before your eyes." The citizens immediately consented, so the Saint attacked the monster, and smote off his head, and commanded that he should be thrown into the green fields, and they took four carts with oxen, and drew him out of the city. Then were fifteen thousand men baptized (without reckoning the women and children), and the king erected a church, and dedicated it to Our Lady and St. George, in which floweth "a founteyne of lyuying water which heleth seeke people that drynke therof." After this the prince offered the champion incalculable riches, but he refused them all, and enjoining the king to take care of the church, to honour the priests, and pity the poor, he kissed him and departed.

Some time after this marvellous event the Emperor Diocletian so cruelly persecuted the Christians, that "twenty-two thousand were martyred in the course of one month," and many others forsook God and sacrificed to idols. When St. George heard this he laid aside his arms, and sold his possessions, and took the habit of a "crysten-man," and went into the midst of the "paynims," and began to denounce their gods as devils. "My God," cried he, "made heaven and earth, He only is the true God." Then said they to him, "How dare ye defame our deities? Who art thou? —what is thy name?"—"My name is George; I am a gentleman and knight of Cappadocia, and I have left all to serve my Lord," replied the Saint. Seeing that the stranger was no common man, the ruler of that district endeavoured to gain him over with fair words, but finding the knight inflexible, he tied him aloft on a gibbet, and caused him to be cruelly beaten; and then, having rubbed salt into his wounds, he bound him with heavy chains and thrust him into a dark dungeon. But our Lord appeared to him that same night and comforted him, "moche swetely," so that the warrior took good heart and feared no torment which he might have to suffer. The chief magistrate, whose name was Dacien, finding he could not shake his prisoner's faith by the infliction of torture, consulted with an enchanter, who agreed to lose his head should his "crafts" fail; and taking strong poison, the wizard mingled it with wine and invoked his gods and gave it to the Saint, who, making the sign of the cross, thanked him kindly, and drank it off without injury. Astonished at the failure of his plan, the magician made a draught still more venomous, and finding that this also had no ill effect on the charmed warrior, he himself acknowledged the might of Christ, embraced St. George's knees, and entreated to be made a Christian,—and his request was immediately granted.

The provost's fury knew no bounds when he witnessed these marvels. He stretched the champion on the rack, but the engine broke in pieces; he plunged him into boiling lead, and lo! the Saint came out "refreshed and strengthened." When Dacien saw this he began to moderate his anger, and again had recourse to flattery, praying the Saint to renounce his faith and sacrifice to the idols, and, much to his surprise, the knight questioned him with a smiling countenance why he had not asked him before, and promised to do his bidding. Then the provost was glad indeed, and assembled all the people to see the champion sacrifice. So they thronged the temple where the Saint was kneeling before the shrine of Jupiter, but he earnestly prayed a while to the true God, entreating Him to destroy those accursed images and convert the deluded Romans,—"and anone the fyre descended from heuens and brente the temple and the ydolles and theyr prestes;" and immediately after the earth opened and swallowed up all the ashes. This last marvel only hardened the ruler's heart and strengthened him in his infidelity; he caused the warrior to be brought before him, and sternly reproved him for his duplicity. "Thenne sayd to him Saynt George, 'Syr, beleue it not, but come wyth me and see how I shall sacrefise.' Thenne said Dacyan to him, 'I see wel thy frawde and thy treachery; thou wylt make the erthe to swalowe me lyke as thou hast the temple and my goddes.'"

Then said St. George, "O catiff, tell me how thy gods help thee when they cannot help themselves?" Then was the provost so enraged that he ran to his wife, and, telling her that he should die of anger if he could not master his prisoner, requested her counsel. "Cruel tyrant," replied his loving spouse, "instead of plotting against this heaven-protected knight, I too am resolved to become a Christian!" "Thou wilt!" returned her husband furiously, and taking her by her flowing tresses, he dashed her against the pavement, when, feeling herself in the agonies of death, she craved of St. George to know her future lot, seeing she had not been christened. Then answered the blessed Saint, "Doubt thee nothing, fair daughter, for thou shalt be baptized in thine own blood." Then began she to worship our Lord Jesus Christ, and so died and went to heaven. Thither the martyr followed her very shortly, for Dacien caused St. George to be beheaded, and "so he perished." But the cruel persecutor did not long survive his victim, for as he was returning to his palace, says the legend, from the place of execution, "fire came down from heaven and destroyed him and all his followers." *

In the Middle Ages the dragon gave a title in Hungary to an order of knighthood, that of "the dragon over-thrown." This was established in the year 1418, to per-petuate the memory of the condemnation of John Huss and Jerome of Prague by the Council of Constance for heresy, and to denote the overthrow of the doctrines these men propagated in Hungary, Bohemia, and else-where in Germany, and for which they were ultimately burnt at the stake. The badge of the order was a dragon prostrate. In China the dragon is the symbol of the Imperial power, and all our readers who are familiar with the appearance of the Celestial pottery, bronzes, and so forth, will readily recall how commonly the form is introduced. Some little time ago the Chinese

* Appendix B.

Government permitted coal-mines to be opened at Kai-
ping, but they were speedily closed again, as it was supposed that their continued working would release the
earth-dragon, disturb the Manes of the Empress, and
generally bring trouble upon the Imperial house and upon
the nation.   Uncharitable people, however, have been
found to declare that the fear of the earth-dragon is all an
excuse, and that, as the Government set its face against
the introduction of railways, so it was equally prepared,
in its rigid conservatism and hatred of innovations, to
forswear the mining operations.   The dragon of the
Chinese designers is of the weirdest forms, and conceived with a freedom and wildness of fancy that puts
to shame our Western attempts, powerful as they often
are.

As a symbol and attribute the dragon is constantly
appearing in mediæval work, as carvings, illuminations,
and the like, and we may remind our readers that in the
term gargoyle, used in speaking of the strange and
monstrous forms often found in our old cathedrals and
abbeys doing duty as water-shoots, we get the dragon
idea again, as the word is derived from an old French
word signifying some such draconic monster.   While,
however, we find ourselves thus classing the dragon
amongst the mythical and arbitrary forms of the stone-
carver or the herald, we must be careful to remember
that its terror had not thus in earlier days lost its sting,
for the workman who sculptured it on a capital or thrust
its hideous form into any other noticeable position not
only regarded it as a symbol, but believed very really
and truly in its veritable existence.   Albertus Magnus
gives a long account of the creature, an account altogether too elaborate for us to here transcribe; but its
capture, according to him, is an easy matter enough if

one only goes the right way to work. It was fortunately
ascertained that dragons are "greatly afraid of thunder,
and the magicians who require dragons for their enchant-
ments get drums, on which they roll heavily, so that the
noise is mistaken for thunder by the dragons, and they
are vanquished." The thing is simplicity itself, and
rather detracts from the halo of heroism that has hitherto
surrounded dragon' vanquishers. A man is scarcely
justified in blowing his trumpet when he has previously
so cowed his antagonist by beating his drum and delud-
ing its dull brains with his fictitious thunder. Pliny says
that the eyes of a dragon, preserved dry, pulverised and
then made up with honey, cause those who are anointed
therewith to sleep securely from all dread of spirits of
the darkness. In a mediæval work we are told that
"the turning joint in the chine of a dragon doth promise
an easy and favourable access into the presence of great
lords." One can only wonder why this should be, all
clue and thread of connection between the two things
being now so hopelessly lost. We must not however forget
that, smile now as we may at this, there was a time when
our ancestors accepted the statement with the fullest
faith, and many a man who would fain have pleaded his
cause before king or noble bewailed with hearty regret
his want of draconic chine, the "turning-point" of the
dragon and of his own fortunes. Another valuable
receipt—"Take the taile and head of a dragon, the haire
growing upon the forehead of a lion, with a little of his
marrow also, the froth moreover that a horse fomethe
at the mouth who hath woon the victorie and prize in
running a race, and the nailes besides of a dogs-feete :
bind all these together with a piece of leather made of
a red deers skin, with the sinewes partly of a stag, partly
of a fallow deere, one with another : carry this about

with you and it will work wonders." It seems almost a
pity that the actual benefits to be derived from the
possession of this compound are not more clearly defined,
as there is no doubt that a considerable amount of
trouble would be involved in getting the various materials
together, and the zeal and ardour of the seeker after this
wonder-working composition would be somewhat damped
by the troublesome and recurring question, Wherefore? Mediæval medicine-men surely must have been
somewhat chary of adopting the now familiar legend
"Prescriptions accurately dispensed," when the onus of
making up such a mixture could be laid upon them.
John Leo, in his " History of Africa " says that the dragon
is the progeny of the eagle and wolf. After describing
its appearance, he says—"This monster, albeit I myself
have not seen it yet, the common report of all Africa
affirmeth that there is such a one." Other writers affirm
that the dragon is generated by the great heat of India
or springs from the volcanoes of Ethiopia ; and one is
tempted to take the prosaic view that this dragon rearing
and slaying is but a more poetic way of dwelling on
some miasmatic exhalation reduced to harmlessness by
judicious drainage ; that the monster that had slain its
thousands was at last subdued by no glittering spear
wielded by knightly or saintly arm, but by the spade of
the navvy and the drain-pipes of the sanitary engineer.
Father Pigafetta in his book declares that " Mont Atlas
hath plenty of dragons, grosse of body, slow of motion,
and in byting or touching incurably venomous. In
Congo is a kind of dragons like in biggnesse to rammes
with wings, having long tayles and divers jawes of teeth
of blue and greene, painted like scales, with two feete,
and feede on rawe fleshe." We cannot ourselves help
feeling that if we saw a dragon like in bigness to a ram

we should so far be disappointed in him. After having had our imagination filled by legend after legend we should look for something decidedly bulkier than that, and should feel that he really was not living up to his reputation. Abundant illustrations of the most unnatural history may be found in the works of Aldrovandus: his voluminous works on animals are very curious and interesting, and richly illustrated with engravings at least as quaint in character as the text. His "Monstrorum Historia," published in folio at Bologna in 1642, is a perfect treasure-house; the various volumes range in date from 1602 to 1668, and are, with one exception (Venice), published at either Bologna or Frankfort. If any of our readers can get an opportunity of looking through them they will find themselves well repaid.

Amongst the Lansdowne MSS. in the British Museum will be found Aubrey's "Gentilisme and Judaisme." His remarks on St. George and the dragon are sufficiently quaint and interesting to justify insertion here. "Dr. Peter Heylin," he says, "did write the Historie of St. George of Cappadocia, which is a very blind business. When I was of Trin. Coll. there was a sale of Mr. William Cartright's (poet) books, many whereof I had: amongst others (I know not how) was Dr. Daniel Featley's Handmayd to Religion, which was printed shortly after Dr. Heylin's Hist. aforesaid. In the Holyday Devotions he speaks of St. George, and asserts the story to be fabulous, and that there never was any such man. William Cartright writes in the margent— For this assertion was Dr. Featley brought upon his knees before William Laud, Abp. of Canterbury. See Sir Thomas Browne's 'Vulgar Errors' concerning St. George, where are good Remarks. He is of opinion that ye picture of St. George was only emblematical. Methinks ye picture of St. George fighting with ye Dragon hath some resemblance of St. Michael fighting with the Devil, who is pourtrayed like a Dragon. Ned Bagshaw of Chr. Ch. 1652, shewed me somewhere in Nicophorus Gregoras that ye picture of St. George's horse on a wall neighed on some occasion."

A vast amount of learning upon the subject of our patron saint may be found in Selden's "Titles of Honour," in which he treats of "The chiefest testimonies concerning St. George in the Western Church, and a consideration how he came to be taken for the patron saint of the English nation." Selden originally inclined to the idea that the saint first stepped into this exalted position in the reign of Edward III., but in "a most ancient Martyrologie" that he afterwards came across—one of Saxon date in the library of one of the Cambridge Colleges—he found a sufficient testimony that the position of the saint as patron of Britain dated from a much earlier time.

Peter Suchenwirt, a German poet of the fourteenth century, gives in one of his poems a very curious and striking illustration of the esteem in which at the battle of Poictiers the English soldiers held their patron saint :—

> " Di Frantzois schrienn ' Nater Dam ! '
> Das spricht Unser Fraw mit nam ;
> Der Englischen chrey erhal ;
> ' Sand Jors ! Sand Jors ! ' "

> " The French shout forth ' Notre Dame,'
> Thus calling on our Lady's name ;
> To which the English host reply,
> ' St. George ! St. George ! ' their battle cry."

The Celtic use of the word dragon for a chieftain

is curious : in time of danger a sort of dictator was appointed under the title of pen-dragon. Hence any of the English knights who slew a chieftain in battle were dragon vanquishers, and it has been suggested that the military title was at times confused with that of the fabulous monster, and that a man thus got an added credit that did not belong to him. The theory is not, however, really tenable, as all the veritable dragon-slayers had the great advantage of living a long time ago, and no such halo of romance could well have attached itself to men of comparatively modern times. In any case, too, the use of the Celtic word is very local, and does not meet the case of a tithe of the histories of such deeds of valour. The red dragon was the ensign of Cadwallader, the last of the British kings. The Tudors claimed descent from this ancient monarch, and Henry VII. adopted this device for his standard at the battle of Bosworth Field. There is a place in Berkshire called Dragon Hill, near Uffington, and the more famous White Horse Hill, that is in local legend the scene of the encounter between St. George and the dragon ; and for full confirmation a bare place is shown on the hillside where nothing will grow, because there the poisonous blood of the creature was shed. We learn, however, in the Saxon annals that Cedric, the West-Saxon monarch, overthrew and slew here the pen-dragon Naud, with five thousand of his men. The name of the hill, therefore, commemorates this ancient victory ; but the common folk of the district, who know nothing of pen-dragons, erroneously ascribe the battle won there to the more familiar St. George.

The dragon of Wantley deserves a passing word, since he supplies a good illustration of how the mythical and the material are often mixed up. Wantley is merely a cor-

ruption of Wharncliffe, a delightful spot * near Sheffield,
and here, of all places in the world, this very objectionable dragon took up his abode.   One ordinarily expects
to hear of such creatures uncoiling their monstrous
forms in some dense morass or lurking in the dark
recesses of some wide-stretching and gloomy forest ;
possibly he may have found the choice of such an
attractive locality may have helped him to an occasional
tourist.   On the opposite side of the Don to the crag
that held the cave of the dragon stood the desirable
residence of More Hall ; and its owner, doubtless feeling
that the presence of such an objectionable neighbour
was a great depreciation of his property, determined one
day to bring matters to a crisis ; so he walked up to the
mouth of the cave clad in a suit of armour thickly covered
with spikes, and administered such a vigorous kick in
the dragon's mouth, the only place where he was vul-
nerable, that the whole transaction was over almost at
once, and he was back again in ample time for lunch.
Dr. Percy, the editor of " Reliques of Antient English
Poetry," holds that we must not accept this story too
seriously ; that, in fact, the old ballad in which it is set
forth is a burlesque, and that the real facts are as follows :—
that the dragon was an overbearing and rascally lawyer
who had long availed himself of his position and influence
to oppress his poorer neighbours, but he capped a long
series of dishonest and disreputable actions by depriving
three orphan children of an estate to which they were
entitled.   A Mr. More generously took up their cause,

---

* Lady Mary Wortley Montagu lived here for some time.   Writing afterwards from Avignon, and dwelling on the exquisite landscape
there spread out before her when standing on the Castle height, she
exclaims that " it is the most beautiful land prospect I ever saw, except
Wharncliffe."

brought all the armoury of the law to bear upon the spoiler, and completely defeated him, and the thievish attorney shortly afterwards died of chagrin and vexation.

" Old stories tell how Hercules
   A dragon slew at Lerna,
With seven heads and fourteen eyes,
   To see and well discern-a ;
But he had a club this dragon to drub,
   Or he had ne'er done it, I warrant ye ;
But More of More Hall, with nothing at all,
   He slew the dragon of Wantley.

This dragon had two furious wings,
   Each one upon each shoulder ;
With a sting in his tayl, as long as a flayl,
   Which made him bolder and bolder.
He had long claws, and in his jaws
   Four-and-forty teeth of iron ;
With a hide as tough as any buff,
   Which did him round environ.

Have you not heard how the Trojan horse
   Held seventy men in his belly ?
This dragon was not quite as big,
   But very near, I tell ye.
Devouréd he poor children three,
   That could not with him grapple ;
And at one sup, he eat them up,
   As one would eat an apple.

All sorts of cattle this dragon did eat,
   Some say he did eat up trees,
And that the forests sure he could
   Devour up by degrees :
For houses and churches were to him geese and turkeys :
   He eat all, and left none behind,
But some stones, dear Jack, that he could not crack,
   Which on the hills you will find.

In Yorkshire, near fair Rotherham,
   The place I know it well ;
Some two or three miles, or thereabouts,
   I vow I cannot tell ;

But there is a hedge, just on the hill edge,
  And Matthew's house hard by it ;
O there and then was this dragon's den,
  You could not chuse but spy it.

Hard by a furious knight there dwelt,
  Of whom all towns did ring ;
For he could wrestle, play quarterstaff, kick and cuff,
  And any such kind of a thing ;
By the tail and the main with his hands twain
  He swung a horse till he was dead,
And that which is stranger, he in his anger
  Eat him all up but his head.

These children, as I told, being eat ;
  Men, women, girls and boys,
Sighing and sobbing, came to his lodging,
  And made a hideous noise :
' O save us all,· More of More Hall,
  Thou peerless knight of these woods ;
Do but slay this dragon, who won't leave us a rag on,
  We'll give thee all our goods.'

' Tut, tut,' quoth he, ' no goods I want ;
  But I want, I want, in sooth,
A fair maid of sixteen that's brisk and keen,
  And smiles about the mouth :
Hair black as sloe, skin white as snow,
  With blushes her cheeks adorning ;
To anoynt me o'er night, ere I go out to fight,
  And to gird me in the morning.'

This being done, he did engage
  To hew the dragon down ;
But first he went, new armour to
  Bespeak at Sheffield town ;
With spikes all about, not within but without,
  Of steel so sharp and strong ;
Both behind and before, arms, legs, and all o'er,
  Some five or six inches long.

Had you but seen him in this dress,
  How fierce he looked and how big,
You would have thought him for to be
  Some Egyptian porcupig :

He frighted all, cats, dogs, and all,
   Each cow, each horse, and each hog ;
For fear they did flee, for they took him to be
   Some strange outlandish hedge-hog.

It is not strength that always wins,
   For wit doth strength excell ;
Which made our cunning champion
   Creep down into a well,
Where he did think this dragon would drink,
   And so he did in truth ;
And as he stooped low he rose up and cried ' boh ! '
   And hit him in the mouth.

Our politick knight, on the other side
   Crept out upon the brink,
And gave the dragon such a crack,
   He knew not what to think.
' Aha,' quoth he, ' say you so, do you see ? '
   And then at him he let fly
With hand and with foot, and so they both went to't,
   And the word it was, hey, boys, hey !

' Oh,' quoth the dragon with a deep sigh,
   And turned six times together,
Sobbing and tearing, cursing and swearing,
   Out of his throat of leather ;
' More of More Hall ! O thou rascal !
   Would I had seen thee never ;
With that thing at thy foot thou hast pricked me sore,
   And I'm quite undone for ever.'

' Murder, murder,' the dragon cried,
   ' Alack, alack, for grief ;
Had you but missed that place, you could
   Have done me no mischief.'
Then his head he shaked, he trembled and quaked,
   And down he laid and cried ;
First on one knee, then on back tumbled he,
   And groaned, and kicked, and died."

We sometimes see allusions in poetry and the press
to the sowing of dragons' teeth. The reference is always
to some subject of civil strife, to some burning question

that rouses the people of a state to take up arms against
each other.

The incident is derived from the old classic legend
of the founding of Thebes by Kadmos. Arriving on
the site of the future city, he proposed to make a sacrifice
to the protecting goddess Athene, but on sending his
men to a not far distant fountain for water, they were
attacked and slain by a terrible dragon. Kadmos thereupon went himself and slew the monster, and at the
command of Athene sowed its teeth in the ground, from
whence immediately sprang a host of armed giants.
These on the instant all turned their arms against each
other, and that too with such fury that all were presently
slain save five. Kadmos invoked the aid of these giants
in the building of the new city, and from these five the
noblest families of Thebes hereafter traced their lineage.
The myth has been the cause of much perplexity to
scholars and antiquaries, but it has been fairly generally
accepted that the slaying of the dragon after it had destroyed many of the followers of Kadmos indicates the
final reduction of some great natural obstacle, after some
few or more had been first vanquished by it. We may
imagine such an obstacle to colonisation as a river hastily
rising and sweeping all before it in its headlong flood,
or an aguish and fever-breeding morass. The springing-
up of the armed men from the soil has been construed
as signifying that the Thebans in after times regarded
themselves as the original inhabitants of the country—
no mere interlopers, but sons of the soil from time
immemorial; while their conflicts amongst themselves,
as their city rose to fame, have been too frequently re-
flected time after time elsewhere to need any very special
exposition.

Another literary allusion in which the dragon bears

its part is seen in the dragonnades, those religious perse-
cutions which drove so many thousands of Protestants
out of France during the Middle Ages. Their object
was to root heresy out of the land. Those who were
willing to recant were left in peaceable possession of
their goods, while the others were handed over to the
tender mercies of the soldiery let loose upon them.
These were chiefly dragoons; hence the origin of the term
dragonnade; and these dragoons were so called because
they were armed with a short musket or carbine called a
dragon, while the gun in turn was so called because it
spouted out fire like the dreadful monsters of the legends
were held to do. On many of the early muskets this
idea was emphasised by having the head of a dragon
wrought on the muzzle, the actual flash of the piece on
its discharge issuing from its mouth.

One naturally turns to Shakespeare for an apt illustration of any conceivable point that may arise. The lover
finds in him his tender sonnets, the lawyer his quillets
of the law, the soldier the glorification of arms, and the
philosopher rich mines of wisdom. The antiquary finds
in him no less a golden wealth of allusion to all the
customs and beliefs of his day. In " Midsummer Night's
Dream " we find the lines—

> " Night's swift dragons cut the clouds full fast,
> And yonder comes Aurora's harbinger."

We get much the same idea again in the line in
" Cymbeline "—" Swift, swift you dragons of the night,"
and in " Troilus and Cressida "—" The dragon wing of
night o'erspreads the earth." " Scale of dragon, tooth
of wolf," and many other horrible ingredients are found
in the witches' caldron in " Macbeth," while in " King
Lear " we are advised not to come " between the

dragon and his wrath." King Richard III. rushes to his fate with the words, "Our ancient word of courage, fair St. George, inspire us with the spleen of fiery dragons." In "Coriolanus" we find another admirable allusion—

> "Though I go alone, like to a lonely dragon that his fen
> Makes feared and talked of more than seen."

In the play of "Pericles" we have the lines—

> "Golden fruit, but dangerous to be touched,
> For death-like dragons here affright thee hard."

And there are other references in "Romeo and Juliet" and other plays—references that it is needless here to give, as enough has been quoted to show our great poet's realisation of this scaly monster of the marsh and forest. In the last extract we have given, that from "Pericles," the golden fruit are the apples of the Hesperides, guarded by the dragon Ladon, foul offspring of Typhon and Echidna. Allusions to this golden fruit are very common amongst the poets, so we content ourselves with quoting as an illustration one that is less well known than many, from a poem by Robert Greene in the year 1598:—

> "Shew thee the tree, leafed with refinèd gold,
> Whereon the fearful dragon held his seat,
> That watched the garden called Hesperides."

The dragon, like the griffin, is oftentimes the fabled guardian of treasure : we see this not only in the classic story of the garden of the Hesperides, but more especially in the tales of Eastern origin. Any of our readers who have duly gone through much of the "Arabian Nights' Entertainments" will scarcely have failed to notice the employment of the dragon as a defender of gold and other hoarded wealth. Guillim, in his quaint

book on heraldry, says that these treasures are committed
to their charge "because of their admirable sharpness
of sight, and for that they are supposed of all other
living things to be the most valiant." He goes on to add
that "they are naturally so hot that they cannot be
cooled by drinking of water, but still gape for the air to
refresh them, as appeareth in Jeremiah xiv. 6, where it
saith that the ' wild asses did stand in the high places,
they snuffed up the wind like dragons.'" Any one who has
been in any mountainous district in hot weather will no
doubt have noticed the cattle fringing the ridges of the
hills like a row of sentinels. When we first observed
this, and wondered at it, in North Wales, we were at once
told that it was a regular habit of the creatures, that
they did it partly to avoid the plague of flies that haunted
the lower levels and the woodlands, but more especially
to get the benefit of any breeze that might be stirring.
While Guillim is willing to admit that even a dragon
can render valuable service to those who are so fortunate
as to be able to procure his kind offices, and induce him
to play the part of watchdog, he very properly regards
him, and such like monsters, as something decidedly
uncanny. "Another sort there is," he says, " of exorbi-
tant Animals much more prodigious than all the former.
Such are those creatures formed, or rather deformed, with
the confused shapes of creatures of different kinds and
qualities. These monsters (saith St. Augustine) cannot
be reckoned amongst those good Creatures that God
created before the transgression of Adam, for those did
God, when He took the survey of them, pronounce to be
valde bona, for they had in them neither excess nor
defect, but were the perfect workmanship of God's
creation. If man had not transgressed the Law of his
Maker this dreadful deformity (in likelihood) had not

happened in the creation of aminals which some Philo-
sophers do call *Peccata Naturæ.*"

The dragon, though, as we have seen, at times induced
to mount guard over other people's property, is ordinarily
a very Ishmaelite; his hand is against everybody, and
everybody's hand against him; yet would he appear, if
we may credit Pliny, to bear an excess and maximum of
ill-will against the elephant. The elephant always strikes
one as being such a great good-natured beast, as one
who could do so much mischief if he would, yet spends
his strength instead for the good of others, that it is
difficult to understand how he should in so pre-eminent
a degree have earned the ill-will of so potent an enemy.
The dragon would appear to be always the aggressor,
and the elephant has to defend himself as well as he
can against the uncalled-for attack : it is satisfactory in
this case to know that the scaly assailant sometimes fully
meets his match. In Book VIII. of Pliny's history we
read that "India bringeth forth the biggest elephants, as
also the dragons, that are continually at variance with
them, and evermore fighting, and those of such great-
nesse that they can easily clasp and wind them round
the elephants, and withall tie them fast with a knot.
In this conflict they die, both the one and the other;
the elephant hee falls downe dead as conquered,
and with his great and heavie weight crusheth and
squeaseth the dragon that is wound and wreathed about
him. Also the dragon assaileth him from an high tree,
and launceth himselfe upon him, but the elephant knowing well enough he is not able to withstand his windings
and knottings about him, seeketh to come close to some
trees or hard rocks, and so for to crush and squeese
the dragon between him and them. The dragons ware
hereof, entangle and snare his feet and legs first with

their taile; the elephants on the other side undoe those knots with their trunke as with a hand, but to prevent that againe, the dragons put in their heads into their snout, and so stop their wind, and withall fret and gnaw the tenderest parts that they find there." One does not quite understand how this last counter-plan of the dragon is effected, but it is evidently to be understood as equivalent to "checkmate."

In the "Bestiare Divin" of Guillaume this antagonism of the elephant and dragon is again referred to, and indeed we find it an accepted belief throughout the Middle Ages. Pliny's work was held for centuries in the greatest admiration, and to add "as Pliny saith" to any statement, no matter how wild, was considered amply sufficient. Guillaume's description of the dragon is as follows—"C'est le plus grand des animaux rampants. Il nait en Éthiopie: il a la gueule petit, le corps long et reluisant comme or fin. C'est l'ennemie de l'éléphant; c'est avec sa queue qu'il triomphe de lui: là est, en effet, le principe de sa force; sa gueule ne porte point venin de mort." The book of Guillaume is a fair type of several books of the sort written by ecclesiastics during the Middle Ages. Such books were an attempt to show that all the works of nature were symbols and teachers of great Scriptural truths; hence, while much that they give is interesting, their statements always require to be received with great caution. If the facts of the case got at all in the way of a good moral, so much the worse for the facts; and if a little or a great modification of the true state of the case could turn a good moral into one much better, the goodness of the intention was held to amply justify the departure from the hampering influence of the real facts. The MS. of Guillaume dates from the thirteenth century, and is at present preserved in the

National Library in Paris. The writer was a Norman priest. The work has been very well reproduced in a French dress by Hippeau, a compatriot of the writer.* As we simply wish in our extract to bring out the belief in the antagonism between the elephant and the dragon, we forbear to add any moral teachings that a more or less morbid symbolism was able to deduct from the supposititious fact; but we shall have occasion to quote again more than once from the " Bestiare," and doubtless the peculiar connection between scientific error and religious truth will have an opportunity of making itself felt in one or more of these extracts.

Referring back to the " 300 Animals," the natural history that was considered good enough for the people living in the year of grace 1786, we find, after the account of the Dart, "so called from his flying like an arrow from the tops of trees and hedges upon men, by which means he stings and wounds them to death," the following description :—" The Cockatrice is called the king of serpents, not from his bigness—for he is much inferior in this respect to many serpents—but because of his majestic pace, for he does not creep upon the ground, like other serpents, but goes half upright, for which cause all other serpents avoid him; and it seems nature de-signed him that pre-eminence, by the crown or coronet upon his head. Writers differ concerning the production of this animal. Some are of opinion that it is brought forth of a cock's egg sat upon by a snake or toad, and so becomes a cockatrice. It is said to be half a foot in length, the hinder part like a serpent, the fore part like a cock. Others are of opinion that the cock that lays the egg sits upon and hatches it himself. These

* Appendix C.

monsters are bred in Africa and some parts of the world."
In England it would appear, so far as we have observed
the matter, that the hens have entirely usurped the egg-
laying department, and we are therefore spared the
mortification of finding that our hoped-for chick has
assumed the less welcome form of a cockatrice, for we
shall see that the advent of a cockatrice is no laughing
matter. The book goes on to tell us that authors differ
about the bigness of it, for some say it is a span in compass and half a foot long, while others, with a truer sense
of the marvellous, realise more fully that bulk is a potent
element in all such matters, and at once make it four
feet long. Its poison is so strong that there is no cure
for it, and the air is in such a degree affected by its
presence that no creature can live near it. It kills, we
are assured, not only by its touch, but even the sight of
the cockatrice, like that of the basilisk, is death. We
read, for instance, in "Romeo and Juliet" of "the
death-darting eye of cockatrice;" and again in "King
Richard III."—"A cockatrice hast thou hatched to the
world whose unavoided eye is murtherous;" while in
"Twelfth Night" we find the passage, "This will so
fright them both, that they will kill one another by
the look, like cockatrices." After this we can scarcely
wonder at a certain vagueness of description, as those
who never saw the animal have full licence of description,
while those, less fortunate, who have had an opportunity
of studying from the life have forfeited their own in
doing so. The only hope of getting an idea of it would
be the discovery of a dead specimen, for we read that
"as all other serpents are afraid of the sight and hissing
of a cockatrice, so is the cockatrice itself very fearful of
a weasel, which after it has eaten rue will set upon and
destroy the cockatrice. Besides this little creature, it is

said there is no other animal in the world able to con-
tend with it." We can well imagine the indignant
astonishment of the cockatrice, after being for years the
monarch of all it surveyed, when the gallant little weasel,
strong in the triple armour which makes a quarrel just,
and duly fortified by the internal application of rue,
charges boldly home and takes him, *monstrorum rex*,
by the throat. At the time that our authorised version of
the Old Testament was made there was a sufficient belief
in the creature to make the translation of some Hebrew
word seem correctly rendered by the word cockatrice,
for we read in the book of Isaiah that one sign of the
millennial peace shall be that the child shall put his
hand, unharmed, upon the den of the cockatrice; and a
little farther on we find the passage, "For out of the
serpent's root shall come forth a cockatrice, and his
fruit shall be a fiery flying serpent." In the fifty-ninth
chapter the workers of iniquity are described as hatching the cockatrice egg, and amongst the judgments pronounced upon the impenitent Jews by the prophet
Jeremiah we find the verse, "Behold, I will send serpents,
cockatrices, amongst you, which will not be charmed,
and they shall bite you." The heraldic cockatrice is
represented as having the head and legs of a cock,
a scaly and serpent-like body, and the wings of a
dragon.

Guillim * in his "Heraldry" says that "the Cockatrice
is called in Latin Regulus, for that he seemeth to be a
little King among Serpents : not in regard of his Quantity,

---

* The reader must notice the near approach to similarity of name in
the Frenchman Guillaume, author of " Le Bestiare Divin," and in the
Englishman Guillim, the writer on heraldry, and at the same time make
due discrimination. They are men of widely different periods, and
approach our subject from wholly different directions.

but in respect of the Infection of his pestiferous and poisonous Aspect wherewith he poisoneth the Air. Not unlike those devillish Witches that do work the Destruction of silly Infants, as also of the Cattel of such their Neighbours whose prosperous Estate is to them a most grievous Eye-sore. Of such Virgil in his Bucolicks makes mention, saying, I know not what wicked Eye hath bewitched my tender Lambs." The belief in the evil eye has been almost universal, and may be found in tribes the most remote from each other either in distance or in time. If it were not that Guillim is so ostentatiously loyal, and, like all heralds, a zealous upholder of rank and state, one might suspect him almost of a touch of bitter sarcasm in ascribing royal rank to the cockatrice, not from his magnanimity, not from his noble bearing, not from his beauty, but from the power of inflicting injuries that he so especially displays. When we consider what sort of a sovereign politically, socially, and every way the second Charles was, Guillim's dedication of his book to him errs somewhat, perhaps, on the side of fulsome and sickening adulation :—" To the most August Charles the Second, King of Great Britain, France, and Ireland, Defender of the Faith, &c. Dread Sovereign, Here is a Firmament of Stars that shine not without your Benign Beam ; you are the Sun of our Hemisphere that sets a splendour on the Nobility : For as they are Jewels and Ornaments to your Crown, so they derive their lustre and value from thence. From your Breast, as from a Fountain, the young Plants of honour are cherisht and nurst up. Your vertuous Atcheivements are their Warrant and Example, and your Bounty the Guerdon of their Merit. And as all the Roman Emperors after Julius Cæsar, were desirous to be called Imperatores and Cæsares after him, so shall all succeeding Princes in this our Albion (in emulation of your Vertues) be ambitious to bear your Name to Posterity."

The Basilisk, to whom also was given the title of king of the serpents, was another of the stern, very stern realities of our forefathers, though, like the cockatrice, it has fallen a victim to the march of intellect. Its royal rank was bestowed upon it not from its pestiferous qualities, but from the crest or coronet it wears, or rather wore, as the species may now be considered extinct. Like the monstrous kraken of the Norway seas and the classic harpy or minotaur, down to the sheeted spectre that clanked its chains last century in churchyard or corridor, it has failed to make good its claims to our credence ; and even the great sea-serpent, that from time to time appears in the columns of the newspapers when Parliament is not sitting, will have to appear very visibly elsewhere as well, or the scepticism of the nineteenth century will disestablish it. The basilisk was by some old writers described as a huge lizard, but in later times it became a crested serpent. Exact accuracy on this point was impossible, as, like the cockatrice, the glance of its eye was death. Pliny says, " We come now to the basiliske, whom all other serpents do flie from and are afraid of ; albeit he killith them with his very breath and smell that passeth from him : yea, and by report, if he do but set his eye on a man it is enough to take away his life." Readers of Shakespeare will recall the passage in King Henry VI., " Come, basilisk, and kill the inno- cent gazer with thy sight ; " and again where the Lady Anne exclaims to Richard III., with reference to her eyes, " Would that they were basilisk's, to strike thee dead." Beaumont and Fletcher, too, in their " Woman Hater," speaks of " The basilisk's death-doing eye." Dryden avails himself of the same old belief, and makes

Clytus say to Alexander, "Nay, frown not so ; you cannot look me dead ; " and in another old poem, King's
" Art of Love," we find the lines, " Like a boar plunging
his tusk in mastiff's gore, or basilisk, when roused, whose
breath, teeth, sting, and eyeballs all are death." The
only way to kill the basilisk was held to be to cause it to
gaze on its own image in a mirror, when its glance would
be as fatal to itself as it had hitherto been to others.
To effect this, however, evidently presents many practical difficulties, and he must have been a bold man who
ventured on so perilous an errand, where the least
nervousness or mismanagement of the mirror would be
literally fatal in bringing the basilisk to a proper state of
reflection.

The basilisk is mentioned by most of the old writers,
by Dioscorides, by Galen, Pliny, Solinus, Ælian, Ætius,
Avicen, Ardoynus, Grevinus, and many others. Aristotle
makes no mention of it. Scaliger gravely describes one
that was found in Rome in the days of Leo IV., while
Sigonius and others are so far from denying the pos-
sibility of such a beast that they have duly set forth
various kinds or sub-species. Pliny, for instance, describes
a thing he calls the Catoblepas, while Ætius gives
details of another called Dryinus, each being only modifications of the basilisk idea. Where, of course, the whole
thing was purely a figment of the imagination, the multiplication of species presents no difficulty at all, and
it really makes little difference whether all the peculiarities and properties be focussed on one creature, or
whether they be divided by a three or a four, and due
distribution of them made to a like number of slightly
varying monsters. There is no doubt but that if Baron
Munchausen had turned his attention to this branch of
natural history, we should have had many more species

D

to record, and some of them probably still more wonderful than any at present described. The very indefiniteness of the descriptions gives them an added charm and affords full scope for romancing. Familiarity is undoubtedly likely to lead to contempt, and probably if the Zoological Society of London are ever able to add a basilisk to their fine collection of reptiles it will be a very disappointing feature.

The Phœnix had what we may be allowed to call a literary existence amongst the Greeks and Romans, but scarcely became a visible creation of the artist until the mythic fowl was accepted by the early Christians as a type of the resurrection of the body—an association of ideas that afterwards rendered its use very common, and Tertullian, amongst other early writers, thus refers to its symbolic use. According to a tale narrated to Herodotus on his visit to Heliopolis, the phœnix visited that place once every 500 years, bringing with it the body of its predecessor, and burning it with myrrh in the sanctuary of the Sun-god ; but the version on which the Christian moral and application is based is somewhat different. It is founded on the old belief that the phœnix, when it arrived at the age of 1461 years, committed itself to the flames that burst, at the fanning of its wings, from the funeral pyre that it had itself constructed of costly spices, and that from its ashes a new phœnix arose to life. This belief, which appears to us so absurd, was for hundreds of years as accepted a fact as any other point in natural history. The home of the phœnix was said to be at that delightfully vague address, somewhere in Arabia.

In Hoole's translation of the " Orlando Furioso " of Ariosto we have both the mystic bird and its very indefinite home thus referred to :—

"Arabia, named the Happy, now he gains;
    Incense and myrrh perfume her grateful plains;
    The Virgin Phœnix there in seek of rest,
    Selects from all the world her balmy nest."

We get the same idea again in Fletcher's poem of
" The Purple Island ":—

" So that love bird in fruitful Arabie,
    When now her strength and waning life decays,
    Upon some airy rock or mountain high,
      In spicy bed (fix'd by near Phœbus' rays),
    Herself and all her crooked age consumes.
    Straight from her ashes and those rich perfumes,
    A new-born phœnix flies, and widow'd place resumes."

These two extracts speak respectively of the virgin
and widowed phœnix. The latter idea can scarcely
be correct; widowhood implies the loss of a mate,
and the phœnix, we are told, is unique and alone
in the world. Pliny and Ovid use the masculine pro-
noun. The former writer's account of him, her, or it
will be found in the second chapter of his tenth book,
and runs as follows :—" It is reported that never man was
knowne to see him feeding; that in Arabie hee is held a
sacred bird, dedicated unto the Sunne; that he liveth
six hundred years, and when he groweth old and begins to decay, he builds himselfe a nest with the twigs
and branches of the cannell or cinnamon and frankincense
trees; and when he hath filled it with all sort of sweet
aromiticall spices, yieldeth up his life thereupon. He
saith, moreover, that of his bones and marrow there
breedeth at first, as it were, a little worme, which afterwards proveth to bee a pretie bird. And the first thing
that this young phœnix doth is to performe the obsequies
of the former phœnix late deceased; to translate and
carie away his whole nest into the citie of the Sunne,

near Panchæ, and to bestow it there full devoutly upon the altar."

It was one of the venerable jokes of our fathers that a man hearing that a goose would live one hundred years, determined to buy one and see whether this really was so; but this simple plan does not seem to have occurred to any of the ancients, for while Herodotus affirms that the phœnix lives five hundred years, Pliny as plumply and roundly asserts as a matter beyond doubt or contradiction that it is six hundred. Another authority, more precise, though perhaps not more accurate, brings it, we see, to just one thousand four hundred and sixty one, the odd unit giving a delightful appearance of extreme accuracy and precision that seems to challenge one to gainsay it if he dare.

In Ovid the fable is given with the fullest detail. The following lines from Dryden's translation let us into the secret of how the whole thing is managed. "Our special correspondent" could hardly be more precise :—

> " All these receive their birth from other things,
> But from himself the phœnix only springs ;
> Self-born, begotten by the parent flame
> In which he burn'd, another and the same ;
> Who not by corn or herbs his life sustains,
> But the sweet essence Amomum he drains ;
> And watches the rich gums Arabia bears,
> While yet in tender dews they drop their tears.
> He (his five centuries of life fulfill'd)
> His nest of oaken boughs begins to build,
> On trembling tops of palms : * and first he draws
> The plan with his broad bill and crooked claws,
> Nature's artificers : on this the pile
> Is formed and rises round : then with the spoil
> Of Cassia, Cynamon, and stems of Nard
> (For softness strewed beneath) his funeral bed is reared.

* Appendix D.

Funeral and bridal both : and all around
The borders with corruptless myrrh are crowned.
On this incumbent, till ethereal flame
First catches then consumes the costly frame ;
Consumes him, too, as on the pile he lies :
He lived on odours, and on odours dies.
   An infant phœnix from the former springs,
His father's heir, and from his tender wings
Shakes off his parent dust, his method he pursues,
And the same lease of life on the same terms renews.
When grown to manhood he begins his reign,
And with stiff pinions can his flight sustain ;
He lightens of his load the tree that bore
His father's royal sepulchre before,
And his own cradle : this with pious care
Placed on his back, he cuts the buxom air,
Seeks the Sun's city, and his sacred church,
And decently lays down his burden in the porch."

The phœnix was a good deal employed during the
Middle Ages, like the griffin, salamander, and other
mythical creatures, as a badge or heraldic device, one
of the most interesting illustrations being its use by
Jane Seymour. Queen Elizabeth then adopted it, and
thereby gave the court poets a grand opportunity of
yielding her that highly spiced flattery that was so much
to her liking. Sylvester, in his " Corona Dedicatoria,"
a poem written at a slightly later period, thus introduces
the title :—

" As when the Arabian (only) bird doth burne
  Her aged body in sweet flames to death,
  Out of her cinders a new bird hath breath,
  In whom the beauties of the first return ;
  From spicy ashes of the sacred urne
  Of our dead phœnix (deere Elizabeth)
  A new true phœnix lively flourisheth."

Shakespeare frequently employs the ideas associated
with the mythical bird in his writings, and seems to
have thoroughly mastered all that could be said on the

subject. Some half‑dozen passages may readily be quoted as illustrations of this. In "As you Like It," for example, we find the line, "She could not love me, were man as rare as phœnix;" and the idea of its unique character is again brought out in "Cymbeline," in the passage, "If she be furnished with a mind so rare, she is alone the Arabian bird." The destruction of the bird on its own funeral pile and the resurrection of its successor therefrom is several times referred to. In 1 Henry VI. we read, "But from their ashes shall be reared a phœnix that shall make all France afeared;" and in 3 Henry VI., "My ashes, as the phœnix, may bring forth a bird that will revenge upon you all;" while as a final example we may quote the line in Henry VIII., "But as, when the bird of wonder dies, the maiden phœnix, her ashes new create another heir."

Richardson ascribes an age of one thousand years to the phœnix, and adds a detail that many of the older writers seem to have missed; according to him the bird has fifty orifices in his bill, and when he has built his funeral pyre he treats the world to a melodious ditty through this novel wind instrument, flaps his wings with an energy that soon sets fire to the pile, and so perishes. There seems a hint of this vocal and instrumental performance in "Paradise and the Peri" where the poet Moore refers to

> "The enchanted pile of that lonely bird,
> Who sings at the last his own death lay,
> And in music and perfume dies away."

The Alchemists employed the phœnix as a symbol of their hopes and vocation, and in Paracelsus and other writers many curious details of its association with alchemy may be found.

In the annals of Tacitus we find references to what is termed the phœnix period. According to him the phœnix appeared on five occasions in Egypt—in the reign of Sesostris, B.C. 866; in the reign of Am-Asis B.C. 566; in the reign of Ptolemy Philadelphos, B.C. 266; in the reign of Tiberius, A.D. 34; and in the reign of Constantine, A.D. 334. It will seem from this that the phœnix cycle consisted of periods of about 300 years (another variation from the estimates of Pliny and other writers quoted). The old monastic writers draw ingenious parallels between our Saviour and the phœnix, both sacrificing themselves when their career is over, and both rising again in glory from their temporary resting-place. The fourth of the dates given above is at once the alleged date of one of these appearances of the phœnix and also that of the great sacrifice on Calvary.

Though it seems a tremendous drop from the mythical phœnix of Arabia and its dissolution in fragrant spices to the old Dun Cow in Warwickshire, yet the latter proved herself, if legends may be credited, a foe fully worthy of the prowess of a right knightly arm, and as deserving of our notice as the dragon-slaying of that valiant brother star of chivalry St. George himself. Sir Guy of Warwick takes a high place amongst the famous ancient champions, and Dugdale and other good authorities hold that the stories connected with his name are not wholly apocryphal, though doubtless the monks and other early chroniclers drew the long bow at a venture sometimes. Dugdale, in his " Warwickshire," A.D. 1730, writes—" Of his particular adventures, lest what I say should be suspected for fabulous, I will onely instance that combat betwixt him and the Danish champion, Colebrand, whom some (to magnifie our noble Guy the more) report to have been a giant. The storie whereof, however it may

be thought fictitious by some, forasmuch as there be
those that make a question whether there was ever
really such a man, yet those that are more considerate
will neither doubt the one nor the other, inasmuch as
it hath been so usual with our ancient Historians, for
the encouragement of after ages unto bold attempts, to
set forth the exploits of worthy men with the highest
encomiums possible ; and therefore, should we be for
that cause so conceited as to explode it, all history of
those times might as well be vilified.* And having
said thus much to encounter with the prejudicate fancies
of some and the wayward opinions of others, I come to
the story." We do not ourselves propose to "come to the
story," though it is all duly set down in Dugdale ; though
if the fact of Guy's Danish antagonist being a giant could
be fully substantiated, he might perhaps claim a place in
our pages. The date of the combat seems to have been
the year 929. The exploits of Guy were long held in
high favour not only in England but abroad ; we find
a French version dated 1525, and the British hero is
referred to in a Spanish romance which was written
almost a hundred years before this. Chaucer evidently
knew the story well, for he tells us that

> " Men speken of romances of price,
> Of Horne Childe and Ippotis,
> Of Bevis and Sir Guy ; "

while Shakespeare, in "King Henry VIII.," makes
one of his characters say, "I am not Samson, nor Sir
Guy, nor Colbrand, to mow them down before me."

In Percie's "Reliques of Antient Poetry" is a long
black letter ballad upon the exploits of Guy. It seems
unnecessary to quote it *in extenso*, so we pick out a verse

---

* Appendix E.

here and there, sufficient at least to show how doughty
a champion our hero must have been :—

" I slew the gyant Amarant
    In battle fiercelye hand to hand :
And doughty Barknard killed I,
    A treacherous knight of Pavye land.

Then I to England came againe,
    And here with Colbronde fell I fought :
An ugly gyant whom the Danes
    Had for their champion hither brought.

I overcame him in the field,
    And slewe him soone right valliantlye ;
Wherebye this land I did redeeme
    From Danish tribute utterlye.

And afterwards I offered upp
    The use of weapons solemnlye
At Winchester, whereas I fought,
    In sight of manye farr and nye.

But first, near Winsor, I did slaye
    A bore of passing might and strength ;
Whose like in England never was
    For hugenesse both of bredth and length.

Some of his bones in Warwicke yet,
    Within the castle there do lye,
One of his shield-bones to this day
    Hangs in the citye of Coventrye.

On Dunsmore heath I alsoe slewe
    A monstrous wyld and cruell beast,
Called the Dun-Cow of Dunsmore heath,
    Which manye people had opprest.

Some of her bones in Warwicke yett
    Still for a monument doe lye ;
Which unto every lookers viewe
    As wondrous strange, they may espye.

A dragon in Northumberland,
  I alsoe did in fight destroye,
Which did both man and beast oppresse,
  And all the countrye sore annoye.

My body that endured this toyle,
  Though now it be consumed to mold ;
My statue faire engraven in stone,
  In Warwicke still you may behold."

The origin of the story of the mythical dun cow is lost in obscurity, but in the north-west of Shropshire will be found an eminence known locally as the Staple Hill, and on this a ring of stones of the rude Druidic type seen in various parts of England, and most notably at Avebury, in Wiltshire. This circle is some ninety feet or so in diameter, and legend has it that this enclosure was used by a giant as a cow-pen. This cow was no ordinary creature, but yielded her milk miraculously, filling any vessel that was brought to her. She seems to have deeply resented the act of an old crone in bringing her a sieve thus to fill, construed it into a direct insult to her powers (though one scarcely sees on what ground), broke loose from her enclosure, and wandered into Warwickshire, doing enormous mischief, until her career was cut short by the redoubtable Guy. Bones of the dun cow may be seen in many places, a circumstance that is explained by telling us that on the victory of the knight over the cow he sent its bones far and wide over the district it had ravaged, as tokens of victory and a manifest proof that the monster was no longer to be dreaded. At Warwick a rib is exhibited : this is some seven feet long, and at Coventry there is a gigantic blade-bone some eleven feet round. In some cases these probably are the bones of whales, and in others of the wild bonasus or urus ; but it must be distinctly understood that they do not give credibility to the legend, but only, in fact, derive an added glory from being associated with it. In the fine old church of Chesterfield is another gigantic rib some seven feet or more in length and a foot in circumference. This rests on the altar-tomb of a now unknown knight, whose marble effigy is represented clothed in a suit of armour, and local tradition has naturally bestowed on the once nameless warrior the proud title of Guy, Earl of Warwick. Another big rib may be seen in the grand church of St. Mary Redcliff at Bristol. Near it used to be suspended a grimy old picture representing a fierce-looking dun cow, and, though the inference was sufficiently obvious, the sexton, in showing people round, used to boldly affirm that this undoubtedly was one of the ribs of the monster slain by Sir Guy. Both rib and picture may now possibly be removed in deference to more modern ideas, but they certainly were there within a very recent period. A third rib may be seen at Caerleon, once a place of much importance, but now an insignificant little town, and chiefly interesting from its association with the history of the great King Arthur. Caerleon boasts a museum containing a very valuable collection of Roman and old British relics, and here too is the rib in question. It has only recently been removed from the church, and it is, by the way, curious to note the association of these bones with churches in almost every case. In the church of Pennant Melangell, in Montgomeryshire, is another gigantic rib said by some of the natives to be that of a giant, while others affirm that it is one of the ribs of St. Monacella, to whom the church is dedicated. As the bone is over four feet long, her stature must have been something considerable altogether. Another big bone is in the church at Mallwyd, in the same county. In Buckland's "Curiosities of Natural History" it is stated that "the ribs of the dun cow at Warwick and the gigantic rib at St. Mary's, Bristol, are the bones of whales;" and in his interesting account of the whale he mentions that he found whale-bones in all parts of the country, one of them being a large blade-bone hanging from a ceiling in Seven Dials. Assuming, as we probably may, that most if not all of these big bones scattered over the country are those of whales, one is still at a loss to know how or why they got so scattered, and more especially why they were placed in the churches. The legend of the dun cow appears to afford a very convenient popular explanation of them, but one feels that there is a mystery that this account does not dissipate.

The Salamander received its full mythical development during mediæval times, though the older writers refer to it occasionally. We see in the writings of such men as Pliny the first steps taken towards the erection of that fabric of fancy and superstition that in the Middle Ages was reared on so slight a foundation. Pliny asserts that the Salamander is made in the fashion of a lizard and marked with spots like stars; that it is never seen during fair weather, but only in heavy rain; and that it is of so cold a nature that if it do but touch fire it will as effectually quench it as if ice were placed thereon. He, moreover, declares its poisonous nature—a nature that, according to later writers, is so noxious that the mere climbing of the tree by the animal poisons all the fruit, so that all who afterwards eat thereof perish without remedy, and that if one enters a river the stream is effectually poisoned, and all who drink therefrom for an indefinite date thereafter must die. Glanvil, a learned English Cordelier monk who lived in the thirteenth century, goes so .

far as to declare roundly, as though undoubted and historic
fact, that 4000 men of the army of Alexander the Great
and 2000 of the beasts of burden were lost through drinking at a stream that had been thus infected. It was in
the Middle Ages an article of belief that the salamander
was bred and nourished in fire, and we have ourselves
been gravely told that if the fires at the ironworks in the
Midland Counties were not occasionally extinguished, an
uncertain but fearful something would be created in them.
When the salamander is represented it is always placed
in the midst of flames. We see that the book to which
we have already frequently referred as that to which our
grandfathers went for instruction puts the poisonous
nature of the salamander in the following graphic way :
—"A man bit by a salamander should have as many
physicians to cure him as the salamander has spots."

The salamander is the well-known device of Francis
I. of France, A.D. 1515–1547, the monarch who met our
own King Henry VIII. at "the field of the cloth of
gold." On this occasion the French Guard had the
salamander embroidered on their uniform, and we also
find the device freely in the sculpture, wall paintings, and
stained glass at Fontainebleau, Chambord, Orleans, in fact
in all the palaces of Francis I. The motto adopted
with it was *Nutrisco et extinguo*, "I nourish and extinguish," a somewhat contradictory saying based on a
somewhat contradictory story, for while we are told on
the one hand that the salamander is reared and nourished
in flame, we are also told that "he is of so cold a com-
plexion that if he doe but touch the fire he will quench it
as presently as if yce were put into it." John, king of
Aragon, had, almost a hundred years before, adopted the
same device, adding to it the motto, *Durabo*, "I will
endure." Asbestos, though really, of course, of a mineral

nature, was, from its incombustible property, held in the Middle Ages to be the wool of the salamander. We are told that the Roman emperors had napkins of this material, and that if they became at all soiled they were thrown into the fire, the fierce heat quickly destroying all foreign matter. As the testing flames purified the good while they destroyed the bad, so we presume King Francis intended to hold himself up as a terror to evil-doers and a rewarder of the loyal and faithful. The motto is none the less faulty, however ; for while we find the king claiming both functions, it will be noticed in the legend that it is the fire which nourishes and the creature which extinguishes.

The writings of Pliny abound in strange ideas ; some of these he evidently set down without putting the statements to the test, but in many cases he shattered the old beliefs by bringing them to the crucial test of experiment. The story of the extreme frigidty of the salamander's body at once putting out the fiercest fire was a matter that he thus brought to the testing-point, the result being that the unfortunate victim of science was quickly shrivelled up and consumed. Another old statement, equally capable of being brought to the trial, was that if even the foot of a man came in contact with the liquid exuded from the skin of the salamander all his hair would fall off. Perhaps the reason why one statement was tested and not the other was that in the first case any ill consequences that might arise would affect the reptile, while the second would come home more closely to the experimenter himself.

In Breydenbach's travels we find a salamander included amongst the other animals, a position that it probably owed to its association with legend, for we also find in the same old author that the unicorn is frankly accepted as a beast that may be met with by the traveller. The book is interesting, too, as giving the first figure that had then been made of a giraffe, or, as he terms it, seraffa.* The existence of the giraffe was long afterwards denied by naturalists, and his seraffa was for a very lengthened period held to be but a myth. Breydenbach was a canon of the cathedral of Mentz, and seems to have been of a somewhat adventurous spirit, for despite all the difficulties of the undertaking—difficulties that in these days of steam-boats, railways, and through bookings we cannot at all realise—we find him visiting Sinai and the Holy Land. His travels were first printed as a folio volume at Mentz in 1486. This was a Latin edition ; but two years later we find one in German, and in less than ten years six different editions were called for in Germany, besides others printed in Holland and elsewhere for the benefit of those to whom both Latin and German were un-known tongues. The book is full of quaint woodcuts, and is altogether a treasure-house of history, natural and unnatural.

The salamander is commonly to be met with in many parts of Europe, but the real and the ideal creature are two very different things—as different as the deer-eyed cows quietly ruminating in their verdant pasturage are to the dun cow that taxed all the heroism of Sir Guy of Warwick, or as old grey Dobbin to Pegasus. The real creature is very similar in form to the newts that are so commonly to be found in ponds, but the salamander of Francis I. is more like a wingless dragon, while some of the mediæval heralds made it a quadruped something

---

* Representations of the giraffe are to be found in the ancient monu-ments of Egypt, the animal being part of the annual tribute brought by the vassal Ethiopians to the king of Egypt. These representations were, we need scarcely say, unknown to the naturalists of the Middle Ages.

like a dog. Such a creature, breathing forth flames, may be seen in the crest of Earl Douglas A.D. 1483.

Shakespearian students will recall how Falstaff rails at Bardolph, calling him the "Knight of the Burning Lamp," "admiral, bearing lantern in the poop," "ball of wildfire," and so forth, all compliments called forth from the effects of strong liquor on the rubicund countenance of Bardolph. He winds up by saying, "Thou hast saved me a thousand marks in links and torches, walking with thee in the night betwixt tavern and tavern, but the sack that thou hast drunk me would have bought me lights as good cheap, at the dearest chandler's in Europe. I have maintained that salamander of yours with fire any time this two and thirty years."

The salamander, like the toad, the slow-worm, or the water newt, is still held to be decidedly uncanny. In our younger days our seeking after such small objects of natural history was always held by wondering rustics as a foolish tempting of Providence, and we have repeatedly been told the most moving stories of the poisonous nature of all such creatures, and especially how newts developed the most alarming properties if interfered with, biting out pieces of the captor's flesh, and then spitting fire into the wound. Prompt amputation or death was the dire alternative offered, though in our own case matters never reached so dread a climax. "Them pisonous effets" were many a time in those by-gone days held in the hand that now guides our pen, The belief in such fatal powers must have a very disquieting influence on the rustics who hold it. When farm animals, as calves or colts, die mysteriously, some one is sure to start the theory that they have been bitten by an effet while drinking; and in view of such a belief even the fetching of a pail of water from the pond that too often supplies the drinking water in country places must appear attended with no little risk. The following graphic and amusing letter from one of the correspondents of the *Field* newspaper shows how the salamander is still regarded in rural France :—

"Returning homeward a few evenings ago from a country walk in the environs of D——, I discovered in my path a strange-looking reptile, which, after regarding me steadfastly for a few moments, walked slowly to the side of the road, and commenced very deliberately clambering up the wall. Never having seen a similar animal, I was rather doubtful as to its properties; but, reassured by its tranquil demeanour, I put my pocket-handkerchief over it, and it suffered itself to be taken up without resistance, and was thus carried to my domicile. On arriving *chez moi*, I opened the basket to show my captive to the servants, when, to my surprise and consternation, they set up such a screaming and hullabaloo that I thought they would have gone into fits.

"'*Oh! la, la, la, la, la!—Oh! la, la, la, la, la!*' and then a succession of screams in altissimo, which woke up the children and brought out the neighbours to see what could be the matter.

"'*Oh, monsieur a rapporté un sourd!*'

"'*Un sourd!*' cried one.

"'UN SOURD!' echoed another.

"'UN S-O-U-R-D!!!' cried they all in chorus; and then followed a succession of shrieks.

"When they calmed down into a mild sample of hysterics, they began to explain that I had brought home the most venomous animal in creation.

"'*Oh! le vilain bête!*' cried Phyllis.

"'*Oh! le méchant!*' chimed in Abigail; 'he kills

E *

everybody that comes near him; I have known fifty people die of his bite, and no remedy in the world can save them. As soon as they are bitten they *gonflent, gonflent,* and keep on swelling till they burst, and are dead in a quarter of an hour.'

"Here I transferred my curiosity from the basket to a glass jar, and put a saucer on the top to keep it safe.

"'*O Monsieur!* don't leave him so; if he puts himself in a rage, nothing can hold him. He has got such force that he can jump up to the ceiling; and wherever he fastens himself he sticks like death.'

"'Ah! it's all true,' cried my landlady, joining the circle of gapers; '*Oh! la la! Ça me fait peur; ça me fait tr-r-r-r-embler!*'

"'Once I saw a man in a haycart try to kill one, and the *bête* jumped right off the ground at a bound and fastened itself on the man's face, when he stood on the haycart, and nothing could detach it till the man fell dead.'

"'*Ah! c'est bien vrai,*' cried Abigail; 'they ought to have fetched a mirror and held it up to the *bête,* and then it would have left the man and jumped at its *image.*'

"The end of all this commotion was that, while I went to inquire of a scientific friend whether there was any truth in these tissue of *bêtises,* the whole household was in an uproar, *tout en émoi,* and they sent for a *commissionnaire* and an ostler with a spade and mattock, and threw out my poor *bête* into the road and foully murdered it, chopping it into a dozen pieces by the light of a stable lantern; and then they declared that they could sleep in peace!—*les miserables!*

"But there were sundry misgivings as to my fate, and, as with the Apostle, 'they looked when I should have swollen or fallen down dead suddenly;' and next morning the maids came stealthily and peeped into my room to see whether I was alive or dead, and were not a little surprised that I was not even *gonflé*, or any the worse for my *rencontre* with a *sourd*.

"And so it turned out that my poor little *bête* that had caused such a disturbance was nothing more nor less than a salamander—a poor, inoffensive, harmless reptile, declared on competent authority to be noways venomous, but whose unfortunate appearance and somewhat Satanic livery have exposed it to obloquy and persecution."

As the French word *sourd* primarily means one who is deaf, we get a curious parallelism of ideas between the salamander deaf to all sense of pity, and insensible to all but its own fell purpose, and the old idea of the deafness of the poisonous adder. "Deaf as an adder" is a common country saying, and the passage in the Psalms of David where we read that "the deaf adder stoppeth her ears, and will not heed the voice of the charmer, charm he never so wisely," naturally rises to one's mind. The deafness, it will be noted, is no mere lack of the hearing faculty, but a wilful turning away from gentle influence. It was an old belief that when the asp heard the voice of the serpent-charmer it stopped its ears by burying one of them in the sand and coiling its folds over the other.

In turning over the quaint pages of the " Bestiary " of De Thaun we find allusion made to a creature that is evidently the salamander again, though we cannot quite make out the reference to King Solomon. Like all such books written in the Middle Ages, everything is introduced to point some moral or religious truth, though it may at first seem difficult for our readers to realise what possible connection there can be between the dreaded "sourd" and any spiritual instruction. The

reference is as follows :—" Ylio is a little beast made like
a lizard.   Of it says Solomon that in a king's house it
ought to be and to frequent, to give an example.   It is
of such nature that if it come by chance where there
shall be burning fire it will immediately extinguish it.
The beast is so cold and of such a quality that fire will
not be able to burn where it shall enter, nor will trouble
happen in the place where it shall be.   A beast of such
quality signifies such men as was Ananias, as was Azarias,
and as was Misael, who served God fairly : these three
issued from the fire praising God.   He who has faith
only will never have hurt from fire." *

Like the salamander, the Griffin was to our forefathers
no mere creature of the imagination.   Ctesias describes
them in all sober earnestness as " birds with four feet,
of the size of a wolf, and having the legs and claws of
a lion.   Their feathers are red on the breast and black
on the rest of the body."   Glanvil says of them, " The
claws of a griffin are so large and ample that he can
seize an armed man as easily by the body as a hawk a
little bird.   In like manner he can carry off a horse or
an ox, or any other beast in his flight."   The creature is,
if anything, still more terrible when met with in the
description given by Sir John Mandeville :—" Thai have
the body upward as an egle, and benethe as a lyoun,
but a griffonne hath the body more gret, and is more
strong than eight lyouns, and more grete and strongere
than an hundred egles such as we have among us.   For
he hath his talouns so large and so longe and grete upon
his fete as though thei weren hornes of grete oxen, so
that men maken cuppes of them to drinken of."   Oriental
writers, who appear to have an especial delight in the

* Appendix F.

marvellous, go even beyond this, and the creature becomes
with them the roc, the terrible creature we read of, for
example, in the wonderful adventures of "Sindbad the
Sailor." Milton introduces the creature very finely in
his noble poem, as for instance :—

> " As when a gryphon through the wilderness
> With wingèd course o'er hill and moory dale
> Pursues the Arimaspian, who by stealth
> Has from his watchful custody purloin'd
> The guarded gold : so eagerly the fiend
> O'er bog, or steep, through strait, rough, dense, or rare,
> With head, hands, wings, or feet, pursues his way,
> And swims, or sinks, or wades, or creeps, or flies."

The Arimaspians were a one-eyed people of Scythia,
who braided their hair with gold and drew their supplies
of the precious metal as best they could from the stores
guarded by the griffins. The griffin has long been employed as a symbol of watchfulness, courage, and per-
severance, on account of this fabled treasure-guarding.
But Browne, who, as we have seen, took great delight in
vivisecting the vulgar errors of his day and generation,
discourses as follows on the matter—" Aristeus affirmed
that neer the Arimaspi, or one-eyed nation, griffins
defended the mines of gold, but this, as Herodotus
delivereth, he wrote from hearsay, and Michovius, who
hath expressly written of those parts, plainly affirmeth
that there is neither gold nor griffins in that country, nor
any such Animall extant, for so doth he conclude, ' Ego
vero contra veteres authores, gryphes nec in illa septen-
trionis nec in alius orbis partibus inveniri affirmarim.' "
Like the dragon, the griffin seems to have been a
good sort of fellow to deal with if you only took him the
right way, and though a terrible monster to encounter
if one had any burglarious intentions, he seems to have

served his masters with a singleness of purpose and bull-dog tenacity that were very much to his credit. In Ariosto's "Orlando Furioso" we read of a griffin-steed that flew through the air with its master on its back, and landed him wheresoever he listed.

The griffin was fabled to be the offspring of the union of the lion and the eagle ; it has the leonine body and stout claws of one parent, the hooked beak, keen eye, and wings of the other. The form is very often met with in heraldry, past and present, either as a crest or as a supporter to the arms. A very familiar example of their employment in this latter service will be seen in the arms of the city of London. It is also a very common form in Roman and Renaissance painting and sculpture. Gryphius, a celebrated French printer, adopted the creature as his device, and on his decease the following epitaph was written :—

> " La grande griffe
> Qui tout griffe
> A griffé le corps de Gryphe."

Though ordinarily written as griffin or griffon, the alternative rendering gryphon is somewhat more correct, as the word is derived from the Greek *grypos*, or hook-nosed, in evident allusion to its eagle-beak. Shakespeare frequently refers to the creature, but the only instance we need here refer to is where a considerable difference in the spelling of the word might lead some of our readers astray. The passage to which we allude will be found in "The Rape of Lucrece," where she

> " Like a white hind under the grype's sharp claws
> Pleads in a wilderness, where are no laws."

In the forests of Bohemia, we are told by Burton in

his "Miracles of Art and Nature," there is a little beast
called the Lomie, "which hath hanging under its neck
a bladder always full of scalding water, with which, when
she is hunted, she so tortureth the dogs that she thereby
easily makes her escape." Elsewhere he tells of four-
footed serpents, strange creatures that, unlike many of
his wonders—only to be found in Peru or India, or such
like distant lands—are to be seen as near home as
Poland. The people of Poland, we are told, are "boys-
terous, rude, and barbarous; nourishing amongst them
a kind of four-footed serpent, above three handfuls in
length, which they worship as their household gods,
tending them with fear and reverence when they call
them out to their repasts; and if any mischance do
happen to any of their family it is imputed presently to
some want of due observations of these ugly creatures."

Vegetable Lambs were another of the wonders of our
forefathers. The credulous Sir John Mandeville says
that in Cathay a gourd-like fruit is found that when ripe
contains "as though it were a lytylle lomb withouten
wolle." In the twenty-sixth chapter of his book the
lamb-tree is duly figured, and its peculiar fruit development
graphically delineated. In many old books of natural
history we find representations of some such creature
under the names of the Scythian or Tartarian lamb.
According to some old writers it was said to be purely
an animal, and although rooted to the ground, was held
to have so deadly an effect on vegetation in its neighbourhood that it effectually prevented the growth of all
herbage within the scope of its baleful influence. So
singular a creature naturally provoked attention and
curiosity, and in the earlier days of the Royal Society
the matter was considered quite worthy of their notice.
Naturally, also, the supply endeavoured to keep pace

*

with the demand, and as the belief in mermaids led to their fabrication and exhibition, so also the myth of the Scythian lamb took visible shape. One of these impositions was formerly preserved in the British Museum, not from any belief in it, of course, but as an illustration of the old belief.*

The reference to the mermaid reminds us that the sea no less than the land bore in ancient and mediæval days its full share of wonders. Of the mermaids we shall

have occasion to say more presently, as we propose to class together all those forms that are more or less human, and to deal with them separately; but the sculptures of classic antiquity or the fancies of the mediæval herald afford us illustrations of the sea-horse, the sea-lion, and many other quaint imaginings. On an antique seal we once even saw a sea-elephant, a creature having the forelegs, tusks, trunk, and great flapping ears of the African

* Appendix G.

elephant, yet terminating in the body of a fish, and duly
furnished with piscine tail and fins. The combination
was of the most outrageous character, and would seem
to indicate the limit possible to absurdity in this direction. When the ancient writers would desire to people
the vast unknown of air or sea their thoughts naturally
turned to those creatures of the land with which they
were more familiar; hence the denizens of the air or
ocean are not really creations at all, but adaptations,
wings or fins being added to horses, lions, and the like
according to the new element in which they were to
figure. Of these, the sea-horses that draw the chariot of
Neptune through the waves and the winged-horse Pegasus
are examples that at once occur to one's mind.

Pegasus or Pegasos, the offspring of Medusa and
Poseidon, was the symbol of poetic inspiration. Its
association with Perseus and Bellerophon, with the fountain of Peirene and the heights of Olympus, may all be
found duly set forth in classic story and engraved or
sculptured on the gems and marbles of antiquity. It is
also introduced in mediæval heraldry, but there seems to
be no reference in any book of this period to lead us to
suppose that it was then regarded as a living verity.
Shakespeare refers to it from time to time, but in one case
it is only as an inn-sign, and in another the very terms
employed indicate that the reference to it must be taken
in a poetic rather than a literal sense. The first of the
two to which we allude will be found in the " Taming of
the Shrew," and runs as follows:—

> "Signior Baptista may remember me,
> Near twenty years ago, in Genoa,
> Where we were lodgers at the Pegasus."

The second will be met with in the first part of " King

Henry IV. ; " it will probably be very familiar to many of our readers :—

> " I saw young Harry, with his beaver on,
> His cuisses on his thighs, gallantly arm'd,
> Rise from the ground like feather'd Mercury,
> And vaulted with such ease into his seat
> As if an angel dropp'd down from the clouds,
> To turn and wind a fiery Pegasus,
> And witch the world with noble horsemanship."

The arms of the Barrister Templars of the present day consist of the Pegasus on an azure shield. The original devices of the Templars were the Agnus Dei, a device that may still be seen carved on the Temple buildings in London, and two knights riding one behind the other on the same horse. This badge or device was originally chosen to denote the poverty of the order in its earlier days, but at a later day, when the symbol was misunderstood, these two rude figures of knights were taken for wings, and hence we get the modern device of the winged steed or Pegasus.

The Vampyre was another of the strange imaginings of our forefathers. It was thought that men and women sometimes returned, body and soul, from the other world after their death, and wandered about the earth doing all kinds of mischief to the living, one of their favourite pursuits being to suck the blood of those who were asleep, and these became vampyres in turn. The superstition took deepest hold in Eastern Europe, and is still an article of firm faith in Hungary and Servia. One reads ghastly stories of men unconsciously entertaining and sheltering vampyres and perishing miserably, of lonely travellers pining suddenly away, of the bodies of the dead being disinterred and the corpse found with the tell-tale stains of blood around its mouth, and the like; and we can easily see how such beliefs as this, or the wehr-wolf or loup-garou of the Germans and French, or the ghoul of the Arabs and Persians, would have a terrible effect on the minds of the superstitious. The vampyre was a terror of the night, since the corpse then, after lying in the stillness of the grave throughout the day, awoke to a fearful vitality. The forms it assumed were not always human, but were believed to be at times those of the dog, frog, toad, cat, flea, spider, and many other innocent creatures. Hence the contemptuous expression one sometimes hears used to deride a needless anxiety, "a mere flea-bite," could have had no counterpart in mediæval days, for the anxiety such a misadventure might create would be of the most alarming and harassing description. In old books one finds the most circumstantial details as to how to detect when one has been bitten, or to prevent further mischief. To this end the grave of the suspected vampyre was opened during daylight when his powers of evil were quiescent, the corpse was decapitated and the head buried elsewhere, a stake was driven through the body, and many other elaborate and horrible precautions were taken to prevent a recurrence of the nightly resurrection. On the whole, we may well congratulate ourselves that we do not live in "the good old times." Even now in country districts and amongst the uneducated one comes across such striking instances of superstitious belief and thraldom as suffice to enable us to faintly realise what it must have been when all alike were enwrapped in a dreadful bondage to unseen powers of evil far more intense than is now possible even to the few.

The vampyre bat, a native of South America, is so called from its blood-sucking propensities. It is the legend of the vampyre that has given the name to the bat, not the habits of the bat that originated the fable of the vampyre, for at the time that these legends of the destroyer were articles of faith in Europe, the American animal was quite unknown. The natural tendency towards exaggeration surrounded the vampyre bat with a mysterious horror, and having once gained its name of ill-omen, it became easy to rear upon it a superstructure of morbid fancy. The researches on the spot of Waterton, Darwin, and other reliable authorities show that the name is not altogether ill bestowed, as both Europeans and natives suffer severely from its attacks during the night, and the horses and cattle that are out in the pastures frequently return in the morning with their flanks covered with blood.

Though the Chameleon, unlike the phœnix, the griffin, or the basilisk, is a living verity, so large a body of fable has grown up around it that the animal is almost as mythical as those creatures of the imagination. The name is derived from two Greek words signifying "ground-lion," a name singularly inappropriate in every way, as it has nothing leonine in look or nature, while its organisation fits it especially for living on trees. When we consider the singularity of its appearance and the peculiarity of its habits, it is by no means surprising that it should have attracted attention; and when we recall the numerous erroneous beliefs current amongst our rustics in England in this nineteenth century in the matter of frogs, newts, slow-worms, and the like, we can hardly wonder at the superstitions that have surrounded it. The eyes of the creature are quite expressionless, and are worked perfectly independently of each other, so that one may be directed upwards and the other downwards at the same time, or turned simultaneously to front and rear. Its exceeding slowness of movement is another curious feature, and though this exposes them to easy capture when seen, for "*un Caméléon aperçu est un Caméléon perdu,*" it has its advantages in another direction, for a creature that takes some hours to advance a yard or so will certainly not attract attention by any sudden movement; and the assimilation in colour of its skin with the surrounding foliage is another great protection. The creature has a singular habit of puffing out its body until it is nearly as large again, and in this state it will sometimes remain for hours. The best known fact, however, is its capacity for changing colour, passing from green to violet, blue, or yellow; but this power of varying the tint has been greatly exaggerated. We have been told that if the creature be placed on any colour, as bright scarlet, it will assume that colour; but this is one of those fragments of unnatural history that will not bear putting to the test. The following lines of Prior convey aptly enough this popular but erroneous notion :— '

> " As the chameleon, who is known
> To have no colours of its own,
> But borrows from his neighbour's hue
> His white or black, his green or blue."

Aristotle was acquainted with the singular motions of the eyes of the creature, and his description may well have been taken from nature. At the same time, these old writers knew nothing of comparative anatomy or dissection and conducted no scientific *post-mortem* examinations; hence in all matters of internal structure they are often ludicrously in error, while the weakness of their statements is only perhaps equalled by the strength with which they are asserted. We are, therefore, not surprised to read in Aristotle that the chameleon has

no blood except in its head.   Pliny re-states all the errors
made by Aristotle, and further adds that it lives without
either eating or drinking, deriving its nourishment wholly
from the air, and that, though ordinarily harmless, it
becomes terrible during the greatest summer heats.
Even Pliny, however, could not believe everything that
was told him, though his powers of imbibing outrageous
notions were of the keenest, and whenever any old writers
deal with something more than usually incredible they
fortify their statement and evade personal responsibility
by adding "as Plinie saith."   Pliny, then, rejects the still
older idea that its right leg artfully cooked with certain
herbs conveys the power of invisibility on the eater, and
will not believe that the thigh of its left leg boiled in
sow's milk will induce gout in any one so injudicious
as to bathe their feet in this peculiar broth.   Neither
will he credit that a man may be made to incur the hatred
of all his fellow-citizens by having his gate-posts anointed
with another nasty preparation of chameleon.   As a set-
off to all this very unusual incredulity he hastens to adopt
the statement of another wise man, Democritus, that it
has the power of attracting to the earth birds of prey, so
that they in turn become the prey of other animals—a
most unselfish proceeding on the part of the creature, as
its own food consists of flies and such like small matters.
Democritus also asserts, and Pliny confirms him in the
assertion, that if the head and neck of the chameleon be
burned on oak charcoal it will cause thunder and heavy
rain.   One is lost in astonishment at the fertility of the
imagination in these old naturalists ; and though it is now
easy when one has once been put on the track of
discovery to surmise that the tail of a chameleon burnt
on walnut charcoal might produce snow or possibly
fog, much of the credit of the discovery should go to

the man who first gave the clue to these physiologico-meteorological influences. Aldrovandus, another man of science gifted with a strong imagination and the power of assimilating the fancies of others, informs us that if a viper passes beneath a tree in the branches of which a chameleon is resting, the latter will eject from its mouth a poisonous secretion that effectually rids the world of the equally venomous snake; and he further adds that elephants sometimes unknowingly eat a chameleon in the midst of the foliage on which they are browsing, a mishap that is rapidly fatal to them unless they can at once have recourse to the wild olive-tree as a remedy and antidote.

Many other strange beasts might engage our attention were it not that we have much new ground yet to explore,

for not only might we discourse of the strange beliefs that have clustered round these monsters, but of the equally strange fancies that have been associated with such familiar creatures as cats and dogs, hares and spiders, goats and mice, while in another section we must dwell on the equally unnatural fancies that have been associated with various plants. Before, however, passing to these we must refer to those strange imaginings, such as the troglodytes, centaurs, and pigmies, that owe more or less to the combination of the human with other forms—a large class that deserves a measure of attention that may well suggest the advisability of opening a new chapter for its benefit.

CHAPTER II.

THE creatures we have hitherto been considering—the griffin, the phœnix, the manticora or the sea-horse—have either been unmitigated monsters of the fancy, or else, like the salamander or the chameleon, so transformed by legend as to be scarcely less monstrous and unreal. Having the fear of Pope's oft-quoted line upon us, "The proper study of mankind is man," we leave for a while these fantastic imaginings, and turn to another class of forms scarcely less grotesque, but all agreeing in this, the presence in them of more or less of the human form and nature. This class of forms readily subdivides itself into three sections, which we propose to deal with in

F

the order in which we enumerate them. The first of these are forms compounded of the human and the animal, as, for example, the sphinx or the centaur ; the second may be considered as human, though distorted, as the one-eyed cyclops, or, " the men whose heads do grow beneath their shoulders ; " while the third class may be held to embrace the fairies, pigmies, and giants, forms that are human, yet in bulk or minuteness bear no semblance to ordinary humanity.

The Sphinx may be considered as more especially an artistic and symbolic creation, though the old Greek myth of Œdipos would seem to show that in very early times there was a real belief in a real monster. The sphinx is composite in nature, being in Greek art and legend ordinarily the combination of the head and bust of a woman with the body of a lion and the wings of an eagle ; while in Egyptian art the creature is always wingless, and its recumbent leonine body is surmounted by the head of a man, hawk, or other creature. Egyptian art is full of such composite monsters, and in cases where such attributes as the courage of the lion or the wisdom of the serpent were to be expressed, it was held that the actual leonine body or the head of the serpent itself would best convey the required characteristics to the eye and mind of the beholder. A reference to Wilkinson, Rosellini, or any other good standard work on Egypt, will reveal an immense variety of these curious composite figures, though, as they are evidently in most cases symbolic merely, they scarcely fall within the limits of our present study. According to some authorities, the well-known type of Egyptian sphinx represented the royal power by its junction in one creation of the highest physical and mental strength. Pliny, however, states that it is to be taken as the representation of the beneficent Nile, as the annual rising took place while the sun was in Leo and Virgo. As the head is masculine in type, and not that of maiden fair, this theory will scarcely meet the case.

The sphinx of classic story, a monster half-woman, half-lion, was sent by Hera to devastate the land of Thebes in revenge for an insult that had been offered to her. Sitting by the roadside, the sphinx put to every passer-by the celebrated riddle, "What creature walks on four legs in the morning, on two legs at noon, and on three in the evening?" As one after another of these luckless travellers was obliged to "give it up" he was cast from the rock on which the monster sat into a deep abyss at its foot. The understanding was, that if any one could solve this conundrum the sphinx should herself perish, a consummation devoutly to be wished. One Œdipos hit upon the happy idea that perhaps it was a man that was meant, his career being traced through crawling infancy to stalwart manhood, and thence to tottering old age. Probably the sphinx had presumed too thoroughly on the badness of the riddle, and thought that its inane character would be her safeguard in this perilous game for forfeits. Lord Bacon * supplies a curious theory in explanation of the Greek legend; he tells us that the creature represented science, her composite nature being the various and different branches of which it is composed; that the female face denoted volubility of speech, while the wings showed the rapidity with which knowledge could be diffused. Her hooked talons are supposed to remind us of the arguments of science laying hold of the mind. Her position on the crag is a hint that the road to knowledge is steep and difficult, while

* Appendix H.

the riddles of science "perplex and harass the mind." Probably our readers have already made up their minds as to the value of this theory of Bacon's; it appears to us that fifty other equally good explanations might be devised, and all equally wide of the mark. Of course after so sweeping a statement we can scarcely be expected to supply one ourselves for the other forty-nine critics to mercilessly dissect.

The Chimæra was, according to Hesiod, a fire-breathing monster compounded of lion, goat, and serpent, having three heads, one of each of these creatures. It is in this form often represented in classic art; but Coats, a great authority in blazonry in the last century, in describing the monster departs somewhat from the ancient type, and in so doing brings the creature within the scope of our present chapter. He speaks of it as "an imaginary creature invented by the Poets, and represented by them as having the Face of a beautiful Maiden, the two Fore-legs and the Main of a Lyon, the Body like a Goat, the hinder-legs like a Griffin, and the Tayl like a Serpent or Dragon turned in a Ring." He does not, however, give his authorities. Though Milton in his "Paradise Lost" gives us the line, "Gorgons, and Hydras, and Chimæras dire," the myth has been received amongst ourselves with so little faith that anything wildly improbable is branded as chimerical, and scouted accordingly.

The Centaurs are said by Virgil and Horace to have dwelt in Thessaly, a land then greatly famed for its breed of horses. Instances, as in the landing of the Spaniards in America, have not been unknown where those to whom the horse was unknown have imagined that the horse and his rider were but one creature. The belief in centaurs is not, therefore, so difficult a myth to trace to its origin as many others. The usual form of representation is the conjoining of the body and legs of a horse and the head, arms, and body of a man so far as the waist, though in some early works, as, for example, in archaic pottery in the British Museum, the legs of the man take the place of the fore-legs of the horse. The celebrated statue in the Louvre known as the Borghese Centaur, a sculpture of the most refined period of Greek art, gives the best idea, perhaps, of the highest treatment the form permits. Other fine examples, fragments of the sculpture of the Parthenon, may be seen in our own national collection in London.* In the works of the earlier writers, as Homer, the centaurs have nothing unnatural in their composition; we read nothing of their being half-horse, half-man, but they are introduced to us as a tribe of men whose home was in the mountains and whose nature was altogether barbarous and ferocious. The contests with centaurs, so favourite a subject in Greek art, have been generally conceived to be the struggle of Greek civilisation with the barbarism of the tribes with which it came in contact in the early Pelasgian period, a struggle that strangely enough finds its memorial not only in the grand sculptures of the matchless Parthenon, but in the delicate beauty of a little English wild flower, the pink centaury.†

Isidore refers to a creature called the Onocentaur, "which has the shape of a man down to the waist, and behind has the make of an ass."

As the centaurs are frequently represented as bearing bows and arrows, the Sagittarius of the heralds (such, for instance, as that assigned as the armorial bearing of King Stephen or the sign of the Zodiac of the same

* Appendix I.   † Appendix J.

name) is ordinarily represented in this half-human,
half-equine form, though it is, of course, obvious on a
moment's consideration of the real meaning and deriva-
tion of the word, that this is but a narrow and arbitrary
limitation, and that Robin Hood, for example, or William
Tell, to say nothing of "A, the archer that shot at a frog,"
might as readily, in fact, be called a Sagittarius as any
Thessalian centaur.

Other partly human, partly animal forms often found
in classic art and literature are those of the Satyrs
and the Fauns. The satyrs are represented as having
bristly hair, ears sharply pointed like those of animals,
low sensual faces, small horns growing out of the top
of the forehead, and a tail like that of a horse or goat.
These satyrs, Greek in their conception, are often
confounded with the fauns of the Romans, creatures
half-man and half-goat, the head, like that of the satyrs,
being horned. Our readers will doubtless recall the
lines in "Hamlet:"—

> "So excellent a king, that was to this,
> Hyperion to a satyr."

These woodland sprites, as attendants on Pan, Bacchus,
and Silenus, are often represented in classic art, and were
a firm article of belief in those early ages. Thorwaldsen
and other modern sculptors have also introduced them in
their work, and they were often a feature in the quaint
processions of the Guilds of the Middle Ages.*

The Harpys, three in number, were creatures employed,
according to the belief of the Greeks and Romans, by the
higher gods as the instruments for the punishment of the
crimes of men. Their bodies were those of vultures, their

* Appendix K.

heads those of women, and it was their evil property to contaminate everything they touched. They are not infrequently represented in classic art ; several examples of their introduction may be seen on vases in the British Museum, and notably on some bas-reliefs from a monument brought from Xanthus, in Lycia, and commonly, from the subjects of these sculptures, called the Harpy Tomb—a monument dating probably from about the sixth century before the Christian era. Homer mentions but one harpy, Hesiod gives two, but all later writers mention three. Milton refers to these creatures in his " Paradise Lost," Book II., in the lines :—

> " Thither by harpy-footed Furies hal'd
> At certain revolutions all the damn'd are brought."

Shakespeare, too, in his " Much Ado About Nothing," Act ii. scene 1, mentions the creature, though in a more indirect way, using the word, as we from time to time find it employed elsewhere, as typical of one who wants to seize on everything and get people into his own power— " a regular harpy." Another reference will be found in the third scene in the third act of the " Tempest," where Ariel in the midst of thunder and lightning enters as a harpy and addresses those before him as follows :—" I have made you mad. . . . I and my fellows are ministers of fate." In " Pericles," again, Act iv. scene 4, we find Cleon exclaiming—

> " Thou art like the harpy,
> Which, to betray, dost with thine angel's face
> Seize with thine eagle's talons."

In the " Monstrorum Historia " of Aldrovandus * we

* Appendix L.

find figured a mediæval rendering of the creature, and Guillim in his " Heraldry " seems to frankly accept the harpy as a real thing, while the lines he quotes in support from Virgil are powerfully descriptive :—

> " Of Monsters all, most Monstrous this : no greater Wrath
> God sends 'mongst Men : it comes from depth of pitchy Hell :
> With Virgin's Face, but Womb like Gulf unsatiate hath,
> Her Hands are Griping claws, her Colour pale and fell."

Virgil, it will be noticed, makes the creature wholly fearful, while Shakespeare makes the horror yet more weird by giving the implacable and destroying monster a face of angelic sweetness.

Upton, another old writer on heraldry, says that in blazoning arms "the Harpy should be given to such persons as have committed Manslaughter, to the End that by the often view of their Ensigns they might be moved to bewail the Foulness of their Offence." This we should imagine, is more simple in theory than in practice, and Upton must have been very simple himself to fancy that any one could thus be induced to blazon their misdoings abroad like that. In the earlier days of heraldry the monarch had two powerful means of rewarding or punishing his nobles in what were termed respectively marks of augmentation and of abatement in their armorial bearings, but in the later times in which Upton lived no such compulsory stigma was possible. We fancy, too, that in the earlier days a good deal of what a modern judge and jury would call manslaughter went on, and was not by any means considered a foul offence to be bewailed over.

The terrible Echidna, half-woman, half-serpent, the mother of the dread chimæra, the fierce dragon of the Hesperides, the gorgons that turned to stone all who gazed on them, the hydra of the Lernean marsh, the vulture that made itself so decidedly unpleasant to Prometheus, and several other children of an equally objectionable type, was another of the monsters once believed in, while the better known Sirens and Mermaids, half-woman, half-fish, will naturally occur to the minds of our readers.

The Sirens were originally nymphs, but Demeter transformed them into beings half-women, half-birds, for reasons that may be found duly set forth in any work on mythology. Ultimately they were again transformed into creatures of which the upper portion was that of a beautiful woman, while the lower was fish-like. These sirens dwelt in the cliffs on the Sicilian shore, and by the sweetness of their voices bewitched passing travellers, who, allured by the charms of their song, were drawn to them, when they were lulled into insensibility and perished. Skeletons lay thickly round their dwelling, but the warning was useless and hopeless, as the sirens were allowed by the gods to retain this cruel power over the hearts of men until one arose who could defy their sweet allurements. Orpheus and Odysseus each fulfilled the conditions, and thus the evil power of the sirens came to an end. Orpheus, by the unsurpassable sweetness of his own music and his hymns of praise to the gods, carried himself and his crew safely past the spot so fatal to others ; while Odysseus stopped the ears of his crew with wax, that they might be deaf to the bewitching music, while he himself was bound to the mast, and incapable, therefore, of yielding to the soft fascination. It has been surmised that the whole story can be explained by the soft beating and melodious murmur of the waves over the hidden shoals and sands that would engulf those who would attempt to land. However this may be, the sirens

were at one time a firm article of belief, and are often
represented in ancient art or referred to in ancient
poetry, while later moralists find the simile an apt one
between the siren-song and its tragic effects and all
earthly pleasures that carry within them the seeds of
death.* A later legend of the same type may be seen
in the myth of the Lurlei, a water-spirit whose home was
in the steep cliff that overshadows the Rhine near St.
Goar, the fairness of whose person was as great as the
unfairness of her conduct in luring to their destruction
the passing travellers.   Here again, of course, matter-of-
fact people have stepped in and explained all away, a
striking echo and a rock on which to strike being all that
is left to us, the moral being, that if people will be so
foolish as to awaken by bugle or song the slumbering
voices of the rocks when they ought to be giving their
whole attention to their steering, what wonder if they
come to grief?   A very good reference to the siren's
lulling song will be found in the second scene in the
third act of the " Comedy of Errors."

Mermaids and Tritons were once fully accepted facts,
and illustrations of them, literary or artistic, abound,
Ariel in the " Tempest " sings of the sea-nymphs, and
Oberon in the " Midsummer Night's Dream " speaks of

> " A mermaid on a dolphin's back,
> Uttering such dulcet and harmonious breath,
> That the rude sea grew civil at her song ;
> And certain stars shot madly from their spheres,
> To hear the sea-maid's music."

Shakespeare seems to have made a very natural error
in confounding the mermaids and the sirens together, for

* Appendix M.

in the "Comedy of Errors" his allusion to the one is
in language more adapted to the other :—

> " Her fair sister,
> Possessed with such a gentle sovereign grace,
> Of such enchanting presence and discourse,
> Hath almost made me traitor to myself.
> But, lest myself be guilty to' self-wrong,
> I'll stop mine ears against the mermaid's song."

Another illustration of this will be found in the third
part of King Henry VI., a passage peculiarly appropriate
to our present purpose, as it embodies in a concentrated
form no less than three of the items of unnatural history
we have already dealt with—the siren's death-dealing
charms, the death-giving glance of the basilisk, and the
changing tints of the chameleon, besides referring to
the hypocritical tears of the crocodile.   The passage will
be found in the second scene of the third act, where
Gloster exclaims—

> " I can smile, and murther while I smile,
> And cry, content, to that which grieves my heart ;
> And wet my cheeks with artificial tears,
> And frame my face to all occasions.
> I'll drown more sailors than the mermaid shall ;
> I'll slay more gazers than the basilisk ;
> I'll play the orator as well as Nestor ;
> Deceive more slily than Ulysses could ;
> And like a Sinon take another Troy :
> I can add colours to the chameleon."

Other references will be found in " Hamlet " and in
" Antony and Cleopatra."

It has been conjectured that the ancients derived their
idea of the mermaid from the Manatees that may be
found on the shores of Africa washed by the Atlantic, or
from the Dugongs of the littoral of the Indian Ocean.
These singular animals have been placed by naturalists

in a class by themselves and called Sirenia. They have
a curious habit of swimming with their heads and necks
above water. They thus bear some grotesque and remote
resemblance to the human form, and may have given rise
to the poetical tales of mermaids and sirens found in
ancient literature. When the female Dugong is nursing
her offspring the position assumed is almost identical
with that of a human mother. The sea-lions and seals
have the same habit of raising themselves in a semi-erect
position in the water, and the intelligent aspect of their
faces gives them at a little distance a close resemblance to
human beings—a resemblance often equally striking when
they are seen recumbent on the rocks. It is but little
strange, that early navigators with all the superstitions of
their race, and having a very slight knowledge of natural
history, should be deceived, when we find in Scoresby's
Voyages the incident narrated of the surgeon of his ship
so deceived by one of these creatures that he reported
that "he had seen a man with his head just above the
surface of the water." At the same time, it appears to us
at least as probable that the mermaid, like the sea-horses
of Poseidon, was purely a creature of the imagination.

From the graceful beauty of the mermaiden to the less
pleasing physiognomy of "Mistress Tannakin Skimker, the
hog-faced gentlewoman." is a great step indeed, yet both
beliefs bear testimony alike to the universal desire after
something wonderful and outside the ordinary course of
nature, a feeling that in its lowest form finds satisfaction
in paying a penny to see a six-legged lamb, while more
cultured minds revel in the wealth of fancy found in the
myths of Hellas. The unhappy lady who has prompted
our present remarks was bewitched at her birth on the
understanding that she should recover her true shape on
being married. She was born, we are told, in 1618 in a

town on "the River Rhyne." Our authority, a book dated
the year 1640, gives various facts, but does not say
whether any one was so courageous as to remove the
spell by offering her marriage. The book is embellished
(or otherwise) with a portrait of the luckless Tannakin.
While referring to the one old book our thoughts naturally
turn to another of a similar type, the "Humana Physiog-
nomonia" of Porta, a book published in the year 1601.
It is full of curious woodcuts showing the great resemblance sometimes seen between the features of men and
those of some of the lower animals.

Old Burton tells us, in his "Miracles of Art and
Nature" (A.D. 1678), of a creature found in Brazil that
had "the face of an Ape, the foot of a Lyon, and all the
rest of a Man," and he almost needlessly adds, "a Beast
of a most terrible aspect." This is not by any means
the only wonder in that vast and distant land, and he
winds up his description by asserting that "it may be
said of Brasill as once of Africk, every day some New
Object of Admiration." In his account of India he tells
us of dog-headed men, while in the Oriental Isles, besides
a river plentifully stored with fish, yet so hot that it scalds
the flesh of any man or beast thrown therein, there are
men with tails.

Numerous other instances might readily be given of
strange combinations of the human form with that of
some animal, but enough has been given as an illustration of the sort of thing to be freely met with in
ancient and mediæval history; so we pass to our second
division of humanity—those who are wholly human, yet
in some way of so marked a departure from the ordinary
type of mankind as to come within the scope of our
strange history. These modifications sometimes arise
from the suppression of some part, as in the case of the

headless people ; in its exaggeration, as in the instance of the men of India whose ears sweep the ground as they walk ; or in the multiplication or subtraction of various members, as in the one-eyed Cyclops or the hundred-armed Briaræus.

One of the most notable beliefs in mediæval times was that in the headless people :—

> " The Anthropophagi, and men whose heads
> Do grow beneath their shoulders."

Of the Anthropophagi we may read in Eden's " Historie of Travayle," a book published in the year 1577. The word in its literal sense means man-eaters or cannibals.* Eden, in the passage to which we have referred, speaks of these as "the wilde and myschevous people called Canibales or Caribes, whiche were accustomed to eate man's fleshe, and called of the old writers Anthropophagi, molest them exceedingly, invading their countrey, takyng them captive, kyllying and eatyng them." Our old author, it will be seen, speaks of still older writers, but these we have been unable to lay hands on.

Halliwell, in his noble edition of Shakespeare's Plays, comments on the opinion of Pope and other writers, that the lines we have quoted from "Othello" were perhaps originally the interpolation of the players, or at best a mere piece of trash admitted to humour the lower class of the audience. He, as we imagine, very justly combats this idea, holding that the case was probably the very reverse of this, and that the poet rather desired to commend his play to the more curious and refined amongst his auditors by alluding here to some of the most extraordinary passages in Sir Walter

---

* From the Greek words *anthropos*, a man ; and *phago*, to eat.

Raleigh's account of his celebrated voyage to Guiana in
1595. Nothing excited more universal attention than the
accounts which Raleigh brought from the New World of
the cannibals, headless people, and Amazons. A short
extract of the more wonderful passages was published
in several languages, accompanied by a map of Guiana,
by Jodocus Hondius, a Dutch geographer, and adorned
with copperplates representing these Anthropophagi,
Amazons, and headless men in different points of view.

Raleigh's book was published in London in 1596, the
year after his return from these wondrous lands. Its
title runs as follows :—" The discoverie of the large,
rich, and bewtiful Empire of Gviana, with a relation of
the great and golden City of Manoa, which the Spaniards
call El Dorado, performed in the year 1595, by Sir W.
Ralegh, Knt." The book is written throughout in a very
fair, honest way, and with an evident desire to gain the
truth, the whole truth, and nothing but the truth. Our
hero shall, however, speak for himself. " Next vnto
Armi there are two riuers Atoica and Coara, and on
that braunch which is called Coara are a nation of
people whose heades appeare not aboue their shoulders,
which, though it may be thought a meere fable, yet for
mine owne parte I am resolued it is true, because euery
child in the prouinces of Arromaia and Canuri affirme
the same : they are called Ewaipanoma; they are reported to haue their eyes in their shoulders, and their
mouths in the middle of their breasts, and that a long
traine of haire groweth backward betwen their shoulders.
The sonne of Topiawari, which I brought with mee
into England, told mee that they are the most mightie
men of all the lande and vse bowes, arrowes, and
clubs thrice as bigge as any of Guiana, or of the
Orenoqueponi, and that one of the Iwarawakeri took

a prisoner of them the yeare before our arriual there, and brought him into the borders of Arromaia his father's countrey. And further, when I seemed to doubt of it hee told me that it was no wonder among them, but that they were as great a nation, and as common, as any other in all the prouinces, and had of late yeares slaine manie hundreds of his father's people and of other nations their neighbors, but it was not my chance to heare of them til I was come away, and if I had but spoken one word of it while I was there, I might haue brought one of them with me to put the matter out of doubt." It appears to us that "Sir W. Ralegh, Knt.," comes out of the matter very much better than "the sonne of Topiawari," who, to say the least of it, and to take the most charitable view, seems to have been under a misapprehension of the facts.

The same year saw the publication of a second book, "A relation of the Second Voyage to Guiana, performed and written in the yeere 1596, by Laurence Keymis, Gent." This was dedicated to "the approved, right valorous and worthy knight Sir Walter Ralegh," and he too refers to this mysterious people, though only on the same terms, information at second hand, not actual inspection. He says, "Our interpreter certified mee of the headlesse men, and that their mouthes in their breastes are exceeding wide." He evidently feels that this is almost as far as he may reasonably expect to gain credence from the folks at home, for he goes on to say, "What I have heard of a sorte of people more monstrous I omit to mention, because it is matter of no difficultie to get one of them, and the report otherwise will appeare fabulous." He nevertheless does mention it, for in a note on the margin he says of these people, "They have eminent heades like dogs, and live all the day time in the sea : they speake the Charibes language." Probably these were some kind of seal or sea-lion, though one does not generally associate with such creatures the idea of linguistic acquirements. He does not seem to have found it so easy to get hold of one of these people as he anticipated ; his book at least gives no hint that he was so far successful. Guiana, like Africke, was in mediæval times a land of wonders, and even Hartsinck, in his work on Guiana, published in 1770, or not very much more than a century ago, gravely asserts the existence of a race of negroes in Surinam whose hands and feet were forked like the claw of a lobster, the hands consisting merely of a thumb and one broad finger, like the gloves of one's tender infancy, while the foot was suggestive of the split hoof of the ox or sheep.

Hackluyt in his " Voyages " dwells on the land Gaora, a tract inhabited by a people without heads, having their eyes in their shoulders and their mouths in their breasts. His book is dated 1598. A similar race of men, called Blemmyes, were said to be found in Africa ; and Sir John Maundeville, in his " Voiage and Travaile, which treateth of the way to Hierusalem and of Marvels of Inde, with other Ilands and Countries," gives an account of these men whose heads do grow beneath their shoulders. The book is altogether a most curious and interesting one, and the quaint illustrations add greatly to its value. The famous " Nuremburg Chronicle " of the year 1493 has a very curious figure of one of these headless men, almost a hundred years before they are mentioned by Sir Walter Raleigh, and in 1534 we find another representation in one of the books of Erasmus.* Raleigh's book, it will be remembered, was published in 1596.

* Appendix N.

G

An extraordinary realisation of these famous and fabulous beings was afforded to the people of Stuttgard at the great Festival held in that city by the Grand-Duke of Wurtemburg on the occasion of his marriage with the Margravine of Brandenburg in the year 1609. The doings of the Festival were illustrated by Balthazar Kuchlein in a volume of 236 plates. A grand procession was a marked feature in the rejoicings, and in this procession we see three of these headless men riding on gaily caparisoned and prancing steeds, besides "Tempus" with his winged hourglass; "Labor," dressed as a rustic, and bearing in one hand a beehive, and in the other a spade; and "Fama," a winged lady-fair on horseback, and bearing scroll and trumpet. In this grand but heterogeneous cavalcade we also find, amongst many others, the counterfeit presentments of Julias Cæsar, Alexander of Macedon, Hector of Troy, Diana, Jupiter, Sol, Prudentia, Justicia, Fortitudo, and Abundancia—a strange medley, but doubtless a pageant well pleasing to the burghers of Stuttgard, and to the countless throngs drawn within their city walls.

Pliny gravely writes of the Fanesii, a tribe in the far north of Scandinavia, whose ears were so long that they could cover up their whole body with them; while the author of "Guerino Meschino" speaks of Indians with feet so large that they carried them over their heads as sunshades. Their means of locomotion must have been, under these circumstances, decidedly curious.

Amongst one-eyed people we have the Arimaspians and the Cyclops. The former were a race in Scythia, and were legendarily supposed to be in constant war with the gryphons, as elsewhere we find recorded the continuous hostilities between the pigmies and the cranes. They are referred to by Milton in his "Paradise Lost."

The Cyclops were giants, whose business it was to forge for Vulcan; their single eye was placed in the centre of their foreheads. Of these the most notable was the great giant Polyphemus, the defeated and blinded foe of Ulysses :—

> " Roused with the sound, the mighty family
> Of one-eyed brothers hasten to the shore,
> And gather round the bellowing Polypheme." *

All the departures from the ordinary human type that we have hitherto considered sink into insignificance when we come to the great Briarœus, the fifty-headed and hundred-handed giant, and his companions :—

> " He who brandished in his hundred hands
> His fifty swords and fifty shields in fight." †

Giants of this overwhelming type may be also met with in the mythology of Scandinavia and India, but space forbids our dwelling at greater length on their charms. Having, therefore, so far done homage to the dictum of Pope, " The proper study of mankind is man," by considering in the first place the combination of the human nature with the animal, and in the second division man himself, yet warped and distorted from the image of God, we now, in the third place, deal with those forms of human mould that owe their departure from the type form to an excess of bulk or the reverse—a class that includes the men of Lilliput and of Brobdingnag, and all their fellows in towering height or microscopic proportion.

The Fairies were held by our ancestors to be a kind of intermediate beings, partaking of the nature both of men

---

* Addison's " Milton Imitated."
† The " Jerusalem Delivered " of Tasso.

and spirits. They had material bodies, and yet possessed the power of rendering themselves invisible at will. They had minds and hearts that could be touched by kindly feelings, and at the same time they delighted in practical jokes of the most pronounced description, while some displayed a cruel and malignant ferocity. The general idea, however, of them seems to have been of a diminutive race possessed with supernatural gifts, animated with joyous spirits, of great beauty, and full of kindliness to the sons of men when not crossed or slighted. We are told, for instance, of an honest farmer who had been reduced by the badness of the seasons to poverty, and was about to return homewards one morning from the fields in despair, having sown what little seed he had, which was not nearly so much as the ploughed land required. While pondering, not knowing what to do, he imagined that he heard a voice behind him saying—

> " Tak'—an' gie
> As gude to me." ¦

He turned round, and perceived a large sack standing at the end of the field, and on opening it he found it to be full of the most excellent seed-oats. Without hesitation he sowed them ; the sample was admirable, and the harvest no less luxuriant. The man carefully preserved the sack, and as soon as possible filled it full of the best grain that his field produced, and set it down on he spot on which he had received the fairy oats. A voice called to him—

> " Turn roun' your back,
> Whill I get my sack."

The farmer averted his face, and then immediately

looked round, but all was gone. Things ever after prospered with him ; for, according to the popular belief—

> " Meddle and mell
>   Wi' the fien's o' hell,
> An' a weirdless wicht ye'll be ;
>   But tak' and len',
>   Wi' the fairy men,
> Ye'll thrive ay whill ye dee."

In the same dearth, and in the same parish, an old woman who was nearly perishing of hunger, having tasted no food for two or three days, was one morning astonished to find one of her pans full of oatmeal. This seasonable supply she attributed to some of her benevolent neighbours, who she imagined had been wishing to give her a little surprise. Notwithstanding the care, however, with which she husbanded her meal, it by-and-by was expended, and she was again almost reduced to starvation. After passing another day without food her pan was again replenished, which was regularly done whenever the supply was exhausted, always allowing her to remain one day without food. Her store was replenished so regularly that at last she became careless, and presumed on the generosity of her invisible benefactors. One day, on receiving her new supply, she baked the whole of it into cakes, and having by some means obtained a little meat, invited all her acquaintances to a treat. The guests were just going to fall to when, to their astonishment, they beheld the cakes turn into withered leaves. After this the store was never renewed.

The origin of the belief in fairies is lost in the mists of time. Some supposed them to be the spirits of those who had inhabited the land before the birth of the Saviour, shut out until the final judgment from the joys of Paradise, yet undeserving of a place amongst the lost

souls in Hades.   Others tell us that they are the Druids
thus transformed because they would not give up their
idolatrous rites, and that they are continually growing
smaller and smaller, until they eventually turn into ants.*
They may be divided into four classes.   1. The white or
good fairies who live above ground, the joyous dancers,
the ethereal beings the poets delight to portray.   2. The
dark or underground spirits, trolds and brownies, a more
irritable race, working in mines and smithies, and doing
good or evil offices in a somewhat arbitrary and uncertain
fashion.   3. The fairy of the homestead, of whom Puck
and Robin Goodfellow are good examples, fond of
cleanliness and order, rewarding and helping the indus-
trious and punishing the idle and careless.   4. The
water-fairies, the more sombre spirits of the woods
and mountains, the Kelpies and Nixies, luring men to
destruction.   We nevertheless find that the fairies of the
sylvan shades interest themselves at times in the affairs
of men, and though it is easy to define four very distinct
classes, we at the same time find that these classes are
blended together a good deal.   The whole thing is so
purely a creation of the imagination, not of one mind
but of thousands, that it is impossible to reduce the
subject to mathematical exactness.

The fairies of the poets are ordinarily those of the
woodland, while those of the legends of the countryside
are at least equally often the fairies of the homestead in
their association with the daily life, the trivial round, the
common task.

The earliest account of the fairies of England will
be found in the writings of Gervase, in the thirteenth
century, and after that date allusion to them may fre-

* Appendix O.

quently be found ; grave chroniclers like Reginald Scot, poets like Chaucer, Spenser, Shakespeare, and Milton, all make mention of them. The first of these, Scot, in his " Discoverie of Witchcraft," tells us that " the faeries do principally inhabit the mountains and caverns of the earth, whose nature is to make strange apparitions on the earth, in meadows or in mountains, being like men and women, soldiers, kings, and ladies, children, and horsemen clothed in green." Many unfortunate women were persecuted as witches during the sixteenth and seventeenth centuries, and their connection with the fairies was often one of the leading charges against them, as we may see in the indictment of Alison Pearson ; she was convicted of associating with the fairies, the definite charge against her being " for haunting and reparing with the Queene of Elfland." Another woman was found guilty of " taking employment from a woman to speak in her behalf to the Queene of Faerie ;" and many other such cases might be brought forward.

Fairies have ordinarily been invisible, and though they have at times permitted mortals to be present at their revels, more frequently they would appear to have resented any intrusion. In Poole's "English Parnassus" the most circumstantial details are given : the robes are of snowy cobweb and silver gossamer ; the lamps are the mystic lights of glowworms ; the minstrelry is the music of the nightingale or the chirp of the cricket. Their emperor was Oberon, and his royal consort and empress was the sweet but mischeivous Mab :—

> " There is Mab, the mistress fairy,
> That doth nightly rob the dairy ;
> And can help or hurt the churning
> As she please without discerning.
> This is she that empties cradles,
> Takes out children, puts in ladles."

The fairies—the good people as they were often
called—were on the whole kindly and beneficent. During
the Middle Ages these little beings had obtained so much
credit that the clergy, who wished to reserve to themselves the power of blessing or banning, grew seriously
jealous, and endeavoured earnestly to disestablish them
from the hearts of men. That this was by no means
in accordance with the feelings of the laity may be
very well seen in the following extract from the " Canterbury Tales " :—

> " I speke of many hundred yeres ago ;
> *But now can no man see non elves mo ;*
> For now the grete charitee and prayeres
> Of limetoures and other holy freres
> That searchen every land and every streme
> As thikke as motes in the sonne beme,
> Blessing halles, chambers, kichenes and bowres,
> Cities, and burghes, castles highe and toures,
> Thropes and bernes, shepines and dairies
> *This maketh that there ben no fairies ;*
> For thir as wont to walken was an elf,
> Their walketh now the limetour himself."

The fairy rings to be seen in the meadows and woodlands were accepted with undoubted. faith as the
scenes of midnight revelry, and in most cases were
regarded with some little dread from the belief that they
were enchanted ground. Hence when people went to
look after their cattle in the morning they were always
careful to avoid walking too near these rings :—

> " Some say the screech-owl, at each midnight hour,
> Awakes the Fairies in yon ancient tower.
> Their nightly dancing ring I always dread,
> Nor let my sheep within that circle tread ;
> Where round and round all night in moonlight fair,
> They dance to some strange music of the air."

The effect produced on those who incautiously entered these charmed circles seems to have been sufficiently startling, if we may credit the old popular beliefs, to justify the greatest precautions and the most open-eyed watchfulness. In some cases the victim of carelessness or short-sightedness would imagine that he had been absent but a few minutes with the fairies, when he had really been away a century or more; while in other cases a man would suppose that he had lived for a long period in Elf-land when he had been but away an hour. Probably in some cases the spirits were alcoholic. We read of a young man who went out one morning and probably trod in one of these rings; however that may be, he was attracted by the especially sweet singing of some unknown bird. After waiting, as he thought, some few minutes, he resumed his journey, when he noticed to his surprise that the fresh and verdant tree in which the sweet songster had been embowered was scathed and leafless. The well-known house to which he was going had disappeared with all its inhabitants, and in its place a new structure had arisen. On going up to it an old man, who was evidently the owner, came out and asked his business, and on learning his name, told him that he had been away a hundred years or more. "I remember when I was a child hearing my grandfather speak of your disappearance one day many years before I was born, and that, after searching for you far and wide, he learned from a wise woman that you had fallen amongst the fairies, and that you would only be released when the sap had ceased to flow in yonder aged tree!" He had scarcely uttered the words when he beheld his long-lost kinsman fall away to a heap of dry dust!!

A popular Welsh legend tells us that two countrymen were one night crossing the mountains, when one of them, thinking he heard some strains of music, lingered a little behind, and could not afterwards be found. After fruitless search, his friends learned from a Seer that he had fallen amongst the fairies, and that the only way to recover him was to go on the anniversary of his absence to the place where he had disappeared, and that they must then pull him out of a fairy ring. Some few bold spiri.s were equal to the occasion, and on going to the place at the stipulated time they discovered their lost relative in the midst of an immense number of very small people, who were all dancing round in a circle. They pulled him out, but he died of exhaustion almost directly, as he had been dancing without intermission for the twelve months he had been missing. Another tradition current in Wales tells us of a young shepherd who peacefully tended his flock on the steeps of Brynnan Mawr. One day setting forth as usual at daybreak from his homestead near the hills, the lofty summit was enveloped in mist, but, as he proceeded, it gradually cleared away towards the Pembrokeshire side, a sure sign of a fine day. Our shepherd felt all the elevation of spirit which youth and the early dawn of a day in the "leafy month of June" might be expected to produce. Whilst trudging on his way gaily up the steep, he discerned the extraordinary spectacle of a party of persons, brilliantly dressed, and in active movement near the summit of the mountain. He gazed for some time before he could be convinced that what he saw was real. He climbed farther and farther, forgetting his sheep and all else in the world at the apparition of so many bright beings at that desolate spot. At last he drew very near the party, whom he was now convinced were either the Fairies, or some kindred sprites, concluding their nightly revels. Bursts of gentle music, like the melodious murmuring of an Æolian harp, ever and anon entranced him with delight. They were comely little beings to behold, and seemed very merry, while their habiliments of white, or green, or red, glistened with more than earthly beauty. The male sex wore red bonnets, and their fair companions flaunted in head-dresses outrivalling the gossamer in their texture; and many either galloped about on tiny white steeds, or pursued each other with the swiftness of the breeze. The greater portion of the party, however, were intently engaged in their favourite sport of dancing in the circle. Our shepherd did not know how it was, but he felt an irresistible inclination to make one of this joyous group, and growing bolder as the actors in the scene became more familiar to him, he at last ventured forward, and being encouraged by the friendly signals from all around, he advanced one step within the ring. The most exquisite melody now filled the air, and in an instant all was changed. Brynnan Mawr, with its well-known scenery, was seen no more. He was suddenly transported to a gorgeous palace radiant with gold and precious stones. Groves of odoriferous shrubs, intermingled with flowers unknown in this world, which might have rivalled those of the Valley of Gardens in "Lalla Rookh," shed around a fragrance excelling that of the "spicy East." Here did our shepherd wander from day to day amidst porphyry halls, and pavilions of pearl. Time sped away, but years seemed insufficient to explore all the wonders of that veritable Fairyland. He was attended in his wanderings by kind and gentle beings, who anticipated every want, and even invented sports and pastimes to amuse him. In the midst of the gardens there was a well of the clearest water, filled with many rainbow-tinted fish. There was but one limitation affixed to his movements and his curiosity:

he was forbidden to drink of this well, on pain of having all his happiness blasted. It might be thought that, surrounded as he was with all that he could desire, there would have been no danger of his violating this command, but the result proved the error of this Utopian way of viewing the probabilities. One day he cautiously advanced toward the forbidden spot, and placing his hand within the well drew forth some water in his palm and drank it. The shrieks of many voices instantly filled the air, all the fair scenes of enchanting loveliness vanished, and the luckless and too curious shepherd found himself on the summit of Brynnan Mawr with his sheep quietly grazing around him in the early morning just as when he had first entered the fairy-ring. Though years apparently had passed away while he was under the magic spell yet it was evident that in reality not many minutes could have elapsed.

Our readers will doubtless recall Shakespeare's reference to these " fairy rings," in the first scene of the fifth act in the " Tempest " :—

> " Ye elves of hills, brooks, standing lakes, and groves ;
> And ye, that on the sands with printless foot
> Do chase the ebbing Neptune, and do fly him,
> When he comes back ; you, demi-puppets, that
> By moon-shine do the green-sour ringlets make,
> Whereof the ewe not bites ; and you, whose pastime
> Is to make midnight mushrooms ; that rejoice
> To hear the solemn curfew ; by whose aid
> (Weak masters though ye be,) I have be-dimm'd
> The noon-tide sun, called forth the mutinous winds,
> And 'twixt the green sea and the azure vault
> Set roaring war."

The flint arrow-heads or celts so dear to antiquaries, and so commonly to be found in and near the tumuli that mark the resting-places of our remote ancestors, are popularly called fairy-darts or elf-bolts. Though the wound of an elf-bolt was supposed to cause instant death to man and beast when directed by an aggrieved or mischievous fairy, the possession of one of these celts secured its owner from all ill consequences. When cattle or horses fell lame without the reason being forthcoming, it was concluded that they had been wounded by these invisible archers, in which case it was only necessary to touch the tender place with another elf-bolt or to make the animal drink the water in which one had been dipped.

Any money found by the road-side was in the same way ascribed by our rustics to the fairies, some kindly spirit having dropped it by the way for the benefit of the battered wayfarer. As a boy cne day in Anglesea was going out just before daybreak, he saw before him in the grey and obscure light a party of little beings dancing, as usual, in a circle. He hastened home in alarm and without making any further investigation, and on his return found a groat on a stone. He often saw the fairies afterwards at the same place, and as regularly found the money laid for him at the same spot. His possession of funds awakened the paternal curiosity, and he at last confessed the whole matter. Ever after this, though he often passed by the scene of the revels and scanned the wayside stone intently, he never saw either fairy frolic or fairy fee again.

Though fairies had the power of making themselves invisible, and generally resented the intrusion of any human spectator, they were willing to show themselves sometimes, it would appear, though frequently the consequences were not altogether agreeable to the person so favoured. One evening the curiosity of a countryman, in his progress homewards, was powerfully excited by a wild though gentle melody which apparently proceeded from amidst some rocks, resting in picturesque confusion on the slopes of the mountain. After listening for some time he lost his track, and suddenly found himself close beside a troop of elves, who were dancing round a mysterious circle of "stocks and stones." Before he had much time for thought the elfin-troop surrounded him and quickly hurried him aloft, one of the party first asking the question whether he would prefer to be conveyed with a high, a moderate, or a low wind? Had he chosen the first, or "above the wind," he would instantly have soared into the most elevated regions; but our poor bewildered farmer unwisely made choice of the low wind, thus rejecting (as is too often the case in life) the middle course, or " with the wind," where he would have enjoyed an easy and pleasant aerial excursion. The mischievous little spirits then hurried him along the surface of the ground, over bog and briar, thorn and ditch, until at last they threw him in a most miserable plight head foremost in the mire.

In Shakespeare's time it was a belief that no one could see the fairies and live, for he makes Falstaff exclaim, " They are fairies, he who looks on them shall die ; " but any one who desires to see them through the eye of a poet should read most carefully the altogether delightful " Midsummer Night's Dream." The temptation to quote liberally from it is extreme, but its beauty requires it to be read in its entirety.

The references in that play to changlings reminds us that we have not yet referred to this notable piece of family practice.

Both the good and the bad fairies used to recruit their numbers by carrying off children, or young men and

women. The malignant race delighted in spiriting away
the unbaptized offspring (for it was only over these that
they had any power) of affectionate parents, particularly
when heirs, that they might produce as much mischief
and vexation as possible; while the benignant fairies
never took any recruits but the orphans of pious parents,
who had no protectors, or were oppressed by cruel and
unjust guardians. Such protégés, or rather naturalised
fairies, were permitted twice to resume their original
state, and appear to their kindred and acquaintance.
The first time was at the end of seven years, when, if
they had been children when they were taken away, they
appeared to their nearest relatives, and declared to them
their state, whether they were pleased with their condition as fairies, or wished to be restored to that of men.
If they had been boys or girls when they were removed
from this upper earth, and had by this time grown to
men or women, they always appeared to persons of a
different sex to themselves, with whom they had fallen
in love, to whom they declared their state and passion,
and, according to circumstances, either wished their lover
to accompany them to Fairyland, or suggested to them
a method whereby to recover them out of the hands of
their elfish lords.

The second appearance, at the end of fourteen years,
was for the same purpose, and on this occasion they
were either rescued from the power of the fairies or
confirmed under their dominion for ever.

When the bad fairies carried off a child, they always
left one of their own number in its place. This equivocal
creature was always distinguished by being insatiable for
food, and if kept, seldom failed to draw its supposed
mother into a consumption.

Whenever a family suspected that a child had been

changed for a fairy, they had recourse to the following strange, but, in the opinion of the country, infallible ordeal. A sufficient quantity of clay was produced from the eastern side of a hill, with which all the windows, doors, and every aperture through the house, excepting the chimney, were built up. A large fire was then made of peats, and the supposed fairy, wrapped in the sheets or blankets of the woman's bed, was laid on the fire when it was at the briskest, while one of the bystanders repeated—

> " Come to me
> Gin mine ye be ;
> But gin ye be a fairy wicht,
> Fast and flee till endless nicht.''

If the child actually was the woman's it instantly rolled off the fire upon the floor ; but, if it was a fairy, it flew away up the chimney with a tremendous shriek, and was never more seen, while the real infant was found lying upon the threshold.

> " Oh, that it could be proved
> That some night tripping fairy had exchanged,
> In cradle-clothes, our children as they lay ;
> And called mine Percy, his Plantagenet !
> Then would I have his Harry, and he mine." *

Spenser also refers to this belief in the following lines :—

> " And her base elfin breed there for thee left,
> Such men do changelings call, so changed by fairie's theft."

In some parts of the country, it is, or perhaps we should more correctly say was, customary to protect a child against fairy influences by tying a red thread round its throat or by letting its head hang down for awhile in the

* Shakespeare, i. Henry IV.

early morning. One does not of course see why either of these remedies should be efficacious against fairies or against anything else ; but any one who has had occasion to talk matters over with rustics will have found that all their remedies, whether for ills spiritual or material, are of the most inconsequent character, and that the gift of faith in them is one of the most necessary accompaniments. This belief in fairy changelings is of great antiquity, for we read in Holingshead's " Chronicles " that the common people, on the death of King Arthur, held that he was not really dead at all, " but carried away by fairies into some place, where he would remain for a time and then return again and reign in as great authority as ever." It was also an old belief that people who had once lived with the fairies never again looked quite like other people, an ingenious way of accounting for any peculiarity in any one. Sir Walter Scott, in speaking of elf-possession, says that even " full-grown persons, especially such as in an unlucky hour were doomed to the execration of parents or of masters, or those who were found asleep after sunset under a rock or on a green hill belonging to the fairies, or finally those who unwarily joined their orgies, were believed to be subject to their power. The accounts they gave of their situation differ in some particulars. Sometimes they were represented as living a life of constant restlessness and wandering by moonlight. According to others, they inhabited a pleasant region, where, however, their situation was rendered horrible by the sacrifice of one or more individuals to the devil every seventh year. This is the popular reason assigned for the desire of the fairies to abstract young children as substitutes for themselves in this dreadful tribute."

Persons, as we have seen, could occasionally be re-

H

covered from the fairies, and if changelings were taken
before dark to a place where three rivers met, the stolen
child would be brought back in the night and the fairy
youngster would return whence it came. A poor woman
who once had twins had them adroitly carried away
soon after birth, and two of these elf-changelings sub-
stituted. For some months the change was not suspected, but as the mother began to perceive that the
children never increased in size her suspicions were
aroused, and she consulted one of the wise men of the
district. This friend in need amply confirmed her suspicions, and in answer to her appeal for help and counsel,
told her that she must get two eggshells, fill them with
wort and hops, place them where these dubious infants
could see them, and then secretly observe what came
next. After a few minutes of watching the children
began to stir, and these sweet little innocents, who were
supposed to be unable to either walk or talk, crept up
to the table, and after studying the matter awhile, one
said to the other, " We were born before the acorn which
produced the oak of which these cottage beams are made,
but this is the first time we ever saw anybody brewing in
an egg-shell!" The secret was now fairly out, and the
woman was so exasperated at the trick played on her,
that she fell on the changelings with the greatest fury,
and only desisted when she got a solemn promise that
her own dear children should at once be returned to
her. One egg-shell story leads to another, and in an old
book we came across the following :—

"My mother lived in the immediate neighbourhood
of a farm-house that was positively infested by fairies.
It was one of those old-fashioned houses among the hills
of Cambria, constructed after the manner of ancient
days, when farmers considered the safety and comfort of

their cattle as much as that of their children and
domestics, and the kitchen and cow-house were on the
same floor adjoining each other, with a half-door over,
so that the good man could see the animals from his
chimney-corner without moving. My mother and the
farmer's wife were intimate friends, and she used often
to complain to her that the fairies annoyed her and her
family to that degree that they had no peace;—that
whenever the family dined, or supped, or ate any meal,
or were together, these mischievous little beings would
assemble in the next apartment. For instance, when
they were sitting in the kitchen, they were at high
gambols in the dairy, or when they were yoking the
cows, they would see the fairies in the kitchen, dancing
and laughing, and provokingly merry. One day, as
there was a great number of reapers partaking of a
harvest-dinner, which was prepared with great care and
nicety by the housewife, they heard music and dancing
and laughing above, and a great shower of dust fell
down, and covered all the victuals which were upon the
table. The pudding in particular was completely spoiled,
and the keen appetites of the party were most grievously
disappointed. Just at this moment of trouble and despair
an old woman entered, who saw the confusion and heard
the whole affair explained. 'Well,' said she in a whisper
to the farmer's wife, 'I'll tell you how to get rid of the
fairies. To-morrow morning ask six of the reapers to
dinner, and be sure that you let the fairies hear you ask
them. Then make no more pudding than will go into
an egg-shell, and put it down to boil. It may be a
scanty meal for six hungry reapers, but it will be quite
sufficient to banish the fairies; and if you follow these
directions you will not be troubled with them any more.'
She did accordingly, and when the fairies heard that a

pudding for six reapers was boiling in an egg-shell there
was a great noise in the next apartment and an angry
voice called out, 'We have lived long in this world.
We were born just after the earth was made, and before
an acorn was planted, and yet we never saw a harvest
dinner prepared in an egg-shell. Something must be
wrong in this house, and we will no longer stop under
its roof.' From that time the disturbances ceased, and
the fairies were never seen or heard there any more."

Some authorities on the subject—and there are no
greater authorities on it than the most superstitious old
crones one can lay hold of—have averred that if any
persons find themselves unwillingly in the company of the
fairies they can cause their instantaneous departure by
drawing out their knives. This acts not as a threat, for
these puny immortals have no need to fear the weapons
of carnal warfare, but from some inherent property in the
cold bright steel.

Many of the fairies are such kindly, genial little souls
that one is rather grieved to find that they are entirely
antagonistic to any religious influence. Many stories
illustrate this unfortunate peculiarity, but to give one
only will suffice. As a village fiddler was returning
home one evening from some festivities that had doubtless owed much of their success to his enlivening
strains, he was met in the darkness by a stranger. This
stranger wished to make a somewhat curious arrangement with him, to the effect that on the following night
at midnight he should bring his fiddle to a certain wild
spot on the moorland, while he promised him ample
reward for so doing. Though the fiddler presently
agreed to do so, the more he thought it over the less
he liked the bargain, and he would have gladly thrown
it up had he dared. In his strait he bethought him of

the minister of the parish, and determined to lay the whole matter before him and take his advice upon it. His clerical adviser liked the look of the affair no better than he did, but he advised him to keep to his bargain, while he strongly cautioned him to play nothing but psalm tunes. The fiddler kept his appointment, but no sooner had the sacred strains arisen than a great shriek rent the air and he was thrown violently down, and after receiving no slight castigation from invisible adversaries he returned home sore and stiff in the early morning. Unbelievers will no doubt say that the germ of truth in the story will be found in the fact, that if the jovial musician so far yielded to the charms of the revels as to be unable to steer a straight course home within reasonable hours, the early morning would probably find him stiff and sore with rheumatism.

The spirits of the mine were as firmly believed in amongst the miners as the woodland and meadow sprites were by the dwellers on the country side. They were generally called knockers, and any sound heard in the stillness of the earth, that was evidently not the work of a fellow-toiler, was at once attributed to supernatural agency. The miners assert that these fairies may be frequently heard assiduously at work in the remoter parts, and that by their knocking they draw the attention of the workmen to the richest veins of ore. In the "Gentleman's Magazine" for 1754 we found a curious letter from a mine-owner, and the extract we give shows that the belief in such beings was not by any means confined to the rude and uncultivated miners, men a great part of whose lives were spent in the bowels of the earth, far removed from the cheering light of day, and who were in an especial degree under the influence of superstition :—

"People who know very little of arts or sciences, or the powers of nature, will laugh at us Cardiganshire miners, who maintain the existence of knockers in mines, a kind of good-natured impalpable people, not to be seen but heard, and who seem to us to work in the mines; that is to say, they are types or forerunners of working in mines, as dreams are of some accidents which happen to us. Before the discovery of the *Esgair y Mwyn* mine, these little people worked hard through day and night, and there are abundance of sober honest people who have heard them. But after the discovery of the great mine they were heard no more. When I began to work at Lwyn Lwyd, they worked so fresh there for a considerable time, that they frightened away some young workmen. This was when they were driving levels, and before we had got any ore, but when we came to the ore they then gave over, and I heard no more of them. These are odd assertions, but they are certainly facts, although we cannot and do not pretend to account for them. We have now (October 1754) very good ore at Lwyn Lwyd, where the knockers were heard to work. But they have now yielded up the place, and are heard no more. Let who will laugh; we have the greatest reason to rejoice and thank the knockers, or rather God, who sends these notices."

In the coal districts one meets with a similar belief in goblin miners. These spirits are ordinarily of a friendly disposition, and perform such kindly offices for their human fellow-workers as assisting to pump up superfluous water or loosening masses of coal. Of course one can readily see that when the men went to their work and found their toil diminished, owing to a heavy fall of coal in the working, supersti-

tion would at once have material to work on. Some
of these spirits would appear to have been of less
amiable disposition, and the sounds heard were at times
the warnings and forerunners of coming disaster. As
the fairies of the household or of the moonlighted forest
glades were of uncertain and variable natures, though
inclining on the whole to beneficence, so the spirits of
the earth were divisible into those of gentle race and
others of fierce and malevolent disposition. In Milton's
"Comus" we find these earth spirits referred to in the
following passage :—

> " No goblin, or swart fairy of the mine,
> Hath hurtful power o'er true virginity ; "

and in Pope's prefatory letter to the " Rape of the Lock "
we find a further allusion—" The four elements are in-
habitated by spirits called sylphs, gnomes, nymphs, and
salamanders. The gnomes, or demons of the earth,
delight in mischief; but the sylphs. whose habitation is
in air, are the best-conditioned creatures imaginable."
A belief in kindly spirits of the household was
widely spread, for besides our own Robin Goodfellow
we find the Nis of Denmark and Norway, the Kobold
of Germany, the Brownie of Scotland, and many others.
Brownie, we may remark, is a tawny, good-natured spirit,
and derives his name from his colour as distinctive
from fair-ie. Robin Goodfellow was a merry domestic
sprite, full of practical jokes, a terror to the lazy, but a
diligent rewarder of industry :—

> " When mortals are at rest,
> And snoring in their nest,—
> Un-heard or un-espied,
> Through key-hole we do glide :
> Over tables, stools, and shelves,
> We trip it with our fairy elves.

And if the house be foule,
Of platter, dish or bowle,
Upstairs we nimbly creepe
And find the sluts asleepe :
Then we pinch their armes and thighes,
None escapes, nor none espies.

But if the house be swept,
And from uncleannesse kept,
We praise the house and maid,
And surely she is paid :
For we do use before we go
To drop a tester in her shoe."

The "shrewd and knavish sprite" and the good luck
he brings to the deserving are referred to very happily
again in the "Midsummer Night's Dream."

Prudent and considerate housewives who wished to
gain the goodwill of these spirits of the night were
careful to leave a bowl of milk on the table for their use.
Milton, in his poem of "L'Allegro"—

" Tells how the drudging goblin swet,
To earn his cream-bowl duly set ; '

the task he set himself in recompense for the attention
shown him being the threshing during the night of as
much corn as would have required the labour of ten men.
What thrifty housewife would grudge a bowl of milk
or cream for so great a reward !

Queen Mab shares with Robin his functions as critic
of household management, for it will be remembered
that in the "English Parnassus" we find her described
as—

" She that pinches country wenches
If they rub not clean their benches;
And with sharper nail remembers,
When they rake not up their embers.
And if so they chance to feast her,
In their shoe she drops a tester."

Housewives would see their account in keeping such a belief vividly before the eyes of their serving-maids, and may even themselves have sometimes dropped a tester where their diligent hand-maidens would fancy it a fairy-reward for their zeal in her service, while the vague threats of fairy vengeance would come in most opportunely in support of their own chidings of the careless and indolent.

We turn, in conclusion, to the fourth class, the evil spirits of the water and the storm. Of such is the Cornish Bucca, a weird goblin of the winds, whose scream was heard amid the roar of the elements as some gallant vessel was hurled to destruction on the rocks. In Ireland the same creature was the dreaded Phoca or Pooka, in Wales the Pwcca, while in Scottish legends it is the Kelpie. The creature sometimes assumed the human form, and at others that of the eagle or the horse ; thus in Graham's "Sketches of Perthshire" we read— "Every lake has its kelpie or water-horse, often seen by the shepherd sitting upon the brow of a rock, dashing along the surface of the deep, or browsing upon the pasture on its verge." The Nech is a similar creature in the folk-lore of Scandinavia. In Wales we meet with the belief in a creature called Cyoeraeth, so named, we are told, from its deadly chilling voice. We find it thus described in an old book :—"The Cyoeraeth is a being in the dress of a female, with tangled hair, a bloodless and ghastly countenance, long black teeth, and withered arms of great length ;" in short, it is invested with a description which conveys to the mind the idea of a blasted tree as compared to the flourishing monarch of the forest, rather than as possessing the similitude of anything human. This being (fortunately for the people) seldom made itself visible, but its scream or shriek at night had a terrible and overpowering effect on all who heard it. It generally foreboded death or fearful disaster, and always occurred when the spirit approached a cross road or drew near to a river or *llyn*, when it would commence to splash and agitate the water with its long bloodless hands, wailing all the time so as to 'make night hideous.' Those who heard its dreary moaning (or thought they did, the case doubtless of the majority) fled in horror, fearing for their reason, while many were really affected in mind, and ever after had the shriek resounding in memory.

In Brecon a romantic gorge called the Cwm Pwcca bears record in its name of the old belief in the phoca. As a justification of its title we read the following story:—A countryman was wandering in the darkest of dreary winter nights in vain endeavour to find the path that would have guided him to his home, when he saw a light before him on the dreary waste, which he naturally took for the lantern of some wayfarer. He quickened his steps and made for it. As he rapidly neared it he was on the point of hailing its bearer when the roar of waters smote his ear in the silence of the night, and, barely arresting his steps in time, he found himself at the edge of a lofty chasm, the awful gulf at the base of which the torrent was sweeping with resistless fury. At this instant the bearer of the lantern took a flying leap to the opposite side of the gorge, burst into a scornful and unearthly peal of laughter, and vanished from the eyes of the affrighted rustic.

The *ignis fatuus*, will-of-the-wisp, or Jack o' lantern was doubtless at the bottom of such a story as this, and in Milton's " Paradise Lost " we find the following power-full illustrative passage, referring both to the natural phenomenon and the myth built upon it :—

> " ' Lead, then,' said Eve.   He, leading, swiftly rolled
> In tangles, and made intricate seem straight,
> To mischief swift.   Hope elevates, and Joy
> Brightens his crest ; as when a wandering fire,
> Compact of unctuous vapour, which the night
> Condenses, and the cold environs round,
> Kindled through agitation to a flame,
> Which oft, they say, some evil spirit tends,
> Hovering and blazing with delusive light,
> Misleads the amazed night wanderer from his way,
> To bogs and mires, and oft through ponds or pool ;
> There swallowed up and lost, from succour far,
> So glistered the dire snake."

In the same author's poem of " L'Allegro " we find the will-of-the-wisp again referred to, this time under the title of " Friar's lantern ;" while Sir Walter Scott in his " Marmion " writes—

> " Better we had through mire and bush
> Been lantern-led by Friar Rush."

Shakespeare in 1 " Henry IV." calls it a " ball of wildfire," and also used the Latin name, *ignis fatuus.*

This bewilderment of the rustics by false fires does not always seem to have been the result of diabolical malice on the part of the fairies, but sometimes assumed the form of a practical joke.   Like most practical jokes, it was probably much more amusing to the joker than the joked, and the benighted wanderer had little cause to thank him of whom it could be said—

> " Whene'er such wanderers I meete
> As from their night-sports they trudge home ;
> With counterfeiting voice I grete
> And call them on, with me to roam
> Thro' woods, thro' lakes,
> Thro' bogs, thro' brakes ;

Or else, unseene, with them I go
　　All in the nicke
　　To play some tricke,
And frolic it, with ho, ho, ho !''

An old legend tells us how on the advent of Christianity great Pan and all the woodland deities deserted
their old haunts and were never seen of men again ; and
in the same way the march of science and the spread of
education must ere now have killed off all the fairies,
except in the most out-of-the-way districts. Once coaxed
and propitiated, or shudderingly dreaded, they now but
serve to make a pleasant fancy for a Christmas-card, or
aid in the grand spectacular effects of the Christmas
pantomime. Those, then, who would see these denizens
of elf-land and all the grace and beauty that even the
very name of fairy-land suggests, will seek them no longer
in the ferny glades of some fair woodland or beneath the
silvery beams of the moon, but reduce the matter to a
prosaic visit to some great theatre, and endeavour to find
in the great array of " supers " and the glowing of coloured
fires the realisation of their fair ideal. The fairies are, in
fact, as dead, as hopelessly defunct, as the proverbial
door-nail, which seems to have been accepted by the
wisdom of our ancestors as the most expressive symbol
of mortality and the stern decrees of irreversible Fate.*

The Pigmies had not the same glamour of romance
about them that was associated with the dwellers in elf-
land. The consideration of them nevertheless comes well
within the same chapter, as, like the fairies, they were a
race of beings of human mould, but differing from the
ordinary standard of humanity by reason of the exceeding smallness of their stature.

References to them will be found in the writings of

* Appendix P.

Herodotus, Philostratus, Pliny, and many other authors, the first allusion to them being in the third book of the Iliad, where the Trojans are compared to cranes fighting against pigmies :—

> " Thus by their leaders' care each martial band
> Moves into ranks, and stretches o'er the land.
> With shouts the Trojans, rushing from afar,
> Proclaim their motions, and provoke the war :
> So when inclement winters vex the plain
> With piercing frosts, or thick-descending rain,
> To warmer seas the cranes embodied fly,
> With noise, and order, through the mid-way sky :
> To pigmy nations wounds and death they bring,
> And all the war descends upon the wing." *

These combats between the pigmies and the cranes were also dwelt on by Oppian, Juvenal, and others ; and what was, to quote an old writer, " only a pleasant figment in the fountain, became a solemn story in the stream.' Strabo in his Geography considered the belief as fabulous, and so also did another old writer, Julius Scaliger ; and even Aldrovandus, though ready to accept almost anything, found a difficulty in crediting it. Albertus Magnus, another of the old and over-credulous writers, found as much difficulty as Aldrovandus, but suggested that probably the belief arose from some big species of monkey having been taken for a diminutive man. Even the home of the pigmies was a point quite open to dispute. Some writers placed them in the extreme north, where the growth of all nature was feeble and stunted, while Aristotle placed them at the head of the Nile ; Philostratus affirmed that they were to be found on the

* " Marking the tracts of air, the clamorous cranes
Wheel their due flight in varied ranks descried ;
And each with outstretched neck his rank maintains,
In marshalled order through th' ethereal void."

banks of the Ganges, and Pliny placed them in Scythia. Even their size was open to question, for some would have us believe that the mounted men in their armies rode on partridges, while others placed them on the backs of rams. If the warrior and his steed bore any due proportion to each other, this seems to point to a considerable divergence of ideas as to the size of a pigmy. They were said to have been found by Hercules in the great desert, and to have assailed him with their bows and arrows as the Liliputians did Gulliver. Their valour, however, in this case seems to have outrun discretion, as the smiling demi-god carried a number of them off in his lion's-skin. Ctesias says that they were negroes, and places a kingdom of them in the centre of India. Shakespeare mentions them, but gives no local habitation. "Will your Grace command me any service to the world's end? I will go on the slightest errand now to the Antipodes that you can devise to send me on: I will fetch you a tooth-picker now from the farthest inch of Asia; bring you the length of Prester John's foot; fetch you a hair off the great Cham's beard; do you any embassage to the Pigmies!" Others of our poets have adopted the myth, though of course without committing themselves to an expression of their belief in it. In Dryden's "Absalom and Achitophel," for example, we find the lines—

> " A fiery soul, which, working out its way,
> Fretted the pigmy-body to decay,
> And o'er informed the tenement of clay "—

and in Young's "Night Thoughts" we read—

> " Pygmies are pygmies still, though perched on Alps ;
> And pyramids are pyramids in vales."

Another English writer whose book is before us does

commit himself to an expression of belief, for his title runs as follows :—" Gerania, a New Discoverie of a Little Sort of People called Pygmies, with a Lively Description of their Stature, Habit, Manners and Customs." The author was one Joshua Barnes, and his book is dated 1675.

Though spelt indifferently as pigmy and pygmy, the latter is the more correct, though perhaps a little pedantic-looking ; the word is derived from the Greek name for them, the Pygmaioi.

Tennant in his work on " Ceylon " makes the following very just remark :—" We ought not to be too hasty in casting ridicule upon the narratives of ancient travellers. In a geographical point of view they possess great value, and if sometimes they contain statements which appear marvellous, the mystery is often explained away by a more careful and minute inquiry." Against the statements of the geographers and historians of antiquity many modern critics have specially delighted to break a lance, condemning them as more or less fabulous and untrustworthy, though in some cases, as that of De Chaillu, the narratives of modern travellers have been almost as mercilessly analysed.

Probably the African race known at the present time as Bosjesmen or Bushmen are the modern representatives of the pigmies, for in their cave-dwelling, reptile-eating, and other peculiarities they agree entirely with those given by Pliny, Aristotle, and Herodotus. The tales of the battles fought with the cranes may have been but a satire on their diminutive size, or they may very possibly have been the records of actual facts. The Maori traditions tell of the contests with the moa and other gigantic birds which formerly inhabited the islands of New Zealand, while the Jesuit missionaries give accounts of enormous birds that were once found in Abyssinia, but are now, like the dodo, extinct. It is, therefore, quite possible that there is more truth in the story of these mannikins and their struggles with their feathered foes than we are at first prepared to admit, and that while many of the details of these old fables are evidently imaginative, there was in more cases than we at once realise a solid foundation of truth at the bottom of them.

Of giants, the opposite extreme in the scale, we need say but little. Probably in many cases the early peoples, who desired to honour their great champions, felt that the marvels they delighted to credit them with must have been the work of men of more than human power and parts. We see much the same feeling in the sculptures of antiquity, the monuments of Egypt and Assyria, where the monarch far outweighs even in mere physical bulk the subjects that surround him. Hence, like Goliath, the champions of old are generally giants; while at other times they themselves are of slender frame, striplings like David, and it is the foes they subdue that are gigantic in bulk. The struggles, for instance, of the gallant few against the crying and mighty wrong of human slavery would have in earlier times been handed down to posterity as a contest with an evil giant; and in the allegories of the Middle Ages we meet, in the same way, with Giant Pope, Giant Pagan, and Giant Despair.

Though in one's earlier years we read the exploits of Jack the Giant-Killer with great complacency, and give him full meed of praise for his valour, on fuller reflection we cannot help seeing that the giants he encountered had intellects that bore no proportion to their bodily bulk, and that it was the easiest thing possible to outwit them; that according to the doctrine which by men of science is called "the survival of the fittest," or in more popular parlance "the weakest going to the wall." their destruction was strictly according to the inexorable laws of nature. While dwarfs have been accredited with a spiteful vindictiveness that served them in some sort as a defence, giants have ordinarily been considered as great good-natured fellows, fully bearing out Bacon's remark about tall houses being often unfurnished in their upper story. Perhaps it is a merciful arrangement of nature that this should be so, for a combination of the maliciousness of the dwarf with the physical strength of the giant would be something altogether *de trop*.

We very early in the Bible narrative meet with references to giants, but it is by no means agreed by commentators that the word nephilim thus translated means men remarkable for their stature. The context in the case of the first reference to them, for instance, seems to render it more probable that these were men not of gigantic stature, but of gigantic wickedness—men who had departed from the true religion, and were sustaining their apostasy by acts of violence and oppression, and endeavouring by these means to gain to themselves power on the earth. At the same time in other passages the references to the size of the couch or the spear clearly implies their ownership by a man of much more than the ordinary stature. According to Jewish tradition Og lived three thousand years, and walked beside the Ark during the deluge, while after his death one of his bones was used as a bridge for crossing a river. According to Moses his bedstead was not quite sixteen feet long, so that it seems the brook that any single bone would span could scarcely have required bridging at all; while the depth at what we may be allowed to term "high water" during the Noachic deluge must have been very much less than all one's preconceived notions would suggest, if

its volume was a thing of indifference to the owner of
this sixteen-feet couch. The nearest approach to a giant
in modern times was an Irishman named Murphy, who
attained to a height of eight feet ten inches. Many of
our readers will remember seeing the Chinese Chang, or
at least hearing of him, as he was exhibited to the curious
in London in 1866 and 1880. His height was eight feet
two inches. Patrick Cotter, an Irishman, who died in
1802, exceeded this by six inches; and one fine youth
named Magrath, an orphan adopted by Bishop Berkeley,
died at the age of twenty, after reaching a height of seven
feet eight inches. There is no absolutely authenticated
instance of any one in modern times reaching nine feet,
though, of course, when tradition and hearsay have taken
the place of the measuring-tape, there is no difficulty in
going considerably beyond that limit. Plutarch tells of
a giant eighty-five feet high, and Pliny of another who
only reached sixty-six. Many of the skeletons of giants
that were then supposed to be found during the Middle
Ages were really the remains of extinct animals. In the
imperfect state of surgical and osteological knowledge,
the leg or blade bone of some gigantic antediluvian
monster was ascribed to some hero of the past, and a
very pretty little giant story promptly built upon it.

Any curious natural phenomena were generally ascribed by our ancestors to diabolical influence, or else
recognised as the labour of giants. The Giant's Cause-
way is a notable and very familiar illustration of this,
and there are few mountains in Wales that are not invested with some fairy tradition or legend of the marvellous. Trichrug, in Cardiganshire, which derives its
name from three united hills, is believed to have been
a favourite resort of the giants, and, like Cader Idris, this
lofty elevation was once the special seat or chair of a

giant whose grave is still pointed out. In a match at quoits which took place here between the giants of Cambria, he of Trichrug is said to have thrown one across St. George's Channel to the opposite coast of Ireland, thus winning the contest triumphantly. His grave was fabled to possess such extraordinary capabilities that it not only adapted itself to the size of any one that lay down in it, but also gifted the individual with greatly renewed strength. All defensive weapons placed in this grave were either destroyed or swallowed up. The rocky fortification, or *carnedd*, on the summit of Cader Idris is in like manner invested by the surrounding peasantry with a mysterious tradition respecting the giant Idris.

The warring of the giants against the rule of Jehovah finds its parallel in the Greek myth of the sons of Tartaros and Ge attempting to storm the gate of heaven and the seat of Zeus, only to meet with signal discomfiture. The common expression for adding difficulty to difficulty and embarrassment to embarrassment, the piling of Pelion on Ossa, refers to this struggle, as the giants piled two mountains of these names on each other as a scaling ladder to reach the heights of high Olympus.

In "Measure for Measure" we find two well-known allusions to giants :—

> " O ! it is excellent
> To have a giant's strength ; but it is tyrannous
> To use it like a giant."

The second of these is equally familiar :—

> " The sense of death is most in apprehension,
> And the poor beetle that we tread upon,
> In corporal sufferance finds a pang as great
> As when a giant dies."

In Matthew Green's play of "The Spleen," written at the beginning of the eighteenth century, we find an evident allusion to the struggle between David and Goliath in the line—

" Fling but a stone, the giant dies."

Coleridge, again, writes—"A dwarf sees further than the giant, when he has the giant's shoulder to rest on." This idea is not, however, his own, for in Herbert's "Jacula Prudentum" we find the line, "A dwarf on giant shoulders sees further of the two ;" and in Fuller's "Holy State" he says—"Grant them but dwarfs, yet stand they on giants' shoulders and may see the further." Many other illustrations might, of course, readily be given of what may be termed the literary existence of giants, but enough has been quoted to show how valuable these personages have in poesy and general literature. In the West "Gulliver's Travels" and in the East the "Arabian Nights' Entertainments" are two examples that at once occur to one's mind.

CHAPTER III.

HILE we find numerous extraordinary beliefs
clustering round the so-called natural history
of various birds, such as the legend of the
pelican nourishing its young with its own
blood, or the eagle teaching its offspring to gaze on the
brightness of the mid-day sun, it is curious to note how
little of absolute myth-creation has been developed in
the direction of strange forms of bird life.   On the other
hand, many of the weird creations of fancy, such as the
dragon or the phoca, have their terrors greatly enhanced

by the gift to them of the essential bird characteristic, the power of soaring in mid-air, and thus gaining a great additional power for evil over their victims. We have already referred, in our first chapter, to the phœnix, and it now only remains to mention some few other mythical bird-forms, less widely known, before we pass to other creations of fancy. Even in heraldry, the home of much that is marvellous and unnatural, the bird forms depart but little from natural types, and the only instance to the contrary that occurs to us is the well-known Martlet, used not only as "a charge" in blazonry, but also as a mark of cadency to distinguish the arms of contemporary brothers in the same family or to identify different branches of the same family connection.*

The martlet is very similar in form to a swallow, but is always represented as without feet, while the French heralds also deprive it of beak. A good early example of its use may be seen in the arms of William de Valence, emblazoned on his shield at Westminster, and dating from the year 1296; later instances of its employment are so common that it is hardly worth while to particularise any special illustration. The martlet, according to Gwillim, in his elaborate treatise on heraldry, "hath leggs exceeding short, that they can by no means go: and therefore it seemeth the Grecians do call them *Apodes, quasi sine pedibus;* not because they do want feet, but because they have not such use of their feet as other birds have. And if perchance they fall upon the ground, they cannot raise themselves upon their feet as others do, and so prepare themselves to flight. For this cause they are accustomed to make their Nests upon Rocks or other high Places, from whence they may easily take their flight, by

* Appendix Q.

means of the support of the Air. Hereupon it came that this Bird is painted in Arms without feet : and for this cause it is also given as a difference of younger Brethren, to put them in mind to trust to their wings of vertue and merit to raise themselves, and not to their leggs, having little Land to set their foot on."

In mediæval days the Bird of Paradise was in like manner thought to be without feet. The error arose in a very natural but most prosaic way, and simply sprang from the fact that the natives who bartered the skins of the birds with the merchants cut off the legs before bringing them, naturally thinking that they were of no value, and that it was for the richness of the plumage alone that the skins were esteemed. The lovers of the marvellous in the West built upon this weak foundation a most poetic superstructure, and believed that the bird was indeed the denizen of paradise, fed upon the dew of heaven, incapable of contact with earth, building no nest, but hatching its eggs in a cavity upon its own back ; ever soaring in the sunlight far above earth, and independent of all mundane association.

Tavernier supplies another explanation, equally prosaic, of their footless condition—one in fact, that entirely removes the poor birds from all poetic association, and reduces them to the "drunk and incapable" state that some other bipeds are prone to indulge in. He tells us in his book that the birds of paradise come in flocks during the nutmeg season to the plantations, and that the odour so intoxicates them that they fall helplessly to the earth, and that the ants eat off their feet while they are thus incapacitated. Moore, in his " Lalla Rookh," thus refers, it will be remembered, to this Tavernier tale in writing of—

" Those golden birds that in the spice-time drop
    Upon the gardens drunk with that sweet food
    Whose scent hath lured them o'er the summer flood."

"The sublime bird which flies always in the air, and never touches the earth," mentioned by the princess in the introduction to "Paradise and the Peri," was the Humma, an altogether fabulous creature. Like the bird of paradise, it was supposed to pass its whole time in the blue vault of heaven, and to have no contact with earth ; it was regarded as a bird of good omen, and that every head it overshadowed would in time be encircled with a crown. The splendidly jewelled bird suspended over the throne of Tippoo Sultan at Seringapatam was an artistic embodiment of this poetic fancy, and we can well imagine that all good courtiers who had any regard for keeping their necks free from the scimitar would take uncommonly good care to avoid that prophetic overshadowing, that would make them the possible rivals and successors of so very resolute an autocrat.

The Huppe, one of the birds believed in by our fore-fathers in mediæval days, seems morally to have been a somewhat peculiar and, on the whole, objectionable com-pound, reminding one in some degree of those uncom-fortable people who attach an immense importance to their own belongings, but whose sympathies towards the members of the clan are scarcely more marked than their antipathy to all beyond this narrow circle. Such, at least, is the idea we should gather from the description of it by De Thaun, for he tells us that "when it sees its father or mother fallen into old age that they cannot see nor fly, it takes them under its wings and cherishes them. The huppe has such a nature that if any shall anoint a man with its blood while he is sleeping, devils will come and strangle him." The huppe was described as being

like a peacock, but it seems impossible to even imagine
how such a belief in its evil powers could ever have taken
root. It would be difficult to conceive such a notion
growing up in connection with any creature whatever,
but when the first cause is itself non-existent the difficulty
is greatly intensified ; one has not even a foothold of fact
as a starting-point. What a picture, again, of cold-blooded
fiendishness does it not open out to us as we see with the
mind's eye the treacherous anointing of some perchance
innocent sleeper with a preparation of *Sanguis huppæ* and
then the operator walking off and posing in the eyes of
the world as an honourable burgess, while his accomplices
from the bottomless pit finish the job off for him while
he has gone to Mass or is engaged on 'Change! It is
worse even than that little affair with the babes in the
wood, bad as that was in many of its details.

The Ibis, beloved as it was by the Egyptians for its
services to them as the destroyer of venomous snakes,
and from its association with the Sacred Nile and the
great deity Thoth, was not altogether allowed to bring
forth its progeny in peace, for it was believed that its
fondness for a serpent diet might so develop in it evil
properties, that its eggs were diligently sought for and
destroyed, lest from them should issue some strange serpentine forms of horror that in their mysterious nature
would be a still greater scourge than the sufficiently
objectionable grey and brown and diversely spotted and
chequered denizens of the desert that coil or glide
unseen amidst the expanses of burning sand, and whose
fangs convey swift death to those unfortunates who come
within reach of their fatal power.

By far the grandest creation of bird-fancy is the Roc.
This fabulous bird was of enormous size, and of such
strength of talon and digestion that it was said to be

able to carry away an elephant to its mountain home, and there devour it at a meal; while one old traveller, not to be outdone in particularity of detail, calculates that one roc's egg is equal in amount to one hundred and forty-eight hens' eggs. The belief in the roc was altogether an Eastern weakness, and those who would know more of it must turn to such romances as that of "Sindbad the Sailor" and the narratives of such-like Asiatic Barons Munchausen. In the Second Voyage of Sindbad he tells us how he saw in the distance some mysterious object, which, on closer inspection, proved to be the egg of a roc. "Casting my eyes," he says, "towards the sea, I could discern only the water and the sky; but perceiving on the land side something white, I descended from the tree, and taking with me the remainder of my provisions, I walked towards the object, which was so distant that at first I could not distinguish what it was. As I approached I perceived it to be a white ball of a prodigious size. I walked round it, to find whether there was an opening, but could find none; and it appeared so even that it was impossible to get up it. The circumference might be about fifty paces. The sun was then near setting; the air grew suddenly dark, as if obscured by a thick cloud. I was surprised at this change, but much more so when I perceived it to be occasioned by a bird of a most extraordinary size which was flying towards me. I recollected having heard sailors speak of a bird called a roc, and I conceived that the great white ball which had drawn my attention must be the egg of this bird. I was not mistaken, for shortly afterwards it alighted upon it and placed itself to sit upon it." He tells us also in this same voyage of the furious strife waged between the rhinoceros and the elephant, a struggle that often continues till the roc, hearing the disturbance, swoops down upon them and seizes them both in his claws and flies away with them, in much the same manner apparently as the schoolmaster who, appearing suddenly in the midst of a fight between two truculent youngsters, chills their martial ardour by his stony glance, and leads off each culprit by ear or collar to his den.

In another of Sindbad's sea-ventures, the fifth, we find an awful warning against trifling with the parental feelings of the roc. In the course of their voyage the crew landed on a desert island, and very soon found a gigantic egg. Sindbad at once recognised what it was, and earnestly advised them not to meddle with it, but his remonstrances were unheeded ; they boldly attacked the mass with hatchets, and on finding a young roc within, cut it into divers pieces and roasted it. These reckless tars had scarcely finished their meal, when two immense clouds appeared in the air at a considerable distance. The captain, knowing by experience what this portended, or haply making a lucky guess, cried out that it was the father and mother of the young roc, and warned all to re-embark as quickly as possible, and so avoid, if possible, the vengeance of the outraged owners of the egg. All accordingly scrambled on board, and sail was set immediately. The two rocs in the meantime rapidly approached, uttering the most frightful screams, which they redoubled on finding the state of their egg, and that their young one was defunct. They then flew away, and a faint hope began to dawn upon the mariners that they had not come so badly out of the business after all, when to their blood-chilling horror the birds again rapidly approached, each with an enormous mass of rock in its talons. When they were immediately over the ship they stopped in mid-air, and one of them let fall the piece of rock he held. The pilot, his wits sharpened by the imminent peril the vessel was in, deftly turned the ship aside, and the great mass plunged into the depths of the sea alongside ; but the other bird, more fortunate in his aim, let his piece fall so immediately on the ship that it smashed it into a thousand pieces, and, with the exception of Sindbad, all the passengers and crew were either crushed beneath tons of stone or drowned in the surging billows that such a monstrous mass created. Lest a suspicion may cross the reader's mind that the gallant sailor and enterprising merchant was romancing somewhat when he narrated these stirring adventures, we hasten to mention that the third calender, in the same veracious history, met with other experiences of an equally surprising nature in which this gigantic bird played as leading a part, all of which may be found duly set forth in the " Arabian Nights."

Another curious belief of the Arabs is in the existence of a bird called the Hameh. This uncomfortable creation of the Arab fancy is said to spring from the blood of a murdered man. Its weird cry is continuously "Iskoonee," a word signifying "give me to drink," and it rests not, day nor night, till its thirst is quenched in the murderer's blood. When the death of the victim is avenged it flies away to some place left altogether indefinite in the Eastern legend, but probably it wends its way to the spirit-land with the welcome news that the victim's blood no longer cries in vain for vengeance. To an Arab already suffering from an evil conscience the belief in the hameh must be a terrible one, as he hears in fancy the troubled air filled with the wailing cry and fierce demand for vengeance, and knows that, day or night, the haunting sound will never leave his ears until the desert feud be avenged and his own life blood be poured out like water upon the burning sand.

The depths of ocean, so impressive in their mystery and vastness, have been peopled by the lovers of the marvellous in all ages with a special fauna of their own, and have been made the home of divers strange and wondrous creatures, some purely reptilian, others fish-like, or still more commonly a weird combination of the two. The depths and recesses of the great tropical forests, as impressive almost in their vastness as the ocean itself, or the far-reaching swamps and morasses in their mysterious shades, have in like manner been tenanted in the imagination of the savage tribes that thread their depths or probe their treacherous surface with forms more wonderful even than those of Nature herself, weird and bizarre as these in tropical regions so frequently are. Hence amongst all savage tribes we find a belief in serpentine forms more terrible even than the boa or python that they have such cause to dread. The widely spreading worship of the serpent, a form of religion that we find in so many lands and throughout centuries of time, is a most interesting subject of study, though we can here only regret that exigencies of space compel us to do no more than merely mention it.

The belief in sea-serpents does not appear in itself to be an unreasonable one, much as it is from time to time ridiculed. Many species of tropical snakes are aquatic in a greater or less degree, and though some naturalists will tell us that a serpent is not adapted by its structure and organs for a purely aquatic existence, one finds in nature so many wonderful adaptations of form to abnormal circumstances, that it is perhaps wiser to feel that in the great and almost boundless expanse of ocean there may be mysterious forms that science has not yet tabulated and described, rather than to at once assert the contrary. Be this as it may, there is no doubt that while the great mystery of the ocean depths has been tenanted by the credulous with impossible creations of the fancy, we have numerous testimonies from sea-captains and others of appearances that cannot always be so lightly dismissed. A Captain Harrington, for instance, commanding the "Castilian," during a voyage from Bombay to Liverpool in the year 1857, sends the following account to the *Times* newspaper :—" While myself and officers were standing on the lee side of the poop, looking towards the island of St. Helena, then some ten miles away, we were startled by the sight of a large marine animal, which reared its head out of the water within twenty yards of the ship, when it suddenly disappeared for about half a minute, and then made its appearance in the same manner again, showing us distinctly its neck and head about ten or twelve feet out of the water. Its head was shaped like a long buoy, and I suppose the diameter to have been seven or eight feet in the largest part, with a kind of scroll or tuft of loose skin encircling it about two feet from the top. The second appearance assured us that it was a monster of extraordinary length, which appeared to be moving slowly towards the island. The ship was going too fast to enable us to reach the mast-head in time to form a correct estimate of its extreme length, but from what we saw from the deck we conclude that it must have been over two hundred feet long. The boatswain and several of the crew, who observed it from the forecastle, state that it was more than double the length of the ship, in which case it must have been five hundred feet. Be that as it may, I am convinced that it belonged to the serpent tribe; it was a dark colour about the head, and was covered with

several white spots. Having a press of canvas on the
ship at the time, I was unable to round to without risk,
and therefore was precluded from getting another sight
of this leviathan of the deep." This precise description
was endorsed by the chief and second officers of the
ship—men, like the captain, of practised vision, and not
at all likely to be deceived by floating sea-weed or any
of the other matters brought forward to cast doubt on
such stories.

It is curious that another apparently well-authenticated
account of some such creature should also hail from
the neighbourhood of St. Helena. Her Majesty's ship
" Dædalus," in August 1848, when on the passage between
that island and the Cape of Good Hope, came into
close proximity with a strange-looking creature that was
travelling through the water at an estimated speed of
ten miles an hour. Captain M'Quahee was unable,
owing to the direction of the wind, to bring the ship
into pursuit, but, as the creature passed within two
hundred yards of them, they were enabled to bring it
well within observation, its form and colour being distinctly visible from the vessel.

Olaus Magnus, Archbishop of Upsal some three centuries ago, was a firm believer in the marvellous, and in
his writings, amongst many other things, he gives details
of a sea-serpent two hundred feet long by twenty feet
thick, having a dense hairy mane and eyes of fire. This
monster, he further tells us, " puts up its head on high
like a pillar and devours men." He also tells of another
kind, that is forty cubits long and no thicker than a
child's arm ; this is blue and yellow in colour. His
writings also furnish a more detailed account of a vast
monster thrown ashore in 1532 on the English coast
near " Tinmouth." This creature was ninety feet long

and twenty-five feet thick, having thirty ribs on each side, a head twenty-one feet long, and two fins of fifteen feet each. This creature, from its proportions, fins, and so forth, was evidently not serpentine in character, though it may fairly be classed amongst monsters of the deep.

A Greenland missionary, Egede, tells in his journal of a frightful sea-monster that he saw on July 6, 1734. It raised itself so high out of the water, he says, that its head overtopped the mainsail. It had a long and pointed snout, and spouted like a whale ; its fins were like great wings. Another very circumstantial account is that given by Captain Laurent de Ferry of Bergen in 1746. His creature had a horse-like head, raised some two feet out of the water ; in colour it was grey, but it had a white mane and large black eyes. Seven or eight coils of the creature were visible, a fathom or so of space between each. De Ferry says that he shot at and wounded the monster, and that the water was reddened with its blood for some time after. He does not specify whether the weapon used was the longbow or not, but it seems highly probable that it was.

Where the account given is so exceedingly definite as it is, for example, in these two last instances, we are placed in the awkward predicament of either having to believe in the monster so graphically described, or to disbelieve the narrators of the stories ; to conclude, in plain words, that Egede, despite his professions, was lying deliberately— a very Munchausen—and that De Ferry was either a credulous idiot himself, or wilfully concluded that the landsmen's credulity might be safely played upon.

It has been suggested that a long line of tumbling porpoises, rolling after each other in the quaint way that they do, may have deceived people into a belief that what they saw were the coils of one of these great mythical monsters of the deep; but, however such an appearance might deceive a landsman, it is evident that those who go down to the sea in ships and occupy themselves in the great waters are too familiar with the appearance of a shoal of porpoises to be thus deceived.

The ribbon fish may in some cases have given rise to the idea of a serpent of the sea, as the appearance of their elongated, band-like bodies swimming through the water with a gentle serpentine or undulatory motion would be very suggestive. They have been known to attain a length of sixty feet; specimens of this size have actually been captured by trawlers, though even yet we are a long way from the sea serpents gravely mentioned by Pontoppidan in his "Natural History of Norway" as being over six hundred feet long.

On the occasion of the reported appearance of the sea serpent to Captain McQuahee, Professor Owen in a letter published in the *Times* suggested that the creature seen may have been one of the larger species of seals found in the Southern Seas. At the Falkland Islands and in the Kerguelen and Crozet groups the sea elephant attains a size of some twenty feet in length, and some such creature as this, swimming rapidly through a calm sea with its head raised, and with a long wake behind it, caused by the action of its paddles, placed at the posterior extremity of the body, like the screw of a steamer, may have been the foundation of some of the stories told of these mysterious monsters of the deep.

A good sea-serpent story is found in Captain Taylor's "Reminiscences." One day, when his ship was lying at anchor in Table Bay, "an enormous monster" about one hundred feet in length was seen advancing with snake-like motion round Green Point into the harbour. The head appeared to be crowned with long hair, and

K

the keener-sighted amongst the observers could see the eyes and distinguish the features of the monster. The military were called out, and after peppering the object at a distance of five hundred yards, and making several palpable hits, it was observed to become quite still, and boats ventured off to complete the destruction. The "sea serpent" proved to be a mass of gigantic sea-weed, which had been undulated by the ground swell, and had become quiescent when it reached the still waters of the bay. Probably if mariners would attack the "monster" in the same manner whenever it is seen, we should hear little more of the sea serpent.

Stories of sea serpents are almost as old as the hills, and in many cases quite as difficult to digest.

In 1808 the body of a great sea monster was cast ashore at Stronsay, one of the Orkneys. This was some fifty feet long, and every one, even the fishermen themselves, declared that the sea serpent had turned up at last. A naturalist, however, decided that it was only an unusually fine specimen of the great basking shark; so we are as far off as ever, after all, from an authentic monster, and seem in every case to have only offered for our acceptance either outrageous hoaxes and impositions, the imaginations of the credulous, or, at the very best, cases of mistaken identity.

Amongst other serpent myths we may certainly place that most uncomfortable creation of the fancy, the Adissechen, a serpent with a thousand heads that, according to the Indian mythology, bears up the universe; and the Iormungandur, the serpent that according to the Scandinavian myth, encircles the whole earth, and binds it together in its flight through space.

It was a very old belief that the serpent's egg was hatched by the joint labour of several serpents, and was

buoyed up into the air by their hissing. Any one so
intrepid as to catch it while thus suspended 'twixt earth
and heaven bore away with him a talisman of mighty
power, giving him strength to prevail in every contest,
and the favour of all whose favour was worth the having.
It could only be captured at the gallop, and even then
the risk of being stung to death was a peril most
imminent. Pliny tells us that he had himself seen one
of these notable proofs of prowess, and that it was about
as large as a moderately large apple.

The Fire-Drake was, according to mediæval fancy,
a fiery serpent or dragon, keeping guard over hidden
treasure. The drake, of course, has no affinity with the
familiar ducks and drakes on the farmer's pool, nor
even with the ducks and drakes that people make of
their money when they burn their fingers in too rash
speculation, but is clearly suggested by the Latin word,
draco, for a dragon. We find an interesting reference
in Shakespeare to the word in his " Henry VIII.," scene 3
of act v.—"There is a fellow somewhat near the door;
he should be a brazier by his face, for, o' my conscience,
twenty of the dog-days now reign in his nose: all that
stand about him are under the line, they need no further
penance. That fire-drake."

De Thaun in his " Bestiary " tells us of the Aspis, "a
serpent cunning, sly, and aware of evil. When it per-
ceives people who make enchantment, who want to
enchant it, to take and snare it, it will stop very well the
ears it has. It will press one against the earth; in the
other it will stuff its tail firmly, so that it hears nothing.
In this manner do the rich people of the world: one ear
they have on earth to obtain riches, the other Sin stops
up; yet they will see a day, the day of Judgment. This
is the signification of the Aspis without doubt." De

Thaun always endeavours to see a religious meaning in everything, and where the moral declines to fit quite accurately to the facts, by a simple process of reversal the facts are made to fit to the moral. The creature that he had in his mind, and which would naturally occur to him from his familiarity with the Bible, is no doubt identical with the deaf adder that we are told in one of the Psalms stoppeth her ear, and refuseth to hear the voice of the charmer. Though the old author avowedly has no doubt as to the signification he assigns to the creature's obstinate refusal to be charmed, one cannot but feel that his explanation is rather halting. A man who would amass riches has at least as much need of his eyes as of his ears, and his transition from the ear stopped up by sin to the awakened eye at the great day of account is also somewhat lame. The transition should have been not arbitrarily from one faculty to another, but in the sharp contrast between the sense first deliberately blunted and lost through sin, to be then at last terribly restored by the trumpet peal of the dread day of doom. Indeed, if it were not that we are all prepared instinctively to place the worst possible construction upon anything a creature so repellent to us may do, it is evident that the allegory might have been equally developed from quite another point of view. Had the dove shown a similar alacrity to bury one ear in the earth while it stuffed its tail into the other, we should have heard nothing of this wilful blunting of the senses to good counsel, but much, *au contraire*, of its determined resistance to temptation and evil.

The ancients believed in a horrible little brute called the Amphisbena, "a small kind of serpent which moveth backward or forward, and hath two heads, one at either extreme." Galen, Pliny, Nicander, and many other early writers gravely describe this especially objectionable little reptile. Ælian, who was so far in advance of his age as to call the Chimera and Hydra fables, believed fully in the amphisbena. Some few serpents really have the power of taking a mean advantage of those they assault by springing at them from directions not always "straight to your front," as the drill sergeants express it,* but none, of course, have an equal facility for moving either backward or forward ; and certainly still more of course, no serpent at present known to science, or likely to be, has a head " at either extreme."

The Kraken is another notable example of the studies in unnatural history of the ancients. Pliny gravely narrates that one of these monsters—the " mountain fish " of the old Norsemen—haunted the ocean off the coasts of Spain and North Africa, but, owing to its bulk, was unable to penetrate through the Straits of Gibraltar into the Mediterranean. According to some old writers the kraken, when floating on the surface of the sea, stretched to a length of about a mile and a half, and appeared like an island. It is a difficult problem to say which would be the most embarrassing position—for a seaman to find himself stranded on the creature's back on its sudden arrival at the surface, or to be engulfed in the whirlpool that would arise from its sinking again into the depths of ocean. One old writer tells us of a party of sailors that, from the tangled sea-weed on the creature's back, took the kraken for an island, and after fishing for some time with some little success in the pools of water in the hollows of his back, proceeded to light a fire to cook their take, and suddenly found themselves engulfed in the sea when the heat became

* Appendix R.

sufficiently great to awaken their animated island from
its nap. Alaus Magnus, archbishop of Upsala, describes
this colossus of the deep as the kraken, but he stops
short at the length of a mile ; while Pontoppidan, bishop
of Bergen, adds that a whole regiment of soldiers could
manœuvre on its back ; while yet a third ecclesiastic,
another bishop, tells us that he did actually erect an altar
on the creature's back and celebrate mass. We are told
that the kraken submitted to the ceremony without
flinching, but no sooner was it over than it plunged into
the depths of the sea, to the great astonishment and peril
of the divine. It may at first seem curious that so many
of these stories should spring from ecclesiastics, but it
must be remembered that they were in these early days
the great repositories of truth, the laity being steeped in
ignorance and superstition.

It has been conjectured that the kraken myth has
sprung from stories of gigantic cuttle-fish or octopus,
the devil fish described so vividly by Victor Hugo in
his "Toilers of the Sea ;" but one can hardly fall in quite
readily with this notion, since the leading idea, so to
speak, in the kraken belief is that of a monstrous and
quiescent mass, suggestive more than anything else of
an island rising from the sea, while the dominant idea
in our minds of the octopus is of a creature armed with
far-stretching and numerous arms that enwrap their
hapless victim in their pitiless embrace. The kraken
would scarcely have been described without any reference to these fearful feelers, armed with double rows of
suckers, if the myth had had the origin that has been
in several directions claimed for it. The belief in the
kraken chiefly springs, probably, from that delight in
something tremendously big that has also given us the
roc carrying away elephants in its talons, or the serpent

that encompasses the world in its folds, so that we need
not then too anxiously strive to find any counterpart of
it in nature.

" They that sail on the sea tell of the dangers thereof,
and when we hear it with our ears we marvel thereat.

" For therein be strange and wondrous works, variety
of all kinds of beasts, and whales created." *

De Thaun describes something very kraken-like, but
he bestows upon it the title of Cetus. *Cetus*, we need
scarcely remind our readers, is a Latin word applied in
a general sense to all kinds of large sea-fish, and though
the whale is strictly speaking a mammal and not a fish
at all, we find the word reappearing in modern use in
the term cetaceous, as applied to all creatures of the
whale kind. The author of the " Bestiary " tells us that
" Cetus is a very great beast; it lives always in the sea.
It takes the sand of the sea, spreads it on its back,
raises itself up in the sea, and will be at tranquillity.
The seafarer sees it, and thinks that it is an island, and
goes to arrive there to prepare his meal. The Cetus
feels the fire and the ship and the people; then he will
plunge if he can, and drown them. When he wants to
eat he begins to gape, and the gaping of his mouth sends
forth a smell so sweet, that the little fish will enter into
his mouth, and then he will kill them, thus will he swallow
them." In a Jewish work entitled " Bara Bathra " we read
of a whale so large that a ship was three days in sailing
from its head to its tail. Of course this would not be
at Cunard liner pace; still it certainly does give one the
idea of a very considerable fish. But this monster of
the deep sinks into insignificance in its length of but a
hundred miles or so when we compare it with the fish

* Ecclesiasticus xliii. vers. 24, 25.

Pheg (mentioned in an ancient Chinese book, the Tsi-hiai), that churns up five hundred miles of blue ocean into silvery foam when it starts its stupendous paddles in motion for a cruise. This is indeed, to quote Polonius, "very like a whale." When any one's credulity finds no difficulty in digesting such a tale as that, their powers of absorption must be well nigh as striking as the narration itself.

> " The imperious seas breed monsters ; for the dish
> Poor tributary rivers as sweet fish." *

According to Jewish tradition the Leviathan was a great fish ; so great, they taught, that one day it swallowed another fish nearly a thousand miles long. Many of the Jewish legends in the Talmud and elsewhere possess little or nothing of graceful fancy, but simply endeavour to excite wonder by gross exaggeration. There were originally two of these leviathans, a male and a female ; but if their numbers had increased beyond this, the world would have been soon destroyed ; so the female was killed, and laid up in salt for the great feast to be held at the coming of the Messiah. Such is the Jewish tradition. Leviathan is mentioned in the Bible in several places, notably in the magnificent description that comprises the whole of the forty-first chapter of the book of Job. It is curious that a very similar legend to that we have just referred to was believed by the Jews in connection with the Behemoth mentioned in the preceding chapter of Job. Any one reading the fine description of the creature there given will have little difficulty in agreeing with most commentators that the hippopotamus is intended ; but the Jews held that behemoth is a huge animal which has subsisted alone since the

* "Cymbeline," Act iv. sc. 2.

creation, and that it is reserved to be fattened for the great rejoicings that are to be held in the days of the advent of the promised Messiah. Every day they believe that he eats up the grass of a thousand hills, and that at each draught, when he is thirsty, he swallows up as much water as the Jordan yields in the course of six months.

It would probably be found that nine out of ten people would at once declare that their idea of the leviathan was that it was a large fish, and the tenth person would have very little doubt either. We do not mean that these typical folk would really believe in its existence as a special monster, but they would be quite prepared to say in an offhand way that the whale was intended under this name. Burton in his "Miracles of Art and of Nature" (A.D. 1678) has a passage that clearly shows this interchange of words, and the evident idea that the two terms, whale and leviathan, are synonymous. He writes, under the description of Norway—"The whales do so terrifie the shores, the Seas being there so deep, and therefore a fit habitation for those great leviathans." He, however, goes on to tell us that "the People of the Sea-coast have found a remedy, which is by casting some water intermixt with Oyle of Castor, the smell whereof forces them immediately to retire, and without this help there were no Fishing on the Coasts." The remedy for the boisterous presence of these great monsters seems at first a feeble one, until we bear in mind how gladly we too in our child-days would have immediately retired, if we could, at the awful odour of the coming castor-oil. "One touch of nature makes the whole world kin."

The beautiful description of the wonders of creation in the 104th Psalm, the stretching firmament and the chariots of cloud, the fowls of heaven, and the trees so full of sap and vigour, concludes with a reference to the leviathan that has no doubt done much to associate the name with the whale,* and which, in fact, could only apply to some such great creature of the waters; so that we can only conclude that the term was used somewhat vaguely by the different Old Testament writers, as it is now tolerably unanimously held that the leviathan of the book of Job is the crocodile.

No creature of the whale tribe inhabits the Mediterranean; neither is the whale clothed in coat-of-mail, nor is it fierce in disposition; but if any one will carefully read the description given of the crocodile in the book of Job they will find point after point of appropriate detail, allowance being made partly for the wealth of Oriental and poetic imagery, and partly for the wonderful difference between assailing the crocodile in these later days with a rifle-ball as against the old sling, spear, or arrow. What a modern sportsman might lightly esteem would be a very different creature indeed to attack when the world was in its youth.

> "Who can strip off his outer garment?
> Who can open the doors of his face?
> Round about his teeth is terror.
> His strong scales are his pride,
> Shut up together as with a close seal.
> They are joined one to another,
> They stick together that they cannot be sundered.
> In his neck abideth strength,
> And terror danceth before him.
> If one lay at him with the sword it cannot avail,
> Nor the spear, the dart, nor the pointed shaft.
> He counteth iron as straw,
> And brass as rotten wood.

---

* " This great and wide sea wherein are things creeping innumerable, both small and great beasts. There go the ships : there is that leviathan, whom Thou hast made to play therein " (Ps. civ. 25, 26).

The arrow cannot make him flee :
Sling-stones are turned with him into stubble.
He laugheth at the rushing of the javelin.
Upon earth there is not his like,
That is made without fear.'

The poetical ideas that clustered during classic times and the Middle Ages round the Nautilus were, after all, as mythical as they were poetic.

" The tender nautilus who steers his prow,
The sea-borne sailor of his shell canoe,
The ocean Mab, the fairy of the sea " *—

has, alas! no foundation in hard fact; and the lesson that Pope would teach when he bids us—

" Learn of the little nautilus to sail,
Spread the thin oar and catch the rising gale "—

is equally impracticable. The sad fiction-dispelling truth is, that in no case does the little argonaut use its arms as sails or as oars. It rises, it is true, occasionally to the surface, as other cuttle-fish forms do, but when there its only means of propulsion are the *jets d'eau* from its funnel, these jets consisting of the water which has been used in respiration. In Pliny's "Natural History," as translated by Philemon Holland, and published in London in 1601, we find that "among the greatest wonders of nature is that fish which of some is called nautilos, of others pompilos. This fish, for to come aloft upon the water, turneth upon his backe, and raiseth or heaveth himselfe up by little and little; and to the end he might swim with more ease as disburdened of a sinke, he dischargeth all the water within him at a pipe. After this, turning up his two foremost clawes or armes, hee displaieth and

* Byron.

stretcheth out betweene them a membrane or skin of a wonderful thinnesse : this serveth him instead of a saile in the aire above water. With the rest of his armes or clawes he roweth and laboureth under water, and with his tail in the midst he directeth his course, and steereth as it were with an helme. Thus holdeth he on and maketh way in the sea, with a fair show of a galley under saile. Now if he be afraide of anything by the way, hee makes no more adoe, but draweth in water to baillise his bodie, and so plungeth himselfe downe and sinketh to the bottome."

While the Dolphin, like the nautilus, has a veritable existence, and may be duly found amongst the works of nature, it has also, like the nautilus again, served as the foundation for a considerable amount of mythical lore. Thus Pliny, in his so-called Natural History, from which we have already drawn so many curious extracts, writes —"The swiftest of all other living creatures whatsoever, and not of sea-fish only, is the dolphin ; quicker than the flying fowl, swifter than the arrow shot out of a bow." The dolphin, so termed, of the mediæval heralds is a purely conventional form, having no counterpart whatever in Nature. "They are much deceived," wrote an authority on natural history a little more than a hundred years ago, "who imagine Dolphins to be of the Figure they are usually represented on Signs ; that Error being more owing to the unbridled License of Statuaries or Painters than to any such Thing found in Fact." A much earlier writer, Gillius, tells us that when he was "in a Ship where many Dolphins were taken, he observed them so to deplore with Groans, Lamentations, and a Flood of Tears their Condition, that he himself, out of Compassion, could not forbear weeping, and so threw one that he observed to groan more than ordinary (the

Fisherman being asleep) into the Water again, as choosing rather to damage the Fisherman than not to relieve the Miserable. But this gave him but little Rest, for all the Others increased their Groans, as seeming, by not obscure Signs, to beg the same Deliverance." Another well-known belief in connection with the dolphin is the imaginary brilliancy of its supposititiously changeful colours when, having failed to find any one, like Gillius, compassionate enough to throw it overboard, it presently succumbs to its hard fate. The idea has been a favourite one with poets in all ages, but one example from Byron's "Childe Harold's Pilgrimage" will suffice as an illustration :—

> " Parting day
> Dies like the dolphin, whom each pang imbues
> With a new colour as it gasps away ;
> The last still loveliest, till—'tis gone—and all is gray."

According to some of the ancient writers, the eyes of the dolphin were in those most unlikely and unserviceable places, their blade-bones ; they were also said to dig graves for their dead on the sandy shores of the sea, and to follow them to their burial in mournful procession. They were, too, an excellent means of travelling when other means of locomotion were not available. Thus the fifty daughters of Nereus travelled in safety on their backs, we are told in classic mythology in the dry-as-dust style of such fountains of knowledge as are available for reference ordinarily; but these statements help us but little to realise the scene that struck the eyes or the imaginations of the ancients when this bevy of charming girls, a good fifty strong, rode hither and thither in happy *abandon* in the brilliant summer sunlight of the azure Mediterranean Sea, their steeds the willing dolphins ; a scene as unlike the frowsy omnibuses, the dreary chariots of moody men and women, that loom through the murk of a London fog, or that fill to suffocation with resentful fellow passengers, when the prolonged drizzle becomes a heavy downpour, as one can possibly imagine.

The dolphin's love of music, again, was a firm article of faith to the ancients, and most of our readers are no doubt acquainted with the story of the sweet singer, Arion, who, forced to leap into the sea to escape the cruelty of the sailors, escaped to land on the back of a dolphin— one of many that had long followed the ship in rapturous appreciation of the sweet melodies of the singer; and how Arion—

> " With harmonious strains
> Requites his hearer for his friendly pains."

Another strange fish believed in by our forefathers was the Acipenser, "a fish of an unnatural making and quality," as an old writer terms him ; and indeed he may very well do so, as we are told that "his scales are all turned towards the head." We are not, therefore, much surprised to learn that "he ever swimmeth against the stream," though we might well be still more astonished if we ever found him swimming at all.

The Remora. This was held to affix itself so firmly to a ship that neither wind nor waves could dislodge it, while its presence (even worse than that of the more prosaic barnacles and other sea impedimenta that plague the modern shipowner by fouling the bottom of his good ship, and so retarding her course) brought the voyage to an abrupt conclusion. Pliny indeed only says that "there is a little fish, keeping ordinarily about rockes, named Echeneis. It is thought that if it settle and sticke to the keele of a ship under water, it goeth the slower by that meanes," whereupon it is called the stay-ship. But all these marvels have a wonderful way of growing more and more marvellous, and subsequent writers, not content with merely impeding the vessels in their increasingly wondrous stories, soon accredited the remora with the much more striking power of altogether arresting their progress. We see a relic and survival of this old belief in the following lines of Ben Jonson—

> " I say a remora,
> For it will stay a ship that's under sail."

And again much more elaborately worked out in Spenser's " Visions of the World's Vanity "—

> " Looking far forth into the ocean wide,
>   A goodly ship, with banners bravely dight,
> And flag in her top-gallant, I espied,
>   Through the main sea making her merry flight ;
> Fair blew the wind into her bosom right,
>   And th' heavens looked lovely all the while,
> That she did seem to dance as in delight,
>   And at her own felicity did smile ;
> All suddenly there clove unto her keel
>   A little fish that men call Remora,
> Which stopt her course, and held her by the heel,
>   That wind nor tide could move her thence away.
> Strange thing me seemeth that so small a thing
>   Should able be so great an one to wring."

We have already seen how Leviathan, according to the Talmud, is to form a feast for the Saints ; and on turning to the Koran we find a very similar belief, for the food of Mohammed's Paradise is to consist, we are there told, of the flesh of the ox Balam and of the fish Nun. To allay any apprehension on the part of the faithful that these viands will not " go round," as a schoolboy would say, we are reassured on reading that the liver alone of the fish Nun will supply an adequate portion for seventy thousand hungry souls.

The vastness and mystery of the depths of the sea has
naturally led to their being peopled at all ages and amidst
almost all peoples with strange and monstrous forms like
the Chilon, fish-like in body, but having the head of a
man; or the Dies, the creature of a day, whose life's span
ran its course in the hours between the rising and the
setting of the sun ; or more rarely with forms of more
poetic beauty, like those sweet water-wagtails, the mer-
maidens we have already alluded to.   Our illustration is
a representation of the sea lion as believed in, or at least

delineated, by the author of one of the mediæval treatises
on more or less natural history that has come under our
notice.   Ælian describes fish having the heads of lions,
rams, and so forth; and it is, of course, sufficiently
evident that when a man has once got upon that train of
ideas there is nothing to hinder his turning the whole
"Zoological Gardens" into the shadowy depths of
ocean, and evolving from his inner consciousness not

only camel-fish or gazelle-fish, but fifty other equally striking creations. Rondelet, in a book published in the year 1554, gives sufficiently strange illustrations of sea-bishops and sea-monks; and another mediæval writer, Francisci Boussetti, represents in all good faith other forms equally bizarre; but the greatest storehouse by far, so far as our own experience of these old authors goes, is to be found in the " Historia Monstrorum " of Aldrovandus, a book most copiously illustrated, and full of the most extraordinary conglomerations of diverse creatures, or of wild imaginings that find no counterpart in any way in Nature at all. Of these we need give but one example, the very peculiar biped here represented.

Most of us, even the veriest landsmen, must have heard of " Davy Jones's Locker," though few could give it a "local habitation" as well as "a name." Almost all superstitious people—and certainly sailors as a body may be classed as such—have a great objection to telling their beliefs to those whom they think will not receive their communications in a sympathetic spirit; hence it is often exceedingly difficult in most cases to arrive at all at a satisfactory conclusion, as, even after an explanation has been given, we find that what we were told was a mere putting off of the matter at issue, and their real

L

belief has all the time been concealed from us. The following explanation of the seaman's phrase we give for what it is worth, which in our humble opinion is not much. We are told that Jones is a corruption of Jonah the prophet, while *deva* or *duffa* amongst the natives of the West India islands is a spirit or ghost. The sailor's locker, we are all aware, is the one place on board where his private possessions are more or less safe, so that when we hear of an unfortunate having gone to Davy Jones's Locker, we may conclude that he is believed to have gone to some far-down place of safe-keeping in the Spirit-world, as Jonah, by inference, did. It is, however, a decidedly weak point in this explanation that Jonah, whatever may have been his experiences in the depths of the sea, soon exchanged his temporary "locker" for dry land again, and was no doubt ultimately gathered to his fathers in the bosom of mother-earth. Smollett, in his "Peregrine Pickle," ignores all reference to the faithless prophet, and, without seeking out the why or the wherefore of the name, goes, we think, very much more directly to the point when he writes—"This same Davy Jones, according to the mythology of sailors, is the fiend that presides over all the evil spirits of the deep, and is seen in various shapes, warning the devoted wretch of death and woe." Like the Irish Church and many other venerable institutions, Davy is now probably disestablished, or shelved like some fine old admiral on the half-pay list, though it would be interesting to hear the opinion of some navy chaplain on the point, as these old superstitions die very hardly, and at times rather clash with more orthodox theology.

The widespread worship of the serpent is a subject of the greatest interest, though it would take us far away from our present subject if we dwelt at length upon it.

The place held by the serpent in ancient mythologies has, however, caused the creature to pass far from the region of commonplace zoological fact into the realm of myth.

. One old belief more precise than nice was that the serpent first vomits forth its venom before drinking, in order that it may not poison itself by swallowing it; while another curious belief was, that sleeping children whose ears were licked by serpents thereby received the gift of foretelling future events. Cassandra was said thus, amongst other less famous personages more or less believed in by the ancients, to have received the gift of prophecy.

In Squier's " Serpent Worship in America " many legends are given that admirably illustrate the feelings of the North American aborigines, the Peruvians, Mexicans, and other dwellers on that continent with regard to the great serpent that typifies to them, as to so many other races, the great Evil Power.

One of these, an Ojibiway legend, we must venture on quoting, for, somewhat lengthy as it is, it supplies an excellent illustration of this belief in the malign power of the serpent, and incidentally gives an echo of the widespread belief in a deluge, a belief extending from the legends of the Far West to those of distant China.

The Indian legend runs as follows :—" One day, on returning to his lodge in the wilderness after a long journey, Manabazho, the great teacher, missed from it his young cousin : he called his name aloud, but received no answer. He looked around on the sand for the tracks of his feet, and he there for the first time discovered the trail of Meshekenabek, the Great Serpent. He then knew that his cousin had been seized by his great enemy. He armed himself and followed on his track : he passed the great river and crossed mountains

and valleys to the shores of the deep and gloomy lake,
now called Manitou Lake, Spirit Lake, or the Lake of
Devils.   The trail of Meshekenabek led to the edge of
the water.   At the bottom of this lake was the dwelling of
the serpent, and it was filled with evil spirits, his attendants and companions.   Their forms were monstrous and
terrible, but most, like their master, bore the semblance
of serpents.   In the centre of this horrible assemblage
was Meshekenabek himself, coiling his voluminous folds
round the cousin of Manabazho.   His head was red as
with blood, and his eyes were fierce and glowed like fire :
his body was all over armed with hard and glistening
scales of every shade and colour.   Manabazho looked
down upon the writhing spirits of evil, and he vowed
deep revenge.   He directed the clouds to disappear
from the heavens, the winds to be still, and the air to
become stagnant over the lake of the Manitous, and bade
the sun shine on it with all its fierceness ; for thus he
sought to drive his enemy forth to seek the cool shadows
of the trees that grew upon its banks, so that he might
be able to take vengeance upon him.

"Meanwhile Manabazho seized his bow and arrows,
and placed himself near the spot where he deemed the
serpents would come to enjoy the shade ; he then transformed himself into the stump of a withered tree, that
his enemies might not discover his presence.   The winds
became still, the air stagnant, the sun shone hot upon
the lake of the evil Manitous.   By-and-by the waters
became troubled, and bubbles rose to the surface, for
the rays of the hot sun penetrated to the horrible brood
within its depths.   The commotion increased, and a serpent lifted up its head high above the centre of the lake
and gazed around the shores.   Directly another came
to the surface, and they listened for the footsteps of

Manabazho; but they heard him nowhere on the face of the earth, and they said one to another, 'Manabazho sleeps,' and then they plunged again beneath the waters, which seemed to hiss as they closed over them. It was not long before the Lake of Manitous became more troubled than before; it boiled from its very depths, and the hot waves dashed wildly against the rocks on its shores. The commotion increased, and soon Meshe-kenabek, the Great Serpent, emerged slowly to the surface and moved toward the shore. His blood-red crest glowed with a deeper hue, and the reflection from his glancing scales was like the blinding glitter of a snow-covered forest beneath the morning sun of winter. He was followed by all the evil spirits, so great a number that they covered the shores of the lake with their foul and trailing carcases. They saw the broken, blasted stump into which Manabazho had transformed himself, and suspecting it might be one of his disguises, one of them approached and wound his tail around it, and sought to drag it down, but Manabazho stood firm, though he could hardly refrain from crying aloud.

"The Great Serpent wound his vast folds among the trees of the forest, and the rest also sought the shade, while one was left to listen for the steps of Manabazho. When they all slept Manabazho drew an arrow from his quiver; he placed it in his bow, and aimed it where he saw the heart beat against the sides of the Great Serpent. He launched it, and with a howl that shook the mountains and startled the wild beasts in their caves, the monster awoke, and, followed by its frightened companions, uttering mingled sounds of rage and terror, plunged again into the lake. When the Great Serpent knew that he was mortally wounded, both he and the evil spirits around him were rendered tenfold more

terrible by their great wrath, and they arose to over-
whelm Manabazho.   The water of the lake swelled
upwards from its dark depths, and with a sound like
many thunders it rolled madly on his track, bearing the
rocks and trees before it with resistless fury.   High on
the crest of the foremost wave, black as the midnight,
rode the writhing form of the wounded Meshekenabek,
and red eyes glared around him, and the hot breaths of
the monstrous brood hissed fiercely after the retreating
Manabazho.   Then thought Manabazho of his Indian
children, and he ran by their villages, and in a voice of
alarm bade them flee to the mountains, for the Great
Serpent was deluging the earth in his expiring wrath,
sparing no living thing.   The Indians caught up their
children, and wildly sought safety where he bade them.

" Manabazho continued his flight along the base of the
western hills, and finally took refuge on a high mountain beyond Lake Superior, far to the North.   There he
found many men and animals who had fled from the flood
that already covered the valleys and plains, and even
the highest hills.   Still the waters continued to rise, and
soon all the mountains were overwhelmed, save that on
which stood Manabazho.   Then he gathered together
timber and made a raft, upon which the men and women
and the animals that were with him all placed themselves.
No sooner had they done so than the rising floods closed
over the mountain, and they floated alone on the surface
of the waters.   And thus they floated many days ; and
some died, and the rest became sorrowful, and reproached
Manabazho that he did not disperse the waters and
renew the earth, that they might live.   But though he
knew that his great enemy was by this time dead, yet
could he not renew the world unless he had some earth
in his hands wherewith to commence the work.   This

he explained to those who were with him, and he said that were it ever so little, even a few grains, then could he disperse the waters and renew the world.

"The beaver then volunteered to go to the bottom of the deep and get some earth, and they all applauded her design. She plunged in, and they waited long: when she returned she was dead; they opened her hands, but there was no earth in them. 'Then,' said the otter, 'will I seek the earth,' and the bold swimmer dived from the raft. The otter was gone still longer than the beaver, but when he returned to the surface he too was dead, and there was no earth in his claws.

"'Who shall find the earth?' exclaimed all those on the raft, 'now that the beaver and the otter are dead?' 'That will I,' said the musk-rat, and he quickly disappeared between the logs of the raft. The musk-rat was gone very much longer than the otter, and it was thought that he would never return, when he suddenly rose close by, but he was too weak to speak, and he swam slowly towards the raft. He had hardly got upon it when he too died from his great exertion. They opened his little hands, and there, closely clasped between the fingers, they found a few grains of fresh earth. These Manabazho carefully collected and dried in the sun, and then he rubbed them into fine powder in his palms, and rising up he blew them abroad upon the waters. No sooner was this done than the flood began to subside, and soon the trees on the mountains were seen, and then the mountains and hills emerged from the deep, and the plains and the valleys came into view, and the waters disappeared from the land. Then it was found that the Great Serpent, Meshekenabek, was dead, and that the evil Manitous, his companions, had returned to the depths of the Lake of Spirits, from which, for the fear of Manabazho, they never more dared to come forth. In gratitude to the beaver, the otter, and the musk-rat, these animals were ever after held sacred by the Indians, and they became their brethren ; and they were never killed nor molested until the medicine-men of the stranger made them forget their relations and turned their hearts to ingratitude."

As we propose to deal, in conclusion, with some few examples of the fabledom that has grown around various plants, we may fitly usher in this new section of our subject with some little account of the old belief that the barnacle-shells of our shores, or, as some writers held, a tree called the barnacle-tree, developed into Solan-geese,* as the transition from the mythical animal kingdom to the fabulous vegetable kingdom will thus be rendered less abrupt.

This barnacle-goose tree was a great article of faith with our ancestors in the Middle Ages. Gerarde, for example, in his History of Plants gives an illustration of it in all good faith—a branch bearing barnacles and by its side a barnacle goose. Following, however, the plan we have adopted throughout of going directly to the fountain-head, Gerarde shall give us his own description , of this wonder of Nature. We may, however, point out before doing so that the error arose from a near resemblance of two distinct words suggesting that there must be an identity of nature in the things so named. A common kind of shell was in the Middle Ages called pernacula, while the Solan-goose, in France called the barnache,

---

* " From the most refined of saints
　As naturally grow miscreants,
　As barnacles turn Solan-geese
　In the islands of the Orcades."
　　　　　　　　—*Hudibras.*

was the bernacula. Both words being popularly corrupted
into barnacle, it was natural that the two things should be
considered as identical. Gerarde saves this crowning
wonder until the end of his book, and then discourses
as follows concerning it :—"Hauing trauelled from the
grasses growing in the bottom of the fenny waters, the
woods, and mountaines, euen vnto Libanus it selfe ; and

also the sea, and bowels of the same, wee are arriued at
the end of our Historie : thinking it not impertinent
to the conclusion of the same, to end with one of the
maruells of this land (we may say of the world). The
historie whereof to set forth according to the worthinesse
and raritie thereof would not only require a large and
peculiar volume, but also a deeper search into the bowels
of nature than mine intended purpose wil suffer me to
wade into, my sufficience also considered ; leauing the
historie thereof rough hewen unto some excellent men,
learned in the secrets of nature, to be both fined and

refined : in the meantime take it as it falleth out, the naked and bare truth, though vnpolished. There are found in the North parts of Scotland and the Island adiacient, called Orchades, certain trees whereon do grow certaine shells of a white colour tending to russet, wherein are contained little liuing creatures, which shells in time of maturitie do open, and out of them do grow those little liuing things, which falling in the water do become fowles, which we call Barnakles ; in the North of England trant geese, and in Lancashire tree geese ; but the other that do fall vpon the land perish and come to nothing. Thus much by the writings of others, and also from the mouths of people of those parts, which may very well accord with truth.

" But what our eyes have seene and hands haue touched we shall declare. There is a small Island in Lancashire called the pile of Foulders, wherein are found the broken pieces of old and bruised ships, some whereof have been cast thither by Shipwracke, and also the trunks and bodies with the branches of old and rotten trees cast up there likewise ; whereon is found a certain spume or froth that in time breedeth vnto certain shels in shape like those of the Muskle, but sharper pointed and of a whitish colour, wherein is contained a thing in forme like a lace of silke finely wouen as it were together, one end thereof is fastened vnto the belly of a rude masse or lumpe, which in time commeth to the shape and forme of a Birde. When it is perfectly formed the shell gapeth open, and the first thing that appeareth is the foresaid lace or string ; next come the legs of the bird hanging out, and as it groweth greater it openeth the shell by degrees til at length it is all come forth and hangeth onely by the bill ; in short space after it commeth to full maturitie and falleth into the sea, where it gathereth feathers and

groweth to a fowle bigger than a Mallard and lesser than
a goose, hauing blacke legs, and bill and beake, and
feathers blacke and white spotted in such manner as is
our magpie, which the people of Lancashire call by no
other name than a tree goose : which place aforesaid and
all those parts adoining do so much abound thereinth
that one of the best is bought for three pence. For the
truth hereof, if any doubt, may it please them to repaire
unto me, and I shall satisfie them by the testimonie of
good witnesses.

"Moreover it would seeme that there is another sort
hereof; the historie of which is true and of mine owne
knowledge : for trauelling vpon the shore of our English
coast betweene Douer and Rumney, I found the trunke
of an olde rotten tree, which (with some helpe that I
procured by fishermen's wives that were there attending
their husbands returne from the sea) we drew out of
the water upon dry land : vpon this rotten tree I found
growing many thousands of long crimson bladders, in
shape like vnto puddings newly filled, which were very
clear and shining : at the nether end whereof did grow
a shell fish fashioned somewhat like a small Muskle,
but much whiter, resembling a shell fish that groweth
vpon the rokes about Garnsey and Garsey, called a
lympit. Many of these shells I brought with me to
London, which after I had opened I found in them
liuing things without form or shape : in others which
were nearer come to ripeness I found liuing things that
were very naked, shaped like a bird : in others the birds
couered with soft downe, the shell halfe open and the
bird ready to fall out, which no doubt were the fowles
called Barnakles. I dare not absolutely avouch euery
circumstance of the first part of this history concerning
the tree that beareth those buds aforesaid, but will leave

it to a further consideration, howbeit that which I have seen with mine eyes and handled with mine hands, I dare confidently avouch and boldly put down for veritie.

"They spawn as it were in March and Aprille : the geese are formed in May and June and come to fulnesse of feathers in the moneth after.

"And thus hauing through God's assistance discoursed somewhat at large of Grasses, Herbes, Shrubs, Trees, and Mosses, and certain Excrescences of the earth, with other things more incident to the historie thereof, we conclude and end our present volume with this wonder of England. For the which God's name be ever honored and praised."

We extract the foregoing from the first edition of "Gerarde's Historie of Plants," published in 1597. After his death Thomas Johnson, "Citizen and Apothecarie of London," brought out another edition in 1633, and he adds the following note to Gerarde's statement: —"The Barnakle, whose fabulous breed my Author here sets downe, and diuers others haue also delieured, were found by some Hollanders to haue another originall, and that by egges, as other birds haue ; for they in their third voyage to finde out the North-East passage to China and the Moluccos about the eightieth degree and eleven minutes of Northerly latitude, found two little islands, in the one of which they found abundance of these geese sitting upon their egges, of which they got one goose and tooke away sixty egges."

Parkinson, in his "Theater of Plants," published in 1640, gives a picture of a barnacle-tree growing by the sea-shore, and several geese swimming beneath it, at the end of the description of the 14th tribe of plants, "Marsh Water, and Sea Plants, with Mosses and Mushromes."

Though the insertion of the woodcut, as our readers will see, would give one at a casual glance the impression that he was a believer, his comments are sufficiently indicative of his state of mind :—"To finish this treatise of sea plants let me bring this admirable tale of untruth to your consideration, that whatever hath formerly beene related concerning the breeding of these Barnakles to be from shels growing on trees, &c., is utterly erroneous, their breeding and hatching being found out by the

Dutch and others in their navigations to the Northward, as that third of the Dutch in Anno 1536 doth declare." As Gerarde's book was published after the Dutch narrative, we can only conclude that he either had not seen it or that he is one more illustration of the old saying that "A man convinced against his will, remains the same opinion still."

In Munster's Cosmography, a book which was several times reprinted between 1550 and 1570, we find an illus-

tration of the wonderful goose-yielding tree, which we
here reproduce in fac-simile. Munster discourses as
follows on the matter :—"In Scotland are found trees,
the fruit of which appears like a ball of leaves. This
fruit, falling at its proper time into the water below, becomes animated and turns to a bird which they call the
tree-goose. This tree also grows in the island of Pomona,
not far distant from Scotland towards the north." Saxo
Grammaticus, another old cosmographer, also mentions

this tree. Æneas Sylvius notices it too ; he says—"We
have heard that there was a tree formerly in Scotland,
which growing by the margin of a stream produced fruit
of the shape of ducks ; that such fruit, when nearly ripe,
fell, some into the water and some on land. Such as
fell on land decayed, but such as fell into the water
quickly became animated, swimming below, and then
flying into the air with feathers and wings. When in
Scotland, having made diligent enquiry concerning this

matter of King James, we found that the miracle always kept receding, as this wonderful tree is not found in Scotland but in the Orcadian isles." Æneas Sylvius, afterwards better known to the world as Pope Pius II., visited Scotland in the year 1448. His book is in the Latin tongue. William Turner, one of the earliest writers on Ornithology, describes the Bernacle goose as being produced from "something like a fungus growing from old wood lying in the sea." He quotes Giraldus Cambrensis as his authority for the statement, but says he, " As it seemed not safe to popular report, and as, on account of the singularity of the thing, I could not give entire credit to Giraldus, I, when thinking of the subject of which I now write, asked a certain clergyman, named Octavianus, by birth an Irishman, whom I knew to be worthy of credit, if he thought the account of Giraldus was to be believed. He swearing by the gospel, declared that what Giraldus had written about the generation of this bird was most true; that he had himself seen and handled the young unformed birds, and that if I should remain in London a month or two he would bring me some of the brood." In Lobel and Pena's " Stirpium Adversaria Nova," published in London in 1570, there is a figure of the " Britannica Concha Anatifera " growing on a stem from a rock, while beneath, in the water, ducks are swimming about. In his description the writer refers to the accepted belief in such a bird, but declines expressing an opinion of his own until he shall have had an opportunity of visiting Scotland and judging for himself. Ferrer de Valcebro, a Spanish writer who wrote a book on birds in 1680, tells the story of the production from a tree of a bird he calls the Barliata, and lectures his countrymen soundly at their want of belief, and more than insinuates that it is not really so much a want of faith as a contemptible jealousy because the wonder is not found on Spanish soil.

A still more wonderful tree must be the Kalpa-Tarou mentioned in the Hindu mythology, since from this can be gathered not only Solan-geese, but what else may be desired. Whether so multitudinous an array of articles as may be included in the idea of whatever any one and every one, no matter how diverse their tastes may be, could desire, all hung exposed to the view, like the varied display on a Christmas-tree, or whether they sprang into existence as called for, we are unable to say. In either case the tree would be a most valuable possession; the housewife would no longer have to wait for the plums or raspberries to ripen for jam-making, but could at once, even in midwinter, replenish her waning stores with an abundant supply all ready-made; while the connoisseur of choice old etchings, the collectors of rare coins, or the schoolboy earnestly desiring a six-bladed knife could all equally go away with their varied requirements met. The tree is also called the tree of the imagination; and it might, we fear, be equally called the imaginary tree, as all the resources of science are strained in vain to tell us anything more definite about it.

Mohammed tells us in the Koran that a Lote-tree stands in the seventh heaven on the right hand of the throne of Allah, an idea derived, no doubt, from that Tree of Life that bloomed a while in earthly Eden, and that shall be found again in the celestial Paradise of God. The mystical tree that passes out of sight in the earliest chapters of the Bible as the woe descends upon mankind, and reappears at its close, is the welcome symbol that the weary ages of sin and sorrow are at an end for ever, that all tears shall be wiped from off all faces, that there shall be no more death, neither sorrow, nor crying : for all the bitter past is over, and the former things are now for ever passed away.

The sacred tree of the Assyrians, so often seen in the sculptures from Nineveh and Kyonjik, the idolatrous groves of the Israelites, the Hindu tree worship, all point to a most interesting symbolism that would be out of place in our present pages, but that will afford matter of the deepest interest to those who care to work the subject out.

Our readers will no doubt remember the reference in Homer's Odyssey to the Lotophagi, the people who eat of the lotus-tree, and in so doing forgot their friends and homes in their far-off land, losing all desire to return to their native shores, and caring for nought but to rest in ease in the benumbing pleasures of Lotusland.

The immortal Amaranth, "a flower which once in Paradise, fast by the tree of life, began to bloom, but soon for man's offence to Heaven removed," must not be omitted from our pages. Clement of Alexandria refers to it as the *Amarantus flos, symbolum immortalitatis*, and it was thus received for centuries. The name is from the Greek word for immortal, and was bestowed upon it from its never-withering flowers of ruby red. Felicia Hemans, amongst others, refers to it in her fine poem on "Elysium : "—

> " Fair wert thou, in the dreams
> Of elder time, thou land of glorious flowers,
> And summer winds, and low-toned silvery streams
> Dim with the shadows of thy laurel bowers !
>   Where, as they passed, bright hours
> Left no faint sense of parting, such as clings
> To earthly love, and joy in loveliest things."

We could not forbear quoting the opening lines, but

M

the reference we seek occurs a few verses farther on, in
allusion to those—

> " Who, called and severed from the countless dead,
>   Amidst the shadowy Amaranth-bowers might dwell
>   And listen to the swell
>   Of those majestic hymn notes, and inhale
>   The spirit wandering in th' immortal gale."

The passage in our New Testament translated " A
crown of glory that fadeth not away " is in the original
Greek " The amaranthine crown of glory."   Milton is
frequently found to use the word ; it occurs several times
in the " Paradise Lost."   The following fine passage
from the third book of that poem will sufficiently well
illustrate his application of it —

> " The multitude of angels, with a shout
>   Loud as from numbers without number, sweet
>   As from blest voices, uttering joy.   Heaven rang
>   With jubilee, and loud hosannas filled
>   The eternal regions.   Lowly reverent
>   Towards either throne they bow, and to the ground
>   With solemn adoration, down they cast
>   Their crowns inwove with amaranth and gold—
>   Immortal amaranth."

This plant Milton represents as " shading the fount of
life," and with its blood-red flowers—

> " With these, that never fade, the spirits elect
>   Bind their resplendent locks."

The Egyptians wreathed their dead in chaplets of the
sacred lotus to prepare their spirits for entrance into the
presence of the great Osiris.   Several other plants, however, were also employed, but whether their employment
was symbolic or not we have no means of ascertaining.
Amongst the various vegetable curiosities and treasures,

—seeds, gums, wood-sections, and the like—preserved in the large Museum at Kew, will be found—though thousands tramp by them unknowingly—what we may almost venture to call some of the most wonderful things in the world. They are but chaplets, wreaths, and garlands of dried leaves and flowers, until presently we realise that we are gazing on memorials of the dead that were buried with them more than a thousand years before the Christian era. The imagination is then awed as our thoughts attempt to bridge over the interval of two thousand years between these present days and that far-off morning in the childhood of the world when the beautiful fresh flowers of the blue lotus of the Nile were placed in the coffin of Rameses II. Almost all the history of the world has been made since those fragile emblems of passing beauty were laid in the tomb. Empires and monarchies have risen, flourished, and decayed in the interval, and yet this very day, within a mile of where we write these lines, remain, with all their solemn teaching, these wreaths of flowers gathered in the sunshine of old Egypt twenty centuries ago.

> " The past is but a gorgeous dream,
> And time glides by us like a stream,
>   While musing on thy story,
> And sorrow prompts a deep alas !
> That like a pageant thus should pass
>   To wreck all human glory."

Changeless in the midst of mighty changes, these delicate petals are far more wonderful even than the great monuments of Egypt, its pyramids, temples, and obelisks, wonderful as these are, for on those Time has worked with its corroding tooth, while on these it has had but little power. Changeless, again, in all their pristine and God-given beauty, while all the fashions of earth have passed through their kaleidoscope changes, "to one thing constant never," these beautiful lilies of the Nile yet expand their petals every year at Kew within a short distance of these dried flowers of the same species that sprang into existence in the far-off river of Egypt in the dim centuries of the mighty past.*

The Asphodel, referred to by Homer and many later poets, was a plant having edible roots that were laid in the tombs of the dead to nourish the departed spirit in its wanderings in the dim world of shadows. Lucian has a very good illustrative passage that we may here quote. The words are put into the mouth of Charon, and are as follows :—" Down here with us there is nothing to be had but asphodel, and libations and oblations, and that in the midst of mist and darkness; but up in heaven it is all bright and clear, and plenty of ambrosia there, and nectar without stint." The plant referred to by the classic poets was supposed to be the narcissus, but in mediæval days the wild daffodil was intended, at least by the poets, while the herbalists were all at sea in the matter, and applied the name to several different plants.

Gerarde, in his " Historie of Plants," refers to Galen as an authority, quoting from his " Faculties of Nourishments " in defence of the plant he selects, but does not seem to have heard of the old belief in its forming a food for the immortals, and can indeed give it no higher effect in staying the ravages of time and decay than that "the ashes of this Bulbe mixed with oile and hens grease cureth the falling of the haire." Parkinson, in his "Theatrum Botanicum," brings the plant down to a still lower level, and not only sees no poetry in it, but rather more than hints at a fraud, for he says—" The

* Appendix S.

countrey people know no other name thereof or propertie
appropriate unto it but knavery, which, whether they
named it so in knavery, or knew any use of knavery
in it, I neither can learn nor am much inquisitive
thereafter."

We may here remark parenthetically that the old
herbals are full of the most delightfully quaint reading,
and are often freely illustrated with pictures at least as
curious, the frontispieces especially being of the most
elaborate and allegorical nature. The " Rariorum Plan-
tarum Historia " of Clusius is now before us as we write,
and we learn from its title-page that it was published at
Antwerp in the year 1601. We have Adam on one side,
in the simplicity of costume of Eden's earliest days, and
on the other Solomon, with crown and royal robes and
sceptre, bearing in his hands a book. Adam is claimed by
the mediæval herbalists as not only a tiller of the ground,
but also as a student of botanical science, while Solomon, we all remember, wrote a treatise that dealt with
plants, from the lordly cedar to the lowly hyssop of the
wall. Above Adam, in a pot, is a Turk's-cap lily, and
by his side is the fritillary, while Solomon has associated
with him the cyclamen and the crown imperial. The
illustrations in the body of the book are very numerous
and quaint, and, though the book, it will be remembered,
is a history of rare plants, include such common things
as the marsh marigold, the bindweed, and the yellow
loosestrife. Clusius, or Charles d'Ecluse, to give him
his true name, was a Dutch botanist, born 1526, died
1609. He was for some time the director of the Botani-
cal Garden at Vienna, and afterwards the Professor of
Botany at Leyden University, where he died.

The Herbal published by Matthiolus at Venice in the
year 1633 is a particularly fine book. The illustrations

are very large, very numerous, and very good. Another interesting book to see is that of Dodoens, translated by Henry Lyte, "Armigeri, Somersetensis, Angli." The title-page of our copy of the work runs as follows :—"A Nievve Herball, or Historie of Plantes : vvherein is contayned the vvhole discourse and perfect description of all sortes of Herbes and Plantes : their diuers and sundry kindes : their straunge Figures, Fashions, and Shapes : their Names, Natures, Operations, and Vertues : and that not onely of those whiche are here growyng in this our Countrie of Englande but of all others also of forrayne Realmes commonly vsed in Physicke. First set foorth in the Doutche or Almaigne tongue, by that learned D. Rembert Dodoens, Physition to the Emperour, and nowe first translated out of French into English, by Henry Lyte, Esquyer. At London by my Gerard Dewes, dwelling in Pawles Churchyarde at the signe of the Swanne, 1578."

Still earlier in time is "The Vertuose Boke of Distyllacyon of the waters of all maner of Herbes, first compyled by Jherom Bruynswyke, and now newly translated out of Duyche, by Lawrence Andrew," the edition before us being published in London in the year 1527.

In 1551 we find the first appearance of Turner's Herbal, a book that was for a long time a standard authority. It is divided into three sections—

(1.) "A New Herball, wherein are conteyned the names of Herbes in Greke, Latin, Englysh, Duch, Frenche, and in the Potecaries and Herbaries Latin, with the properties, degrees, and naturall places of the same, gathered and made by Wylliam Turner, Physicion unto the Duke of Somersettes Grace, imprinted at London, by Steven Mierdman, Anno 1551.

(2.) A Book of the natures and properties as well as

of the bathes of England as of other bathes in Germany
and Italy, etc., by William Turner, Doctor of Physik,
imprinted at Collen, by Arnold Birckman, in the year
of our Lorde, MDLXII.

(3.) A most excellent and perfecte homish apothe-
carye, etc., translated out of the Almaine Speche into
English, by John Hollybush, imprinted at Collen by
Arnold Birckman, MDLXI."

The latter part of this "homely physick booke for all
the grefes and diseases of the bodye" was really the
work, so far at least as translation went, of Miles Cover-
dale, the notable divine and translator of the Bible,
Hollybush being merely a pseudonym.

The only other quaint old tome that we need here
refer to, though, of course, it must be clearly understood
that we have named but a few of the delightful old books
on plant-lore that have come down to us, is the somewhat
specialised work of Newton. Its title is as follows :—

"An Herbal for the Bible, containing a plaine and
familiar exposition of such Similitudes, Parables, and
Metaphors, both in the Olde Testament and the Newe,
as are borrowed and taken from Herbs, Plants, Trees,
Fruits, and Simples, by observation of their vertues,
qualities, natures, properties, operations and effects : and
by the Holie Prophets, Sacred Writers, Christ Himselfe,
and His blessed Apostles usually alledged, and into their
heauenly Oracles, for the better beautifieng and plainer
opening of the same, profitably inserted. Drawen into
English by Thomas Newton, imprinted at London by
Edmund Bollifant, 1587."

The Ambrosia often referred to by the old writers and
by more modern poets was originally the food of the gods,
nectar being the drink. It is in this sense referred to by
Homer and Ovid, though afterwards the two ingredients

of the Olympian bill of fare became a good deal confused together; thus in the beautiful fable of Cupid and Psyche, in the "Golden Ass" of Apuleius, we find Jupiter conferred on Psyche the gift of immortality by giving her a cup of ambrosia to drink. The term was also sometimes used as descriptive of anything delicious to the taste, fragrant in perfume, or welcome to the eye, from the idea that whatever was used by the immortals, associated with them as an attribute, or that would be grateful in any way to them must be surpassingly excellent. Thus we read in the Iliad of the "ambrosial curls" of Zeus, a somewhat extreme case of departure from the ordinarily limited sense in which the word was most commonly used.* As the word ambrosia means literally "not mortal," it could evidently in this more extended sense be applied by Homer with perfect propriety to the curls or aught else that pertained to the ruler of Olympus.

In the South Kensington Museum may be seen a picture by Francis Danby, bearing the title of "The Upas-tree of the Island of Java." The whole picture is exceedingly dark, but one can just discern in the centre of it the form of a tree, and around this are human bodies and skeletons. The myth of the upas has been created on the very smallest data, and furnishes a striking example of how great a structure of error, not to say gross and wilful exaggeration, can be reared on a basis of truth. The neighbourhood of the tree is unhealthy, not on account of anything in the tree itself, but because it grows in the hot and humid valleys of Java, rank with

---

" * He spoke, and awful bends his sable brows,
  Shakes his ambrosial curls, and gives the nod,
  The stamp of fate and sanction of the god :
  High heaven with trembling the dread signal took,
  And all Olympus to the centre shook."
  —*Iliad*, Book I. lines 683-87.

malaria and fever. A Dutch physician, named Foersch, published in 1783 a narrative of his visit to the island, and amongst his wild statements we find that where the upas grows "not a tree or blade of grass is to be found in the valley or the surrounding mountains, not a bird, beast, reptile, or living thing lives in its neighbourhood." He adds that "on one occasion 1600 refugees encamped within fourteen miles of it, and all but 300 died within two months:" this might easily arise from the malarial vapours, but his picture of the tree standing in the midst of the desolation it had itself created is utterly at variance with the facts. So entirely do the actual facts belie the legend that nothing prospers in its neighbourhood, it is found in the midst of the rich vegetation of the tropics, while the birds perch in its ample branches, and the wild beasts prowl beneath them. So far is it from being the case, to quote one of our own poets, that "Fierce in dead silence on the blasted heath fell upas sits, the hydra tree of death,"—the last relic of the marvellous is gone, when we recall the fact that thousands of holiday-makers have passed harmlessly through the hothouses at Kew, where a specimen of the plant may be seen, and that the refugees from London more or less permanently encamped within a mile or two of it have so far escaped damage from its proximity. The Upas belongs to the same family as the invaluable breadfruit and cow-tree, but, instead of possessing their beneficent properties, yields, when wounded, a thick milky fluid of a very poisonous nature, and which is employed by the natives on their arrows and spear-heads with deadly effect.

The first published account of the Upas-tree will be found in De Brys "India Orientalis," but the scanty particulars of the earlier author become considerably amplified in Sir Thomas Herbert's book of travels,

published in London in the year 1634, and entitled
"Relations of some yeares Travaile." A little later
on, in 1688, we find the tree again referred to in the
" Description historique du Royaume de Macaçar" of
Father Gervaise. The author, who had really resided in
Macassar for several years, affirms that the mere touch or
smell of some of the poisons produced by the natives is
sufficient to produce death, and one of the most deadly
of these was said by him to be produced from the sap of
the Upas. He tells us that arrows dipped in this juice
were as fatal in their effects twenty years afterwards as
at their first preparation. In Kœmpfer's book, published
in the year 1712, we have the plant again described; a
large mixture of fable is at once apparent, but much of
this he gives on the authority of the natives, and he takes
occasion to express his strong doubts of their veracity.
According to him, or them, the collection of the sap is
attended with imminent peril, for not only must the
seeker after the tree penetrate far into places infested
with wild beasts, but he must, when he has found the
object of his search, be careful to pierce it on the side
from whence the wind blows, or he would quickly be
suffocated by the noxious effluvia given forth when the
tree is wounded.

> " Lo ! from one root, the envenomed soil below,
>   A thousand vegetative serpents grow ;
>   In shining rays the scaly monster spreads
>   O'er ten square leagues his far-diverging heads ;
>   Or in one trunk entwists his tangled form,
>   Looks o'er the clouds and hisses in the storm.
>   Steeped in fell poison, as his sharp teeth part,
>   A thousand tongues in quick vibration dart ;
>   Snatch the proud eagle towering o'er the heath,
>   Or pounce the lion, as he stalks beneath ;
>   Or strew, as marshall'd hosts contend in vain,
>   With human skeletons the whitened plain."

Apart from the evil influence exerted on Europeans by climatic and miasmatic drawbacks, the mountain of mystery that has been reared around the dread name of Upas has but little foundation in fact. Its juice is very plentifully yielded, and is of a virulently poisonous character, and even its smell is injurious. In clearing ground near the Upas the natives dread to approach it on this account; but unless the trunk is severely wounded or the tree felled the injurious effects are in the imagination only, and the tree may be approached or ascended with impunity. The Upas is one of the largest of the forest trees of Java, and it is surrounded as other trees are with the usual sturdy vegetation of the tropical wilderness.

The Rev. Dr. Parker, a well-known missionary in Madagascar, gives a description of two trees that recall in their detail much that has hitherto in an especial degree been ascribed to the Upas. In both these species the leaf is spear-head shaped, dark green in colour, very glossy in surface, and very hard and brittle to the touch, and both exude a thick milky juice, while the fruit is like a long black pod, the end being red. One species is a tree with large leaves and a somewhat peculiar stem, as the bark hangs down in long flakes and shows a fresh growth of bark forming beneath and preparing to take the place of the old bark as it falls. The other species is a shrub, with smaller leaves, and the bark not peeling off the stem. Both species are said to possess the power of poisoning any living creatures that approach them, the symptoms of poisoning being severe headache, bloodshot eyes, and a delirium that is presently hushed in death. These trees are natives of Zululand, and only a few persons are believed to have the power of collecting the fruits of the Umdhlebi, and these dare not approach the tree except from the windward side. They also sacrifice a goat or sheep to the demon of the tree. The fruit is collected for the purpose of being used as an antidote to the poisonous effects of the tree from whence they fall, for only the fallen fruit may be collected. As regards habitat, these trees grow on all kinds of soil, but the tree-like species prefers barren and rocky ground. In consequence of the fears of the natives the country around one of these trees is always uninhabited, although in other respects fertile and desirable.

In Persia, we are told, there is a plant, the Kerzereh flower, that loads the air with deathly odour, and that if a man inhales the hot south wind that passes over these flowers during June and July it kills him. Moore, in his Poem of "The Veiled Prophet of Khorassan," alludes to this belief in the lines—

> " With her hands clasp'd, her lips apart and pale,
> The maid had stood, gazing upon the veil
> From whence these words, like south winds through a fence
> Of Kerzrah flowers, came filled with pestilence."

The Mandrake, a plant belonging to the same natural order as the deadly night-shade, henbane, and thorn-apple, had in the Middle Ages many mystic properties assigned to it. The roots are often forked, and when either by nature or art they could be supposed to roughly resemble a man it was looked upon as a talisman securing good fortune to its possessor. The belief in the narcotic and stupefying properties of the plant is referred to in Shakespeare's "Antony and Cleopatra," in the lines—

> " Give me to drink mandragora
> That I might sleep out this great gap of time
> My Antony is away "—

and again in "Othello"—

> " Not poppy, not mandragora,
> Nor all the drowsy syrups of the world
> Shall ever medicine thee to that sweet sleep."

The victories of the Maid of Orleans over the English were ascribed to her possession of a mandrake root. Gerarde, writing in the year 1633, says that the root is long and thick, and divided into two or three parts; but as to its resemblance to a man, " it is no otherwise than in the roots of carrots, parsnips and such like forked or divided into two or more parts, which nature taketh no account of. There hath been many ridiculous tales brought up of this plant, whether of old wiues or some runnagate Surgeons or physicke-mongers I know not, but sure some one or more that sought to make themselves famous and skilful aboue others were the first broachers of that error. They adde further, that it is never or very seldome to be found growing naturally but under a gallows.* They fable further and affirme that he who would take vp a plant thereof must tie a dog there unto to pull it up, which will giue a great shreeke at the digging vp, otherwise if a man should do it he should surely die in short space after. All of which dreames and old wiues fables you shall from henceforth cast out from your books and memory, knowing this that they are all and euery part of them false and most untrue, for I my selfe and my seruants also have digged up, planted and replanted very many and yet could neuer perceiue shape of man. But the idle drones that have little or nothing to do but to eat and drink have bestowed some

---

* " It is supposed to be a creature having life, engendered under the earth of some dead person, put to death for murder."—Thomas Newton, " Herball to the Bible."

of their time in carving the roots of Brionie, which falsifying practice had confirmed the errour amongst the simple and unlearned people who haue taken them upon their report to be the true Mandrakes." *   Parkinson in like manner, in his "Theater of Plants," published in 1640, writes, after describing the plant :—"Those idle forms of the mandrakes which have beene exposed to view publikely both in ours and other lands and countries are utterly deceitful, being the work of cuning knaves, onely to get money by their forgery : do not misdoubt of this relation no more than you would of any other plant set downe in this booke, for it is the plaine truth whereon everyone may relie."   The cry of the mandrake is several times referred to by Shakespeare and others of our poets ; thus in "Romeo and Juliet" we get the line—

" Shrieks like mandrakes torn out of the earth "—

and in the second part of "King Henry VI." Suffolk exclaims—

" Would curses kill, as doth the mandrake's groan."

It was believed that a small dose of the mandrake made persons proud of their beauty, but that a larger quantity deprived them of their senses still more completely, and made them yet more effectually idiots.

Dr. Browne, in his gallant crusade against popular errors, says that the resemblance of the mandrake to the human form "is a conceit not to be made out by ordinary inspection, or any other eyes than such as re-

* " Like a man made after supper of a cheese paring ; when he was naked he was for all the world like a forked radish, with a head fantastically carved upon it with a knife."—Second part of " King Henry IV.," Act iii. scene 2.

garding the clouds behold them in shapes conformable
to pre-apprehension ;" and as to the danger of gathering
the plant, he justly holds it "a conceit not only injurious
unto truth and confutable by daily experience, but somewhat derogatory to the providence of God : That is, not
only to impose so destructive a quality on any plant, but
conceive a vegetable whose parts are useful unto many
should in the only taking up prove mortall unto any. To
think he suffereth the poison of Nubia to be gathered,
yet not this to be moved ! That he permitteth arsenick
and minerall poisons to be forced from the bowells of
the earth, yet not this from the surface thereof ! This
were to introduce a second forbidden fruit and inhance
the first malediction ; making it not only mortal for
Adam to taste the one, but capitall unto his posterity to
eradicate the other."

The orthodox way of plucking up the mandrake was
to stand to the windward of it and, after drawing three
circles round it with a naked sword to dig it up with
one's face looking to the west ; the shrieks that would
follow were in any case a trial to weak nerves, and at
an earlier period were held to be fatal to the hearer.
Philip de Thaun gives the following stratagem as the
only available way of becoming the possessor of it :—
"The man who is to gather it must fly round about it,
must take great care that he does not touch it, then
let him take a dog and let it be tied to it, which has
been close shut up, and has fasted for three days, and
let it be shewn bread and called from afar. The dog
will draw it to him, the root will break, it will send forth
a cry, and the dog will fall down dead at the cry which
he will hear. Such vertue this herb has that no one can
hear it but he must always die, and if the man heard it
he would directly die. Therefore he must stop his ears,

and take care that he hear not the cry lest he die, as the dog will do which shall hear it. When one has this root it is of great value for medicine, for it cures of every infirmity except only death, where there is no help." The office of the herbalist was no sinecure when such a task could be expected of him, as great care had to be exercised not to touch the plant. The tying-up of the dog to it must have been particularly risky, and the consequences of the dog making a premature rush for the bread before the man had time to stop his ears were especially alarming. The writings of De Thaun are full of interesting matter, but his great object was to see in nature figures and symbols of religious truths, hence his narratives have often a somewhat forced character. Thus he tells us that "in India there is a tree of which the fruit is so sweet that the doves of the earth go seeking it above all things, they eat the fruit of it, seat themselves in the tree, they are in repose as long as they are sheltered by it. There is a dragon in the earth which makes war on the birds; the dragon fears so much the tree, that on no acconnt dare it approach it or touch the shadow, but it goes round at a distance, and, if it can, does them injury. If the shadow is to the right then it goes to the left, if it is to the left the dragon goes to the right. The doves have so much understanding which are above in the tree when they see the dragon go all around, which goes watching them, but it does them no harm, nor will they ever have any harm as long as they are in the tree, but when they leave the tree and depart, and the dragon shall come then, it will kill them. This is a great meaning, have it in remembrance." This Indian tree stands not obscurely for the Saviour of the world, while the doves are His faithful ones sheltered in Him from the wiles of the Evil One. When we read story after story all equally *apropos*, we cannot help feeling that a pious fraud has now and then been indulged in, and the comely whole has been attained by a little judicious pruning in one direction, and a little forcing in another, and thus we lose faith in them, at least as examples of the current beliefs of our forefathers.

The Arabs call the mandrake the devil's candle, from a belief that the leaves give out at night a phosphorescent light; and Moore, with his usual felicity, has introduced the idea in his poem of the " Fire-Worshippers:"—

> " How shall she dare to lift her head,
>   Or meet those eyes, whose scorching glare
> Not Yeman's boldest sons can bear?
>   In whose red beam, the Moslem tells,
>   Such rank and deadly lustre dwells,
>   As in those hellish fires that light
>   The Mandrake's charnel leaves at night."

Another old name for the plant was the Enchanter's nightshade, though that very suggestive and rather awe-inspiring title has in these later days become somehow transferred to a very insignificant weed that is common enough in some old gardens and on waste ground, but which is all too small to bear so formidable a title.

The Hebrew word *Dudaim* has, in Genesis and in the Song of Solomon, been translated in the Authorised English Version of the Bible as the mandrake, but this would appear to be nothing more than a guess, various commentators, Calmet, Hasselquist, and others who have written on the subject, not being by any means unanimous. Some tell us that the term is a general one for flowers, while others translate it as lilies, violets, or jessamine, or as figs, mushrooms, bananas, citrons, or melons. Whence we may fairly conclude that no one really knows, and that the whole matter resolves itself into a guess,

N

fortified more or less by dogmatic assertion as a make-weight for the missing knowledge.

One of the most interesting of the old books on our shelves is the " Miracles of Art and Nature, or a Brief Description of the several varieties of Birds, Beasts, Fishes, Plants and Fruits of other Countreys, together with several other Remarkable Things in the World, By R. B. Gent." The author's name thus modestly veiled is Burton, and the date of the book is 1678. In his preface he says—" I think there is not a chapter wherein thou wilt not find various and remarkable things worth thy observation," and this observation of his is strictly within the truth. He arranges his short chapters geo-graphically, but in the most arbitrary way—not alphabeti-cally, not according to the natural grouping together of the countries of which he treats, nor indeed according to any settled method. In fact, he is sufficiently conscious of this, for, to quote his preface again, he says—" 'Tis probable they are *not* so Methodically disposed as some hands might have done, yet for Variety and pleasure sake they are pleasingly enough intermixed." We open the book at random and find " Chap. XX., Castile in Spain; XXI., Norway; XXII., Zisca of Bohemia; XXIII., Assiria ; XXIV., Quivira in California." Adopting his own random and haphazard way of going to work, we will pluck from his quaint pages some few of his botani-cal facts and fancies. His opening chapter deals with Egypt, and in his description of the palm-tree he refers to a very old belief that we may allow him to set forth in his own words :—" It is the nature of this tree though never so ponderous a weight were put upon it not to yield to the burthen, but still to resist the heaviness, and endeavour to raise itself the more upward. For this cause planted in Churchyards in the Eastern Countrys as an Emblem of the Resurrection." A little further on, in his description of Sumatra, we read of "a tree whose Western part is said to be rank poyson and the Eastern part an excellent preservative against it," and of "a sort of Fruit that whosoever eateth of it, is for the space of twelve hours out of his Wits." Travellers' tales have sometimes proverbially been difficult of belief, and it must have been some such as these that procured them their evil report, for we read too that in this same island "there is a river plentifully stored with Fish, whose Water is so hot that it scalds the skin," and that "the cocks have a hole in their backs, wherein the Hen lays her Eggs and hatches her young ones." A few pages further on we read of a tree in Peru, "the North part whereof looking towards the Mountains, brings forth its Fruits in the Summer only; the Southern part looking towards the Sea, fruitful only in Winter." Our old author evidently delights in sharp contrasts. It is curious, however, that the Coca-leaf, which has within the last few years been highly commended for those who have exhausting exercise, is in this book of over 200 years old fully referred to:—"The leaves whereof being dried and formed into little pellets are exceedingly useful in a Journey; for melting in the mouth they satisfie both hunger and thirst and preserve a man in his strength, and his Spirits in Vigour; and are generally esteemed of such sovereign use, that it is thought no less than 100,000 Baskets full of the leaves of this tree are sold yearly at the Mines of Potosia only. Another plant they tell us of, though there is no name found for it, which if put into the hands of a sick person will instantly discover whether he be like to live or dye. For if on the pressing it in his hand he look merry and cheerful it is an assured sign of his recovery, as on the other side of

Death, if sad and troubled." A few pages further on we find ourselves at Sodom and the Dead Sea :—" If but an Aple grow near it, it is by Nature such that it speaks the Anger of God : for without 'tis beautiful and Red, but within nothing but dusty Smoak and Cinders." This belief is a very ancient one. We find it, for instance, in the writings of Tacitus, and it has supplied moralists in all ages with an illustration. In "The Merchant of Venice," for instance, we find the lines—

> " A goodly apple rotten at the heart.
> O, what a goodly outside falsehood hath !"—

and again in " Childe Harold "—

> " Like to the apples on the Dead Sea's shore, all ashes to the taste."

The apple has indeed entered largely into history and legend. According to some writers the forbidden fruit of Eden was a kind of apple, and the *pomum Adami* in one's throat may be accepted as a record of the old belief. " The fruit of that forbidden tree, whose mortal taste brought death into the world, and all our woe." Our readers, too, will recall the golden apple of discord that created strife alike on high Olympus and amongst the sons of men, and that led to the fall of Troy. On the other hand, we read of the apple of perpetual youth in Scandinavian mythology, the food of the gods ; and in the "Arabian Nights" of the apples of Samarkand that would cure all diseases. The apples of Istkahar were all sweetness on one side, all bitterness on the other ; while Sir John Mandeville tells us that the pigmies were fed with the odour alone of the apples of Pyban. Amidst this maze of fancy and legend it would perhaps be scarcely fair to even mention the more historic apple that fell at Woolsthorpe at the feet of Newton, and set his mind thinking on the problem of gravitation.*

At Crete our old author, Burton, finds a plant called Alimos, which it is only necessary to chew to take away all sense of hunger for a whole day; but this wonder pales before those of the flora of Nova Hispania, the country we now call Mexico. " Amongst the Rarities of Nova Hispania, though there be many Plants in it of Singuler Nature, is mentioned that which they call Eagney or Meto, said to be one of the principal : a Tree which they both Plant and Dress as we do our Vines ; it hath on it 40 kinds of leaves, fit for several uses ; for when they be tender they make of them Conserves, Paper, Flax, Mantles, Mats, Shoes, Girdles and Cordage, upon them they grow divers prickles so strong and sharp that the people use them instead of Staws." What Staws may be we cannot say, so we must be content to know that Meto thorns make a very efficient substitute, and are for all practical purposes as good as having the real thing. " From the top of the Tree cometh a Juice like Syrrup, which if you Seeth it will become Honey ; if purified, Sugar ; the Bark of it maketh a good plaister and from the highest of the Boughs comes a kind of Gum, a Soveraigne Antidote against poysons." The tree furnishes

---

* We remember some time ago an interesting article by Dr. Adolf Dux, entitled " La tombe du Savant " appearing in the " Pester Lloyd." The savant was Bolyai, professor of mathematics and physics at Maros-Vásárhely. No statue, no marble mausoleum with sides covered with laudatory inscriptions, marks the place where he lies, but the tomb, by its occupant's strict direction, is overshadowed by the boughs of an apple-tree—" En souvenir des trois pommes qui ont joué un rôle si important dans l'histoire de l'humanité, et il désignait ainsi la pomme d'Ève, et celle de Pâris qui réduisirent la terre à l'esclavage, et la pomme de Newton, qui la replaça au rang des astres." Strangely enough, when Dr. Dux visited the tomb there hung on the tree just three apples—" ni plus ni moins."

at once costume and confection, antidote and rope, and
we can hardly wonder at the people of New Spain setting
considerable store by it.

It would be curious to see the forms of the forty leaves ;
we can well imagine that a plant suggesting about equally
by its foliage the rose, palm, bullrush, buttercup, cactus,
horse-chestnut, and thirty-four other plants would give
our botanists some little difficulty before it got definitely
assigned its just place.

Brazil, like Mexico, is a very large place, and a very
long way off, and two hundred years ago the Royal Mail
Steam-Packet Company was a thing of the far future ;
there was therefore abundant room for play of the
imagination ; thus we read of a kind of corn " which is
continually growing and always ripe ; nor never wholly
ripe, because always growing ; " and of another plant that
yields so sovereign a balm that " the very beasts being
bitten by venomous Serpents resort to it for their cure."
It is interesting, amongst the other strange wonders,
animal and vegetable, that are duly set forth, to come
across a plant that must be very familiar to most persons,
the sensitive plant, the *Mimosa sensitiva* of Brazil, though
in his description of it our author cannot resist an added
touch of the marvellous, imputing to it a power of
observation that later writers would hesitate to confirm,
for he says—" The herb Viva when roughly touched will
close the leaves, and not open them again until the man
that had offended it had got out of sight." We must
not, however, devote more attention to " R. B. Gent,"
great as the temptation to do so may be, for his book is
a perfect mine of the marvellous. Another curious old
book to ponder over awhile is the English Dictionary
of Henry Cockeram, as he certainly produces some extraordinary illustrations of unnatural history. The book

was published in the year 1655, and did not profess to deal with scientific matters alone, but was, to use the author's own language, "an interpreter of hard English words, enabling as well ladies and gentlewomen, young scholars, clerks, merchants, as also strangers of any nation, to the understanding of the more difficult authors already printed in our language, and the more speedy attaining of an elegant perfection of the English tongue." Amongst these hard English words sadly needing an interpretation we will select but five as a sample of the whole :— "Achemedis, an herb which being cast into an army in time of battle causeth the soldiers to be in fear." This probably would be some kind of runner. "Anacramseros, an herb, the touch thereof causeth love to grow betwixt man and man." "Hippice, an herb borne in one's mouth, keeps one from hunger and thirst." "Ophyasta, an herb dangerous to look on, and being drunke it doth terrifie the inside with a sight of dreadful serpents, that condemned persons for fear thereof do kill themselves." "Gelotaphilois, an herb drunk with wine and myrrh, causeth much laughter."

Amidst the mist of error some few men declined to believe quite all that they were told, but exercised for themselves the right of individual judgment. The book we have just referred to was published, as we have seen, in the year 1655, and abounds in strange imaginings ; yet five years before this we find a still better-known book, "the Pseudodoxia Epidemica, or Enquiries into very many Received Tenants and commonly Presumed Truths" of Dr. Browne. The list of commonly presumed truths he ventures to dispute is a very long one, and includes such items of faith as that a diamond is made soft if placed in the blood of a goat, that a pailful of ashes will contain as much water as it would with-

out them, that the two legs on one side of a badger are
shorter than the two on the other side, and so on. As
he approaches the vegetable kingdom he prefaces his
remarks as follows:—"We omit to recite the many vertues
and endlesse faculties ascribed unto plants which sometimes occur in grave and serious authors, and we shall
make a bad transaction for Truth to concede a verity in
half. Swarms of others there are, some whereof our
future endeavours may discover ; common reason I hope
will save us a labour in many whose absurdities stand
naked in every eye, errors not able to deceive the Emblem
of Justice and need no Argus to descry them. Herein
there surely wants expurgatory animadversions whereby
we might strike out great numbers of hidden qualities,
and having once a serious and conceded list we might
with more encouragement and safety attempt their
Reasons." On turning to the list of "vertues" in any
old Herbal, we find, as Browne says, "endlesse faculties
ascribed, and many of them of a character that woulde
we should have imagined have been, during even the
darkest ages, difficult or impossible of credence." Thus
in Gerarde's herbal published in 1633, we find amongst
our British plants one available "against the biting of the
Sea-dragon," two more "a remedy against the poyson of the
Sea-hare," one "against vaine imaginations," another "an
especial remedy against the nightmare," and no less than
thirty-eight preservatives "against the bitings of serpents."
We will, however, confine ourselves to three illustrative instances of the way in which the author of these inquiries
into various received beliefs proceeds to demolish them.
He says, in the first place, that "many things are delivered
and believed of plants wherein at least we cannot but
suspend. That there is a property in Basil to propagate
scorpions and that by the smell thereof they are bred

in the brains of men is a belief much advanced by Hollerius, who found this insect in the brains of a man that delighted much in this smell. Wherein besides that we finde no way to conjoin the effect unto the cause assigned herein the moderns speak but timorously, and some of the Ancients quite contrarily. For according unto Oribasius, physitian unto Julian, the Africans, men best experienced in poisons, affirm whosoever hath eaten Basil although he be stung with a Scorpion shall feel no pain thereby; which is a very different effect, and rather antidotally destroying than promoting its production." Pliny and other ancient writers mention the old belief that the bay-tree, the tree of Apollo, was a preservative against thunder, or rather against lightning; hence Tiberius and some other of the Roman Emperors wore a wreath of bay as an amulet; and in an old English play we find the lines—

> " Reach the bays,
> I'll tie a garland here about his head,
> 'Twill keep my boy from lightning."

Browne discourses on the point as follows:—" That Bayes will protect from the mischief of lightning and thunder is a quality ascribed thereto, common with the fig tree, eagle and skin of a seale. Against so famous a quality Vicomercatus produceth experiments of a Bay-tree blasted in Italy, and therefore although Tiberius for this interest did wear a Laurell about his temples yet did Augustus take a more probable course, who fled under arches and hollow vaults for protection." A most unimperial picture this, great Cæsar deserting his throne and shutting himself up in his wine-cellar when he heard the distant rumbling of the coming storm. " If we consider the three-fold effect of Jupiter's Trisulk, to burn, discusse, and terebrate, and if that be true which is commonly

delivered, that it will melt the blade yet passe the
scabbard, dry up the wine yet leave the hog's head
entire, though it favour the amulet it may not spare
us ; it will be unwise to rely on any preservative, 'tis no
security to be dipped in Styx or clad in the armour of
Ceneus." *

There are many curious legends associated with plants
in classic mythology, such as the metamorphoses of various
lucky or unlucky persons who gained the favour or in-
curred the wrath of the gods, and were in consequence
punished or rewarded by finding themselves laurel-bushes
and the like ; but all this is duly set forth in any mytho-
logical dictionary, and may be there hunted up quite
readily by the curious.

Other legends are associated with religious symbolism,
such as the belief that the palm-tree cannot be bowed
down to earth, but stands erect, no matter how heavily
weighted ; but if we were once to enter upon this most
interesting subject, the preceding pages of our book
would be but a small fragment indeed of all that it would
be possible to introduce.

A very good illustration of the symbolic use of the
palm-tree may be seen on the frontispiece of the "Eikon
Basilike," published in the year 1648. The "Royal
Martyr" kneels before a table on which is placed a
Bible. In his hand he has taken a crown of thorns,
marked "Gratia ; " at his feet is the royal crown of
England, with the inscription "Vanitas," while in the
air above him is a starry crown marked "Gloria." Outside the room we see a landscape. Conspicuous in the
foreground is a palm-tree standing erect with two heavy
weights tied to it, and the legend, "Crescit sub pondere

* Appendix T.

virtus;" while beyond this is a raging sea and a rock rising from its midst, with the legend, "Immota triumphans." The sky is black with rolling clouds, and on either side of the rock we see dark faces in the clouds blowing vehemently against it. Beneath is the "Explanation of the Embleme" in two columns, the one

Latin and the other in the vulgar tongue. The English is as follows :—

> " Though clogged with weights of miseries
> Palm-like depressed I higher rise.
> And as th' immoved Rock outbraves
> The boist'rous Windes and raging waves,
> So triumph I. And shine more bright
> In sad Affliction's Darksom night.
> That Splendid, but yet toilsom Crown
> Regardlessly I trample down.
> With joie I take this Crown of Thorn,
> Though sharp yet easie to be born.

That Heavenlie Crown, already mine,
I view with eies of Faith Divine.
I slight vain things and do embrace
Glorie, the just reward of Grace."

This belief in the impossibility of depriving the palm-tree of its power of upward growth made it a rather popular emblem with those who thought themselves rather "put upon" by fortune or the lack of appreciation from their fellows. Mary Stuart, for example, selected as one of her badges the palm-tree, with the motto, "Ponderibus virtus innata resistit," and other illustrations of the old belief might readily be brought forward.

As these plants, too, whether associated with mythology or religious or other symbolism, are not in themselves fabulous, but are actual laurels, palms, or the like, they need scarcely be dwelt upon at any length in these pages, as our purpose has been rather to deal with forms wholly mythical 'than to enter with any degree of fulness into the mythical beliefs that have grown round forms in themselves natural.

We cannot, in conclusion, do better, we are sure, than transfer bodily to our book the appeal to the reader that appears on the title-page of a quaint little black-letter treatise published in the year 1548—the "Boke of Husbandry" by one Fitzherbert :—

"Go thou lytell boke, with due reuerence
And with an humble hert, recommend me
To all those, that of theyr beneuolence
Thys lytell treatyse doth rede heare or se
Wherewith I praye them contented to be,
And to amende it in place behouable
Where as I haue fauted or be culpable—

For herde it is, a man to attayne
To make a thynge perfyte at the first sighte
But whan it is red and well ouer seene
Fautes may be founde that neuer came to lyght
Though the maker do his diligence and might
Praying them to take it as I haue intended
And to forgiue me yf I haue offended."

APPENDIX.

APPENDIX.

——✦——

A.

THE life and death of St. George, as generally accepted, are so different to the details given by Gibbon in his " History of the Decline and Fall of the Roman Empire," that we give, as a foil, a sketch of the latter as well. From Gibbon it would appear that George, surnamed the Cappadocian, was born in Cilicia in a fuller's shop, that he raised himself from this obscure origin by his talents as a parasite, and that those whom he so shamelessly flattered and assiduously fawned on repaid their worthless dependent by procuring for him lucrative contracts to supply the army with bacon and other stores. Herein he accumulated, as some other army contractors have done since, a vast sum of money by the basest acts of fraud and corruption, until matters became so bad and his shortcomings so notorious that he absconded with his ill-gotten gains. After the disgrace attached to this had in some measure subsided, we next find him embracing, with real or affected zeal, the doctrines of Arianism, and on the death of the Archbishop Athanasius the prevailing faction

O

promoted the ex-contractor to the vacant chair. He had scarcely been established in this high and responsible office ere he sullied the dignity of his position by acts of the greatest cruelty against those who differed from him, and by the development anew of the keenest avarice. He asserted for himself the right to various important monopolies, and impoverished the State while he enriched himself by alone supplying salt, paper, and various other necessaries. The people at length rose in rebellion, and on the accession of Julian he lost the high support that had hitherto, by aid of the civil and military power of the State, maintained him in his position. He was ignominiously dragged in chains to the public prison, and the mob, impatient of the delays of the law, or apprehensive that he might use his wealth and influence to stifle inquiry, presently forced open the gates and tore him to pieces. The Church was at that time an arena of fierce dissension between the Arians and Athanasians, and his followers, conveniently ignoring the facts of his life, asserted that the rival party in the Church had stirred up the strife against him. He received the just reward of his tyranny, or possibly the saintly crown of the martyr for his faith, in the year 361, and in 494 Pope Gelasius formally and officially admitted his claim to a position amongst the saints of the Church. We find him held in great reverence in the sixth century in Palestine, Armenia, and Rome. His fame was brought home from the East by the Crusaders, and his popularity in England dates from that time. So much party feeling has clustered around the matter, and so many learned authorities have been drawn up on one side or the other, that we can only feel that no real verdict one way or the other is now possible.

B.

As we have already in the body of the text given in full detail the accepted prose version of the conflict of St. George with the dragon, it seemed scarcely advisable to repeat these details in metrical form. As we feel, at the same time, that such old ballads will probably possess interest for some, at least, of our readers, we, instead of banishing the story from our book entirely, dismiss it to the Appendix merely, where it can be equally readily read or ignored in accordance with individual tastes. The ballad, as given in Dr. Percy's "Reliques," is based on ancient black-letter copies in the Pepys Collection. In the original the poem is forty-four verses long, but we content ourselves with those that relate to the combat with the dragon, and leave out those that affect what may be termed the politics of the court, the promise of the maiden to the hero, the subsequent endeavours to evade the bargain, and the various consequences to St. George and others that arose from this breach of faith :—

" Of Hector's deeds did Homer sing,
    And of the sack of stately Troy,
What griefs fair Hélena did bring,
    Which was Sir Paris' only joy :
And by my pen I will recite
    St. George's deeds, an English knight.

Against the Sarazens so rude
    Fought he full well and many a day ;
Where many gyants he subdued,
    In honour of the Christian way :
And after many adventures past
    To Egypt land he came at last.

Now as the story plain doth tell,
  Within that countrey there did rest
A dreadful dragon fierce and fell,
  Whereby they were full sore opprest,
Who by his poisonous breath each day,
  Did many of the city slay.

The grief whereof did grow so great
  Throughout the limits of the land,
That they their wise men did entreat
  To show their cunning out of hand ;
Which way they might this fiend destroy,
  That did the country thus annoy.

The wise men all before the king
  This answer framed incontinent ;
The dragon none to death might bring
  By any means they could invent :
His skin more hard than brass was found,
  That sword nor spear could pierce nor wound.

When this the people understood,
  They cryed out most piteouslye,
The dragon's breath infects their blood,
  That every day in heaps they dye :
Among them such a plague it bred,
  The living scarce could bury the dead.

No means there were, as they could hear,
  For to appease the dragon's rage,
But to present some virgin dear,
  Whose blood his fury might assuage ;
Each day he would a maiden eat,
  For to allay his hunger great.

This thing by art the wise men found,
  Which truly must observed be ;
Wherefore throughout the city round
  A virgin pure of good degree
Was by the king's commission still
  Taken up to serve the dragon's will.

Thus did the dragon every day
  Untimely crop some virgin flower,
Till all the maids were worn away,
  And none were left him to devour :
Saving the king's fair daughter bright,
  Her father's only heart's delight.

Then came the officers to the king
  That heavy message to declare,
Which did his heart with sorrow sting ;
  She is, quoth he, my kingdom's heir :
O let us all be poisoned here,
  Ere she should die, that is my dear.

Then rose the people presently,
  And to the king in rage they went ;
They said his daughter deare should dye,
  The dragon's fury to prevent :
Our daughters all are dead, quoth they,
  And have been made the dragon's prey :

And by their blood we rescued were,
  And thou hast saved thy life thereby ;
And now in sooth it is but faire,
  For us thy daughter so should die.
O save my daughter, said the king ;
  And let ME feel the dragon's sting.

Then fell fair Sabra on her knee,
  And to her father dear did say,
O father strive not thus for me,
  But let me be the dragon's prey ;
It may be for my sake alone
  This plague upon the land was thrown.

'Tis better I should dye, she said,
  Than all your subjects perish quite ;
Perhaps the dragon here was laid,
  For my offence to work his spite :
And after he hath sucked my gore
  Your land shall feel the grief no more.

What hast thou done, my daughter dear,
  For to deserve this heavy scourge ?
It is my fault, as may appear,
  Which makes the gods our state to purge :
Then ought I die, to stint the strife,
  And to preserve thy happy life.

Like madmen, all the people cried,
  Thy death to us can do no good ;
Our safety only doth abide
  In making her the dragon's food.
Lo, here I am, I come, quoth she,
  Therefore do what you will with me.

Nay stay, dear daughter, quoth the queen,
  And as thou art a virgin bright,
Thou hast for vertue famous been,
  So let me cloath thee all in white ;
And crown thy head with flowers sweet,
  An ornament for virgins meet.

And when she was attired so,
  According to her mother's mind,
Unto the stake she then did go ;
  To which her tender limbs they bind :
And being bound to stake and thrall
  She bade farewell unto them all.

Farewell, my father dear, quoth she,
  And my sweet mother meek and mild ;
Take you no thought nor weep for me,
  For you may have another child :
Since for my country's good I dye,
  Death I receive most willinglye.

The king and queen and all their train
  With weeping eyes went then their way,
And let their daughter there remain,
  To be the hungry dragon's prey ;
But as she did there weeping lye,
  Behold St. George came riding by.

And seeing there a lady bright
   So rudely tyed unto a stake,
As well became a valiant knight,
   He straight to her his way did take :
Tell me, sweet maiden, then quoth he,
   What caitiff thus abuseth thee ?

And, lo, by Christ his cross I vow,
   Which here is figured on my breast,
I will revenge it on his brow,
   And break my lance upon his chest :
And speaking thus whereas he stood,
   The dragon issued from the wood.

The lady that did first espy
   The dreadful dragon coming so,
Unto St. George aloud did cry
   And willed him away to go ;
Here comes that cursed fiend, quoth she,
   That soon will make an end of me.

St. George then looking round about,
   The fiery dragon soon espied,
And like a knight of courage stout,
   Against him did most fiercely ride ;
And with such blows he did him greet,
   He fell beneath his horse's feet.

For with his lance that was so strong,
   As he came gaping in his face,
In at his mouth he thrust along,
   For he could pierce no other place ;
And thus within the lady's view
   This mighty dragon straight he slew.

The favour of his poisoned breath
   Could do this holy knight no harm ;
Thus he the lady saved from death,
   And home he led her by the arm :
Which when King Ptolemy did see,
   There was great mirth and melody."

C.

In Hippeau's comments on the non-reliability of much of the natural history of Guillaume he points out that not only was it difficult for these early writers to ascertain the truth, but that the truth in its lower sense was not really much striven after or valued. He says—" N'oublions pas que les pères de l'Église se préoccupèrent toujours beaucoup plus de la pureté des doctrines qu'ils avaient à développer, que de l'exactitude scientifique des notions sur lesquelles ils les appuyaient. L'object important pour nous, dit Saint Augustin (Ps. cii., àpropos de l'aigle, qui disait-on, brise contre la pierre l'éxtrémité de son bec devenue trop long) est de considérer la signification d'un fait et non d'en discuter l'authenticité.

" Dans la vaste étendue des Cieux, au sien des mers profondes, sur tous les points du globe terrestre, il n'est pas un phénomène, pas une étoile, pas un quadrupède, pas un oiseau, pas une plante, pas une pierre, qui n'éveille quelque souvenir biblique, qui ne fournisse la matière d'un enseignement moral, qui ne donne lieu à quelqu' effusion du cœur, qui n'ait à révéler quelque secret de Dieu."

D.

The palm was by old writers called the phœnix-tree, and in Greek the same word is used to express both the bird and the tree.

" *Sebastian.* Now I will believe
　　　　　　That there are unicorns ; that in Arabia
　　　　　　There is one tree, the phœnix' throne ; one phœnix
　　　　　　At this hour reigning there.

Antonio.　　　　　　　　　　I'll believe both ;
　　　　　　And what does else want credit come to me,
　　　　　　And I'll be sworn 'tis true ; travellers ne'er did lie,
　　　　　　Though fools at home condemn them."—*Tempest.*

E.

" The story of Guy is so obscured with fable that it is
difficult to ascertain its authenticity. He was the hero of
succeeding Earls of Warwick. William Beauchamp called
his eldest son after him. Thomas by his last will bequeathed
the sword and coat-of-mail of this worthy to his son.
Another christened a younger son after him, and dedicated
to him a noble tower, whose walls are ten feet thick, the
circumference 126, and the height 113 feet from the bottom
of the ditch. Another left as an heirloom to his family a
suit of arras wrought with his story. His sword and armour,
now to be seen in Warwick Castle, were by patent, 1 Henry
VIII., granted to William Hoggeson, yeoman of the battery,
with a fee of 2d. per day. In the porter's lodge at the castle
they still show his porridge-pot, flesh-fork, iron shield, breast-
plate and sword, horse furniture, walking staff nine feet
high, and even a rib of the dun cow which he pretended to
have killed on Dunsmore Heath. In short, his fame and
spirit seem to have inspired his successors, for from the
Conquest to the death of Ambrose Dudley there was scarce
a scene of action in which the Earls of Warwick did not
make a considerable figure."—*Camden's Britannia*, vol.
ii., 1806.

F.

Of the " Bestiary " of Philip de Thaun only one copy of
the MS. is known, that in the Cottonian Collection, though
of another of his quaint treatises, the " Livre des Créatures,"
there are seven copies extant. Three of these are in the
Vatican Library, and in England one may be seen in the
Sloane Library, and another in the Cottonian. The author
had as his great patron Adelaide of Louvain, the second
queen of King Henry I. He dedicates his " Bestiary " to
her in the following lines :—

> " Philippe de Thaun into the French language
> Has translated the Bestiary, a book of science,
> For the honour of a jewel who is a very handsome woman,
> Aliz is she named, a queen is she crowned,
> Queen is she of England, may her soul never have trouble."

His poems are the earliest examples extant of the Anglo-
Norman language ; we give herewith an illustration of it,
the translation being from the excellent reproduction of the
book by Thomas Wright, F.S.A. :—

> " En un livre divin, que apelum Genesim,
> Iloc lisant truvum quæ Dés fist par raisum
> Le soleil e la lune, e esteile chescune.
> Pur cel me plaist à dire d'ico est ma materie,
> Que demusterai e à clers e à lai,
> Chi grant busuin en unt, e pur mei perierunt.
> Car unc ne fud loée escience celée ;
> Pur ço me plaist à dire, ore i seit li veir Sire ! "

> " In a divine book, which is called Genesis
> There reading, we find that God made by reason
> The sun and the moon, and every star.
> On this account it pleases me to speak, of this is my matter,
> Which I will show both to clerks and to laics,
> Who have great need of it, and will perish without it.
> For science hidden was never praised ;
> Therefore it pleases me to speak, now may the true Lord be with it."

G.

As the limited space at our disposal prevents anything like an exhaustive account of the wonders narrated by Mandeville and others, we give the titles of some few old works, in case the reader may care to dive into them at greater length than is here at all possible. The first we would mention is Richard Hackluyt's black-letter folio, published in 1589. Its full title runs as follows :—" The Principal Navigations ; Voiages and Discoveries of the English Nation, made by Sea or over Land to the most remote and farthest distant Quarters of the earth at any time within the compasse of these 1500 yeeres." Another is " Purchas his Pilgrimage, or Relations of the World, Asia, Africa and America and the Ilands adiacent," published in London in the year 1614 ; a very quaint and interesting old book. The " Ortus Sanitatis " is another very curious old black-letter volume, dealing with animals, plants, &c., and richly illustrated with very remarkable woodcuts. To these we may add Marco Polo's travels in the thirteenth century, detailing the observations of this early traveller on many remarkable places and things seen or heard of by him, chiefly in the East. Struy's " Perillous and most Unhappy Voyages through Moscovia, Tartary, Italy, Greece, Persia, Japan," &c., is another interesting old volume. It was published in the year 1638, and is illustrated by divers curious plates. To this list we need only add the " Natvrall and Morall Historie of the East and West Indies," by Joseph Acosta ; 1604. " Intreating of the Remarkable things of Heaven, of the Elements, Mettalls, Plants, and Beasts which are proper to that Country." Where we have given a date it is simply that

of the copy that has come under our own cognisance : many
of these works were of sufficient popularity to run through
several editions, sometimes several years apart ; nevertheless
the. dates we give will give an approximate notion that is
decidedly better than nothing.   This list might readily be
extended tenfold.

H.

The sphinx is described in Bacon's book, " The Wisdom
of the Ancients, Written in Latin by the Right Honourable
Sir Francis Bacon Knt. Baron of Verulam and Lord
Chancellor of England, and done into English by Sir Arthur
Gorges Knt." After narrating the story, he expounds it
as follows :—" This Fable contains in it no less Wisdom than
Elegancy, and it seems to point at Science, especially that
which is joyn'd with Practice, for Science may not absurdly
be call'd a Monster, as being by the ignorant and rude
Multitude always held in Admiration. It is diverse in
Shape and Figure by reason of the infinite Variety of
Subjects wherein it is conversant. A Maiden Face and
Voice is attributed unto it for its gracious Countenance and
Volubility of Tongue. Wings are added, because Sciences
and their Inventions do pass and fly from one to another,
as it were in a Moment, seeing that the Communication of
Science is as the kindling of one Light at another. Ele-
gantly also it is feigned to have sharp and hooked Talons,
because the Axioms and Arguments of Science do fasten so
upon the Mind, and so strongly apprehend and hold it, as
that it stir not nor evade, which is noted also by the Divine

Philosopher—The Words of the Wise are as Goads and Nails driven far in.

Moreover, all Science seems to be placed in steep and high Mountains, as being thought to be a lofty and high thing, looking down upon Ignorance with a scornful Eye. It may be observed and seen also a great Way, and far in compass, as things set on the Tops of Mountains.

Furthermore, Science may well be feigned to beset the High-way, because which way soever we turn in this Progress and Pilgrimage of Human Life we meet with some Matter or Occasion offered for Contemplation. Sphynx is said to have received from the Muses divers difficult Questions and Riddles, and to propound them unto Men, which remaining with the Muses are free (it may be) from savage Cruelty; for, so long as there is no other end of Study and Meditation than to know, the Understanding is not racked and imprisoned, but enjoys Freedom and Liberty, and even Doubts and Variety find a kind of Pleasure and Delectation. But when once these Enigmas are delivered by the Muses to Sphynx, that is, to Practice, so that it be sollicited and urged by Action and Election and Determination, then they begin to be troublesome and raging, and unless they be resolved and expedited they do wonderfully torment and vex the Minds of Men, distracting, and in a manner rending them into sundry Parts.

Moreover, there is always a twofold Condition propounded with Sphynx her Enigmas. To him that doth not expound them, distraction of Mind, and to him that doth, a Kingdom, for he that knows that which he sought to know hath attain'd the end he aim'd at, and every Artificer also commands over his Work.

Moreover it is added in the Fable, that the Body of

Sphynx, when she was overcome, was laid upon an Ass, which indeed is an elegant Fiction, seeing there is nothing so acute and abstruse but, being well understood and divulged, may be well apprehended by a slow Capacity. Neither is it to be omitted that Sphynx was overcome by a Man lame in his Feet ; for when Men are too swift of Foot and too speedy of Pace in hasting to Sphynx, her Enigmas, it comes to pass that, she getting the upper Hand, their Wits and Minds are rather distracted by Disputations than that ever they come to command by Works and Effects."

I.

The spaces in the frieze of the Parthenon, known architectively as the metopes, were filled with sculptures illustrating the struggle between the Lapithæ and the Centaurs. Thirty-nine of these slabs remain in their original position in the temple, while seventeen are in the British Museum and one in the Louvre. In their beauty and bold design they are some of the grandest monuments of Greek art. Other very fine examples may be seen in the fragments in our national collection from the frieze of the temple of Apollo Epicurius, near Phigalia, and the Theseum at Athens. There are also two very fine single statues of centaurs in the Capitoline Museum.

J.

Centaury is so called from an old myth that Chiron, the centaur, cured himself from a wound given by a poisoned arrow by using some plant that Pliny, therefore, calls *Centaurium ;* but whether it was this plant, or a knapweed, or any plant at all, or whether there even ever was a centaur named Chiron, or a centaur named anything else, are points we must be content to leave. Linnæus called the plant the *Chironia;* its modern generic name merely signifies red, as most of the flowers in the genus have blossoms of some tint of red ; but in the specific name *Centaurium* we recognise that the old myth still finds commemoration. In some parts of England the rustics corrupt centaury into sanctuary, and the Germans call it the *tausend-gulden-kraut.* This strange name is built upon another corruption, some of the old writers having twisted *Centaurea* into *Centum aurei,* and the Germans have lavishly multiplied by ten the hundred golden coins. The centaury is said to be a good and cheap substitute for the medicinal gentian, and, as a hair-dye, was for a long time held in repute for the production of a rich golden yellow tint.

" My floure is sweet in smell, bitter my iuyce in taste,
Which purge choler, and helps liuer, that else would waste."

The centaury still figures largely in rustic medicine and in the prescriptions of the herbalists ; we have seen the country agents of these latter with armfuls of centaury as large as they could carry. Into all its accredited virtues in mediæval times we need not here go ; in fact, if our readers will make out at random a list of some twenty of the ills of suffering mortality, and boldly assert that such ills need not exist at all in a world that also produces centaury, they will be sufficiently near the mark for practical purposes.

K.

A good illustration of this may be seen in Brathwait's book, published in 1621, and entitled " Nature's Embassie, or the Wilde-Man's Measures danced by twelve Satyres," the dance itself being very quaintly represented on the curious old woodcut title.

L.

An old author whose voluminous works on natural history are very interesting and curious, and richly illustrated with engravings at least as quaint in character as the text. The " Historia Monstrorum," was published in folio at Bologna in 1642, and is full of the most extraordinary animal forms. His various works range in date from 1602 to 1668, and are, with one exception—Venice—published either at Bologna or Frankfort. All are very curious, and will well repay our readers if they can get an opportunity of seeing them.

Another book of very similar character is Boiastuau's " Histoires Prodigeuses," published in Paris in 1561, a strange assemblage of curious and monstrous figures.

M.

Bacon, in his " Wisdom of the Ancients," writes as follows :—" The Fable of the Syrens seems rightly to have been apply'd to the pernicious Allurements of Pleasure, but in a very vulgar and gross manner. And therefore to me it seems that the Wisdom of the Ancients have with a farther reach or insight strained deeper Matter out of them, not unlike the Grapes ill press'd; from which though some Liquor were drawn, yet the best was left behind. This Fable hath relation to Men's Manners, and contains in it a manifest and most excellent Parable. For Pleasures do for the most proceed out of the Abundance and Superfluity of all things, and also out of the Delights and jovial Contentments of the Mind; the which are wont suddenly as it were with winged Inticements to ravish and rap Mortal Men: But Learning and Education brings it so to pass as that it restrains and bridles Man's Mind, making it so to consider the Ends and Events of Things as that it clips the Wings of Pleasure. These Syrens are said to dwell in remote Isles: for that Pleasures love Privacy and retired places, shunning always too much Company of People. The Syren's Songs are so commonly understood, together with the Deceits and Danger of them, as that they need no Exposition. But that of the Bones appearing like white Cliffs, and descry'd afar off, hath more Acuteness in it; for thereby it is signify'd that, albeit the Examples of Afflictions be manifest and eminent, yet do they not sufficiently deter us from the wicked Enticements of Pleasures.

As for the Remainder of this Parable, tho' it be not over mystical, yet it is very grave and excellent: For in it we set out three Remedies for this violent enticing Mischief: to wit, Two from Philosophy, and One from Religion. The first Means to shun these inordinate Pleasures is to withstand and resist them in their Beginnings and seriously to Shun all Occasions to entice the Mind, which is signified in that stopping of the Ears; and that Remedy is properly used by the meaner and baser sort of People, as it were Ulysses Followers or Mariners; whereas more heroick and noble

P

Spirits may boldly converse even in the midst of these seducing Pleasures, if with a resolved Constancy they stand upon their Guard and fortify their Minds; and so take greater Contentment in the Trial and Experience of this their approved Virtue, learning rather thoroughly to understand the Follies and Vanities of those Pleasures by Contemplation, than by Submission. Which Solomon avouched of himself when he reckoned up the Multitude of those Solaces and Pleasures wherein he swam, doth conclude with this sentence—Wisdom also continued with me. Therefore these Heroes, and Spirits of this excellent Temper, even in the midst of these enticing Pleasures, can shew themselves constant and invincible and are able to support their own virtuous Inclination against all heady and forcible Perswasions whatsoever; as by the Example of Ulysses, that so peremptorily interdicted all pestilent Counsel as the most dangerous and pernitious Poysons to captivate the Mind: But of all other Remedies in this Case that of Orpheus is most predominant : For they that chaunt and resound the Praise of the Gods confound and dissipate the Voices and Incantations of the Syrens, for Divine Meditations do not only in Power subdue all sensual Pleasures, but also far exceed them in Swiftness and Delight."

N.

"A Scorneful Image or Monstrous Shape of a Marvellous Strange Fygure called Sileni Alcibiadis presentyng ye state and condio of this present world, and inespeciale of the Spirituallte how farre they be from ye perfite trade and life of Criste, wryte in the later tonge by that famous Clerke Erasmus and lately translated into Englyshe." A rare old black-letter book.

O.

" All those airy shapes you now behold
  Were human bodies once, and clothed with earthly mould ;
  Our souls, not yet prepared for upper light,
  Till doom's-day wander in the shades of night."
  —DRYDEN, *The Flower and the Leaf.*

P.

Before finally dismissing the Fairies we would just refer our readers to a very curious book amongst the Lansdowne MSS. (No. 231) in the British Museum. It was written by John Aubrey, in the year 1686, and is entitled " Remaines of Gentilisme and Judaisme." The title, however, is no guide whatever to the character of the book, which seems to be merely a note-book for the writing down, without any apparent system or order, of any curious matters that came before him. Scattered throughout these notes are various references to the Fairies ; and though they naturally, to a certain extent, repeat what we have already written, they are perhaps sufficiently interesting to quote, as they were the popular notions current at the time. We can only give them in the disjointed way in which we find them, as they are mixed up with all kinds of other matter.

" Not far from Sr Bennet Hoskyns there was a labouring man that rose up early every day to goe to worke ; who for a good while many dayes together found a ninepence in the way that he went.   His wife wondering how he came by so much money was afraid he gott it not honestlye ; at last he told her, and afterwards he never found any more."

"They were wont to please the Fairies, that they might doe them no shrewd turnes, by sweeping clean the Hearth and setting by it a dish of fair water half sad breade, whereon was sett a messe of milke sopt with white bread.   And on the morrow they would find a groat of which if they did speak of it they never had any again.   Mrs H. of Hereford had as many groates or 3^{ds} this way as made a little silver cup or bowle of (I thinke) 3^{lbs} value, wh her daughter preserves still."

"In the vestry at Frensham, on the N. side of the chancel, is an extraordinary great kettle or caldron, which the inhabitants say, by tradition, was brought hither by the fairies, time out of mind, from Borough hill, about a mile from hence.   To this place, if any one went to borrow a yoke of oxen, money, &c., he might have it for a year or longer, so he kept his word to return it.   There is a cave, where some have fancied to hear musick.   On this Borough hill is a great stone lying along, of the length of about six feet : they went to this stone and knocked at it, and declared what they would borrow and when they would pay, and a voice would answer when they should come, and that they should find what they desired to borrow at that stone. This caldron, with the trivet, was borrowed here after the manner aforesaid, but not returned according to promise, and though the caldron was afterwards carried to the stone it could not be received, and ever since that time no borrowing there.   The people saw a great fire one night not long since, the next day they went to see if any heath was burnt there, but found nothing."

"Some were led away by the Fairies, as was a third riding upon Hackpen with corn led a dance to ye Devises. So was a shepherd of Mr Brown of Winterburn-Basset, but never any afterwards enjoy themselves. He sayd that ye ground opened, and he was brought into strange places underground, where they used musicall Instruments, Viols and Lutes, such (he sayd) as Mr Thomas did play on."

"Virgil speakes somewhere (I think in ye Georgiques) of Voyces heard louder than a Man's. Mr Lancelot Morehouse did averre to me that he did once heare such a loud laugh on the other side of a hedge, and was sure that no Human voice could afford such a laugh."

"In Germany old women tell stories received from their Ancestors that a Water-monster, called the Nickard, doth enter by night the chamber, and stealeth when they are all sleeping the new-born child, and supposeth another in its place, which child growing up is like a monster and commonly dumb. The remedy whereof that the Mother may get her own child again—the mother taketh the Suppositium and whipps it so long with the rod till the sayd Monster, the Nickard, bringes the Mother's own child again, and takes to him the Suppositium, which they call Wexel balg."

In another curious old book on our shelves, the "Philosophical Grammar" of Benjamin Martin, published in 1753, we find another allusion to the belief in Fairies. The book is written in the question and answer style once so popular, and after a long dissertation on the Animal Kingdom, we come at last to the question, "Pray before we leave this survey of the Animal Creation let me ask your opinion of Griffins, the Phœnix, Dragons, Satyrs, Syrens, Unicorns, Mermaids and

Fairies. Do you think there really are any such things in Nature?" The answer is so far to the point, and so interesting in itself as showing the state of mind on the whole subject, that we give it in all its fulness.

The *Phœnix* is mentioned by *Pliny*, and other Antients, more credulous than skilful; but has long since been rejected as a vulgar Error. The *Griffin* and *Harpy* have had a Place given them in Modern Histories of Nature, but not without great Reproach and Ridicule to the Authors. *Satyrs*, *Syrens*, and *Fairies*, are all Poetical Fictions. The *Scripture* makes mention of the *Dragon* and the *Unicorn*, and most *Naturalists* have affirmed that there have been such Creatures, and given Descriptions of them; but the Sight of these Creatures or credible Relations of them, having been so very rare, has occasioned many to believe there never were any such Animals in Nature; at least it has made the History of them very doubtful. As to *Mer-men* and *Mermaids*, there certainly are such Creatures in the Sea as have some distant Resemblance of some Parts of the Human Shape, Mien, and Members; but not so perfectly like them, 'tis very probable, as has been represented. In all such ambiguous Pieces of History 'tis better not to be positive, and sometimes to suspend our Belief, rather than credulously embrace every current Report, or vulgar Assertion which may perhaps expose us to Ridicule.

It makes but little for the Credit of the Histories of *Dragons*, *Unicorns*, *Mer-maids*, &c., that their names are not to be found in the Transactions of our celebrated Royal Society, who, 'tis well known, derive their Intelligence at the best Hand from almost all Parts of the World. At least, I can find no mention of any such Creatures in the seven Volumes of Abridgments by *Lowthorp*, *Eames, and Jones*.

2. The *Histoire Naturelle de l'Universe* gives an Account of several Persons who have described the *Unicorn;* and particularly Father *Lobos*, in his Voyage to the *Abyssine Empire*, says, that this Animal is of the Shape and Size of a fine-made and well-proportion'd Horse, of a bay Colour with a black Tail and Extremities; he adds, that the Unicorns of *Tuacua* have very short Tails; and those of *Ninina* (a Canton in the same Province) have theirs very long, and their Manes hanging over their Heads. *Vol.* IV. *Page* 3.

3. *Du Mont* says, he saw the Head of a Dragon which was set up over the *Water-Gate* in the City of *Rhodes;* this Dragon was 33 Feet long, and wasted all the Country round, 'till it was slain by *Deodate de Gozon*, a Knight of *St. John.* He says, the *Head* was like that of an Hog, but much larger; its *Ears* were like a Mule's, but cut off; the *Teeth* were extraordinary sharp and long; the *Throat* wide; its *Eye* hollow, and burning like two Coals. It had two little Wings on its Back; its *Legs* and *Tail* like those of a Lizard, but strong, and arm'd with sharp and venomous Talons. His Body was cover'd with Scales which was Proof against Arms. See the Manner of his being kill'd in the *Atlas Geigraphicus*, Vol. III. Page 43, 44.

4. *Ludolphus*, in his *Ethiophic* History, tells us, that in the *Abyssine Empire*, there are voracious scaly Dragons of the largest Size, tho' not venomous or hurtful otherwise than by the Bite, and they look like the Bark of an old Tree. *Atlas Geographicus*, Vol. IV. Page 614.

5. The *Stories* of *Mer-maids*, *Satyrs*, &c. had undoubtedly their Original from such Animals as have in some Respects a Likeness to the *human Shape* and *Features*. Among these the *Monkey* Kind, the *Orang-Outang*, and the *Quoja Morron*

are the chief on Land ; and the Fish call'd the *Mermaid* (tho' it has nothing of the *Human Form*) and some other unusual Animals in the Sea."

Q.

Where several sons are contemporaneous, and all have the right to bear the paternal arms, they are thus distinguished —the eldest son adds to them what is known as a label. the second, a crescent ; the third, a five-pointed star ; the fourth, a martlet ; the fifth, an annulet ; the sixth, a fleur-delys ; the seventh, a rose ; and so on. A very good and easily accessible example of this " differencing " of the arms may be seen in those borne by the Prince of Wales, the silver label stretching across the top of the shield, blazoned in all other respects like those of the Queen, marking the relationship.

R.

Bruce tells us, for instance, that the horned viper, or Cerastes, the " worm of Nile " that was the cause of the death of Cleopatra, has a way of creeping until it is alongside its victim, and then making a sudden sidelong spring at the object of its attack. In his book he narrates a curious instance that came under his notice at Cairo, where several of these reptiles had been placed in a box. "I saw one crawl up the side, and there lie still, as if hiding himself, til one of the people who brought them to us came near him, and though in a very disadvantageous position, sticking as it were perpendicularly to the side of the box, he leaped near the distance of three feet, and fastened between the man's forefinger and thumb."

S.

Amongst the things displayed in the case a re portions o a wreath from the coffin of Rameses II. (1100–1200 B.C.), composed of sepals and petals of *Nymphæa cærulea* on strips of leaves of the date-palm, and another wreath made from the *N. Lotus.*

Another wreath is from the coffin of Aahmes I. (1700 B.C.), composed of leaves of willow and flowers of the *Acacia Nilotica.*

There are also two garlands from the tomb of the Princess Nzi Khonsou (1000 B.C.), composed in the one case of willow leaves and the flower heads of the *Centauræa depressa,* and in the other of the *Papaver Rhœas,* the common scarlet poppy so familiar to every one who has ever seen an English cornfield or railway embankment in summer.

There are, in addition, leaves of the wild celery and of the olive and vine, all quite clearly distinguishable.

The ancient Egyptians were exceedingly fond of flowers, and even made rare plants a portion of the tribute exacted from dependent or conquered territories. One old writer tells us that "those flowers, which elsewhere were only sparingly produced, even in their proper season, grew profusely in Egypt at all times, so that neither roses, nor any others, were wanting there, even in the middle of winter." Their living rooms were always adorned with bouquets or growing plants, and the stands that served for holding them have been found in the tombs. On the arrival of guests at a banquet servants came forward with garlands of flowers and placed them round their necks, a custom we may see graphically depicted in the mural painting in the tombs, while a single lotus flower was often placed in the hair.

T.

The Bay enters very largely into the various extraordinary compounds—astrological, medicinal, and the like—of the ancients. Thus—to quote but one instance out of many that might be given—Albertus Magnus, in his treatise "De Virtutibus Herbarum," tells us that if any one gathers some bay leaves and wraps them up with the tooth of a wolf, no one can speak an angry word to the bearer ; while, put under the pillow at night, it will bring in a vision before the eyes of a man who has been robbed, the thief and all his belongings. He further goes on to tell us that if set up in a place of worship, none who have broken any contract or agreement will be able to quit the place till this most potent combination be removed. "This last is tried and most true."

INDEX.

"So essential did I consider an Index to be to every book, that I proposed to bring a Bill into Parliament to deprive an author, who publishes a book without an Index, of the privilege of copyright, and, moreover, to subject him to a pecuniary penalty."
—Campbell's *Lives of the Chief-Justices of England.*

PRINTED BY BALLANTYNE, HANSON AND CO.
EDINBURGH AND LONDON.

www.ingramcontent.com/pod-product-compliance
Lightning Source LLC
Chambersburg PA
CBHW030758020726
47499CB00006B/1672